Contents

Editorial

The demise of HMV just after New Year was met with similar levels of shock, sympathy and sentimentality that greeted the death of Woolworth's at the beginning of the current financial crisis four years ago. TV news showed archive film of Nipper the dog and his gramophone, followed by interviews with downcast customers expressing their surprise considering how much they themselves bought from HMV each year.

However, for those in the retail sector, the hand-wringing sounded a little hollow. HMV has been a basket case for at least 15 years, stumbling from one refinancing, restructuring and management buyout to another. The real surprise is that it lasted so long. The digital revolution had already done for photography, Jessops, the very last man standing in a once vibrant sector, succumbing within days of HMV.

The crumb of comfort for bookworms like ourselves is that Waterstones, formerly an integral part of the HMV empire, was disposed of a couple of years ago, saving it from going down with the sinking ship. However, in reality, things aren't too rosy there either.

Following the death of Borders, Waterstones is effectively our last 'quality' national book chain. With around 60 shops (many of which are specialist academic), Blackwells lacks geographic reach. And one word no publisher or customer would ever use about WH Smith's approach to bookselling would be *quality*...

Russian oligarch, Alexander Mamut, bought Waterstones from HMV two years ago, hiring London indie bookseller James Daunt as the man to turn things around. Many promises were made; redirecting investment from advertising to store refurbishment, an end to heavily discounted 3 for 2 style offers (which many felt devalued the product and unfairly penalised independents unable to compete), a return to range buying (smaller quantities of a wider selection of books) and moving head office into the top floors of its flagship Piccadilly store to save cash.

The shop refurbishment is underway. In *Gutter's* hometown, Glasgow, both the Argyle Street and Sauchiehall Street stores look fresh and engaging. The head office switch happens this month. However, January, traditionally the dead zone for booksellers, heralded a Buy-One-Get-One-Half-Price promotion across many paperbacks. And, as *Gutter* went to press, Waterstones confirmed another massive round of redundancies after it suffered a near £40m loss last year.

Equally worrying, Waterstones has stopped stocking books. Go into the stores and there's what can only be described as an airy feel to the shelving. A chat with Waterstones staff and Scottish publishers confirms that the company has slashed the stock it is ordering. Where it would previously order hundreds of a title, buyers are now taking tens and sometimes single figures. And when those few books they do order are sold, they are not being restocked.

Needs must in a fight for survival. But it seems that customers are deserting Waterstones as they did HMV and Jessops. *Gutter* believes that the Great (but convenient) Satan, Amazon, will soon triumph once more. Any shopkeeper will tell you that when it comes retail, convenience wins every time, no matter how good the competition is 20 yards up the road. Waterstones is also burdened with an estate that was built in the good times, with rent and rates way beyond what anyone would pay now.

However, all is not lost. While the High Street book chains implode, the independent sector is holding its own, with numbers of indie book shops staying relatively stable despite the economic climate. Many are making small but important innovations, such as introducing cafes and wi-fi. Those not old enough to remember ABBA first time around may not realise that the national book chain was an invention of a man called Tim in the mid 1980s. Before then bookselling was dominated by independent regional firms, usually with one or two flagship stores in their home cities, alongside a legion of smaller owner-managed shops. Remember the original John Smith's in Glasgow or James Thin's in Edinburgh?

Some may believe that face-to-face bookselling is as doomed as the photographic print and the music CD. However, we disagree. Books have the advantage of being physical objects of beauty, where the material is as much part of the experience as the content. The most important factor in the preservation of the printed word, and therefore the bookseller, is that a huge proportion of books are bought as gifts. Borders in Glasgow used to take around 70% of its annual turnover in the 5 weeks before Christmas. Have you ever tried to wrap an e-book?

There has been much talk of zombie companies in the press, about how sick and ailing businesses that will never recover, because they subscribed to now broken business models, should do the decent thing and commit hara-kiri so time and investment can be devoted to those with a future. We wouldn't wish that on Waterstones. However, if and when they do pass on to the great High Street in the sky, across the nation a return to small, independent, vibrant bookselling is likely.

*

Comedy performance of the month goes to James Kelman, whose stand-up routine at the Saltire Book Awards just before Christmas brought the house down. Kelman is without doubt a leading contender for the title 'our greatest living writer' but, as is often the case with genius, allowances have to be made. Having been awarded Book of the Year and a £5000 cheque, Kelman reverted to his now default response of biting the hand.

Having spent five minutes robustly criticising the audience (and nation) over its ignorance of Scottish culture, one heckler

was foolish enough to complain about the industrial language (haven't they read any of his books!?). They were swatted away with an appropriately contemptuous growl. However, when another shouted "stop patronising us, Jim" the interruption was ignored.

Kelman's often repeated complaint of how little he makes from his writing (£15,000 last year, he told us) was met with embarrassed bottom-shifting. While the debate on a national endowment for literature continues (something we have supported in previous editorials), in a room packed with writers with full or part-time jobs, there was a palpable fear that someone might stand up and point out that in this age of austerity, it seems there's no such thing as a free lunch.

*

The word patronising also came to mind when we travelled to an otherwise hugely enjoyable and well-attended performance night in Edinburgh a few weeks ago. Another national treasure, who has lived, worked and published outside Scotland for the vast majority of her career, regaled the audience with crowd-pleasing, couthy poetry soaked in the semi-ironic 'crivens, help-ma-boab' Scots of yesteryear. While any writer or poet is welcome to do what the hell they want, one can't help feel the ecstatic response that the turn received was partly a function of our collective deference to those who have 'made it' in England rather than the work itself which seemed a little disconnected from the way anyone has spoken in Scotland for the last eighty years. If folk keep telling us we're a bunch of quaint, small-minded provincials, it seems, eventually we come both to believe it and to love them for it too.

*

We are encouraged by the continuing high standard of poetry submissions. Acting poetry editor Patricia Ace looked for clarity: poems in which the sense was clear and which displayed a certain fluidity of expression did well. A sense of rhythm and musicality were appreciated, an eye for striking imagery or an unusual take on the world also impressed us, and we enjoyed poems that made us laugh as well as those that had the power to move us. Natural themes began to emerge, such as Biblical/ Myth and Gender/Family/Relationships, and we looked for poems that spoke to each other within and across these thematic boundaries. We weren't thwarted in our aim to represent as many different voices as possible within a limited space, as well as a variety of styles and approaches, all of which proved the wealth and vitality of Scottish poets writing today. We're delighted to be publishing work from David Kinloch for the first time, along with some contemporary comment from Graham Fulton and quirky insight from A C Clarke and Alison Flett.

Gutter 08 also sees great variety in terms of prose selected. We're delighted to welcome back former Macallan/*Scotland on Sunday* Short Story Competition winner Rob McClure Smith, who provides some stateside campus black comedy, a beautiful Hebridean tale from former Sceptre Prize winner, John Jennett, last published by us in *Gutter 01*, a new piece from Vicki Jarrett, author of the acclaimed debut novel *Nothing is Heavy*, also set in a fast food joint, more middle-aged misadventure from Brian McCabe and a memorable, unsettling story set in Papua New Guinea from Kirsten Zhang. We have a number of intriguing novel extracts, from Nick Brooks, author of *My Name is Denise Forrester* and *The Good Death*, from Simon Biggam, whose debut *These Are Only Words* was published by the wonderful but brief imprint, Chroma, and also from journalist, broadcaster and playwright, Neil Mackay, from his forthcoming debut novel *All the Little Guns Go Bang Bang Bang*, about two psychopathic eleven year-olds rampage through 1980s Northern Ireland.

We're also delighted to announce that Helen Sedgwick, review editor since *Gutter's* inception and most recently also acting prose editor for the last two issues, has agreed to become managing editor of *Gutter*. To date Helen has been indefatigable in her work for the magazine and she will be helping drive its development over the next few years.

'Easy reading is damn hard writing.'

Nathaniel Hawthorne

Rain on the Roof
Kirstin Zhang

MAY TO DECEMBER is the monsoon season, but this year the rains have not come. Smoke rises from the bushfires on the hills surrounding the city.

Epi's boss is standing in the shade of the frangipani tree listening to the news on a portable radio; army helicopters are bringing in sea water to douse the fires and a government minister is being investigated for payments to a rain doctor.

'But why is rain so bad?' asks Epi stamping the dusty soil around a juna bush.

Mr Tierney turns down the volume on the radio and begins to explain about the upcoming elections and the misuse of public money, but after several minutes his voice trails off. 'Thank God, there's no wind,' he finally says.

They sink the last of the bushes and Epi spreads a layer of chicken manure for good measure. Mrs Tierney is worried about robbery. People are coming in from the villages where the crops have failed, looking for food. They walk in single file along the highway or sit in little groups around the missions. Mrs Tierney wants high fences with barbed wire, but Epi has persuaded her that this would spoil the beauty of the garden and she has agreed to a compromise of thirty thorny juna bushes planted around the perimeter of the property.

'Let's just hope they keep the buggers out,' says Mr Tierney. He is already knocking the dirt from his boots on the bottom step of the veranda. At the top he lets the mesh door slam behind him.

Epi stands to survey their work, shifting his weight from one leg to the other to disperse the flies which have gathered round his ankles.

A face appears above him over the latticed fence. It is Jonah who keeps garden for the Haldanes next door. Jonah wrinkles his nose, 'Ah, yes, I like that chicken shit too,' he says. 'Yes, Yes. And now my flowers are growing tall, growing sweet, like my children.' Jonah's two sons come to help him with the garden when they are not at school.

Epi scowls. 'Bloody rubbish children.' He has no sons, only a daughter, Evie, with skinny legs.

Jonah, who does not appear to have heard, is leaning casually over the fence, fingering a withered flower head. Epi feels an urge to hiss, to strike away that hand from his flowers. Who is he to decide what should stay or go in his garden?

'Okay,' says Jonah raising his long arms wearily, 'I am taking a little nap now. Yes, yes, it is very tiring work to win such a big prize.'

Epi does not raise his head, but his thin body grows rigid.

For four years running he has taken silver at the Sir Hubert Murray Gardening Prize; Jonah has taken bronze for two. This year, however, there is talk that Jonah will not only take the silver, but might even rob Epi of a chance at the gold.

The next morning school is cancelled because there is no water to flush the toilets. Jonah's sons are in the next garden, shirtless and sweating, turning over the soil beneath the papery hibiscus. Epi, who is trying to secure

➤➤

the drooping head of an orchid with a wooden stake, can hear them chanting, 'One stone, two stone, three stone, four...'

His daughter, Evie, is chasing the Tierney's dog around the yellowing lawn. She tosses a ball. 'Fetch!' The old dog totters after it, panting hard.

'My grass!' calls Epi.

It is now against the law to water before seven in the evening, and even then one is allowed to spray for only fifteen minutes. Hammering at the wooden stake he mutters, 'Suppose it doesn't rain? Suppose it doesn't rain?'

By mid-morning his back is aching and he is tired of the banter from the next door garden. 'Evie,' he calls, 'let us run some errands. Let us get ourselves cool.'

Mrs Tierney has an old run-around, a yellow Sunbeam, which he is allowed to use for errands if she does not need it. They drive to Trudi's Cash and Carry, with the air-conditioning on high, to buy a new rake with a rubber grip, two tins of mackerel for the dog and an ice cream for Evie. As an afterthought he plucks two Gerry cans from the shop floor and adds them to the cart.

'I will get us some water,' he says. 'Plenty, plenty water.' He wonders why he has not thought of it before.

On the stretch between Borehoho and Four Mile they pass two men, whom Epi knows, pushing a cart full of ragged tires. The cart lurches wildly on the potholed road. He rolls down the window and toots his horn, 'Some slowcoaches going to get themselves killed,' he shouts.

The two men raise their fists and laugh.

When they reach Waigani Junction, Epi follows the road ahead, past the army barracks, towards the wetlands. Once they leave the road the windscreen is soon covered with a thick film of red dust. He turns on the window wipers but they refuse to budge. He gropes at levers as they make a slow zig zag through the bush.

'Papa,' Evie shrieks.

He is forced to drive with his head half out of the window, coughing and spitting, until the wipers finally begin to screech and scrape across the glass.

The dust gives way to knobbled clumps of weed and rush. In the distance is the Owen Stanley Range. All this, he tells Evie, his right hand making a wide arc, belonged to his grandfather. When he was a boy they would hunt wild boar and cuscus here. The swamp was full of talapi and eel. 'Big, big fish.' For a moment he takes both hands from the steering wheel to show her how big.

Evie is licking with little enthusiasm at the melting ice cream. 'But it isn't his now?'

Epi leans back into the plastic covered seat, his fingers tight once more around the wheel. 'No,' he says quietly and brings the car to a halt.

Ahead of them is a notice painted in red. 'Danger. National Sanitation Project. Do Not Enter.'

Epi climbs out of the car, Evie following. The remains of the ice cream is beginning to run down her arms, drip from her elbows. Epi is standing very still, watching a bulldozer lumber across a shallow pool of brackish water. Two diggers are pulling up nipa palm and wild fig trees. Large plastic pipes lie amongst the devastation.

Epi stamps at the ground, 'Shit. Shit. Everywhere I am finding only shit!'

'Papa,' says Evie.

'Eya, what?!' he shouts, turning.

Evie is standing, her little legs trembling. 'Papa,' she says. 'I think I am having a belly ache.'

Later, he is washing out the car, thinking about the wetlands. The fumes of the disinfectant are making his eyes water. He blinks and shakes his head. Only when Mr Tierney taps on the roof does he realise he is there.

'The missus is complaining about the heat,' he says, dabbing at his face with a handkerchief. 'She wants to go up to Rouala Falls for a couple of days.'

Epi nods absentmindedly, squeezing out the sponge.

'But with the worry of robbery...' Mr Tierney puffs out his cheeks, and glances up at the house. 'She doesn't want to leave the place unguarded.'

It is the weekend of the annual sing sing down at Koki. Evie has been looking forward to it for weeks. Epi's wife has been sewing her a dress. And shoes. They have bought Evie new shoes.

He blinks as if he does not understand.

Mr Tierney's face grows redder. 'I just thought that with the competition so close... you'd want to be around.' He waves his handkerchief in the direction of the fence.

Epi stands straight. Opposite, he sees Jonah tending a weeping cherry. Its slender branches arch towards a patch of grass that is still vibrant, still green.

'Yes,' he sighs and drops the sponge back into the bucket. 'I will look after the house.'

Mr Tierney smiles widely and lays a twenty dollar bill on the roof of the car. 'Good fella,' he says. 'There's plenty of beer in the fridge. Don't get thirsty.'

The next evening a small crowd is waiting at the bus stop on the edge of the shanty town where Epi lives. The women are admiring each other's clothes. Evie is wearing her new dress, but her voice is unhappy, small, whining, like a mosquito bothering in his ear. 'Why is he not coming?' 'Why must he stay?'

Jonah is standing near the front of the queue with his wife. The boys are playing scissor, paper, rock. Their hair is slick with coconut oil and their smooth cheeks are shiny. Evie sniffs, kicks at the dirt with her new shoes, scuffing the polished toes. Epi slaps at her. It is not hard, a flick with his hand, but she glares at him. Once on the bus she keeps her eyes fixed firmly on the seat in front of her, refusing to look down at him, refusing to wave goodbye, despite her mother's prompts.

On his arrival at the Tierney's Epi goes straight to the fridge and takes out a beer. He drinks it there in the kitchen, his face puckering with the bitter coldness, listening to the whir of Mrs Tierney's fishtank. He takes a second bottle from the fridge and stirs the water in the tank with his fingers, scattering the fish and causing the miniature shipwreck on the bottom to float up to the surface. With a third and a fourth bottle in his hands he goes

out onto the veranda and stands, looking down at the garden. The juna bushes are like silent warriors in the dark, the Haldane's weeping willow is a powerful sorcerer. 'What magic is keeping you alive, eh, when everything else is dying?'

For several hours he drinks beer and thinks about the prize, thinks of how he will put an end to Jonah's ambition. But what should he do? A machete is too obvious and weed killer will take time. He goes to bed, the beer gurgling in his stomach, his head tired with scheming. He has considered witchcraft, blackmail, vandalism, murder. He thinks of his wife and his daughter at the sing sing, of the music and dancing. He remembers the feasts when he was a boy, heating up a hundred round stones to line the cooking pit, lifting them one by one from the fire. It was a tiring job. He is counting the stones as he falls asleep.

At first he thinks he is still sleeping. Drip, drip. Still dreaming. Drip, drip. Then there is a crackle like gunfire, a wild drumming. He throws back the thin sheet, and stands. His head is woozy. For a moment he is still, one hand on the doorframe, letting the blood settle, listening.

Outside, he hears children in the street. 'Rain, rain,' they sing. 'Rain, rain.'

'Yes,' he answers them. 'Rain, rain.' He has prayed for it. Offered up his daughter's happiness for it. He pulls on his trousers and steps outside the door. The rain pummels his cheeks and bare chest. He puts up his hands to shield his eyes.

The striped awning at the edge of the house is straining beneath the weight of the water, bulging like a pregnant belly. But the earth, too hard, too long, will not easily yield. Already rivers are forming. They run between the houses carrying away basketballs, plastic bins, banana plants. The wooden stake he has raised only yesterday to secure the orchids has been wrenched from the ground, the green vine mangled. The fence between the Tierney's and the Haldane's is beginning to buckle. The twisting planks make a long, low groan. He lets

➤➤

out a cry of sympathy. Through the gaping slats,
he sees the weeping cherry. Around its base a
whirlpool is forming and the thin branches flail
in the water like a drowning man.

Liberation Street
Rodge Glass

BEATA SAYS IT'S like rescuing an orphan. Feeding it. Giving it shelter. Wrapping a shawl around its shoulders. It just so happens, she says, that this particular orphan gives me a good hard seeing to five times a week. And you'd be amazed what zest gratefulness can add to a man's lovemaking. That kind of logic allows Beata to explain away drawing six figures a year from a so-called 'green' charity. The absence of any job at all keeps me floating up and down this yellow strip of a Tuesday afternoon, ordering cocktails and wondering how it's all going to end. Meanwhile, my old friend's face – colourful, youthful, freshly fucked – haunts me as if she were dead. All week Beata has been fighting environmental fires in Poland, bounding between meetings with politicians and strategists, a tigress freed from the zoo. Stop being so selfish, her last email said, and give something back to the world. She signed off with a smiley face. She's fifty-seven.

Here, I wear the ring you bought me, the one with the narrow score round the outside, on the traditional wedding finger. It took some work to wrench the thing from its old place on what my father used to call *the why-no-wedding-yet finger* and shift it next door. It had been snug for years. Now the damned thing stares at me day and night, asking questions. *What exactly do I think I'm playing at?* it says. *What have I done to deserve this sudden upgrade?* The ring flops around loosely on the finger, threatening to jump down a plughole when I'm in the shower, or leap into the dark when I'm walking back to my room. It's only a matter of time before I notice my hand has no

ring on it, and it's too late, and I end up on the mud path back from the beach, after sunset, begging sunburned English whales with whale husbands and screaming whale children to help me look for a ring with a narrow score round the outside. I'd like to pop that ring into my navel like a coin. Have it die with me. Survive long after both of us, lying on its own in a single pot holding our ashes, sucking up the dust. Still, what I want doesn't count for much. I didn't want your skull shattered by a thief either, I didn't want to wake to the sound of it, but no one consulted me over the issue. So I mourn the ring now to save myself the trouble later. And in the meantime it does its job, keeping interested parties informed of my current status: HARD TO GET. By the way, the ring has left an indent on either side of the why-no-wedding-yet finger (even now I can't say it without shaking my head), also a small band of white skin that hasn't seen sunlight since we were teenagers. Maybe I should just move the fucking thing back to where it came from and stop living a lie.

But it's tempting to keep on like this when the lie is leading to new truths. Yesterday, Hassan clocked the ring and asked, *Does your husband treat you well, Christine?* His cheeks are a child's. His eyes are a man's. I answered, *Like a queen.* And I was convincing. No, it's not quite the truth, but few husbands reach two decades' service these days, and no towel boy could make me feel more like royalty than you did, every day, every year. I blame you, Jonathan, for loving me so well. If only

➤➤

you'd slowly crushed me as some men do their women with the passing years – a chilly comment here, an infidelity there, pregnant sighs, broken promises – if only I'd survived all those ordinary things women put up with, leaving them grateful and dependent in middle age – then perhaps I wouldn't be getting cravings now. Half these dizzy widows never had a genuine compliment in their lives, so they don't have to notice the difference. I have no such luxury.

There's not much to discover here. For a start, locals are not allowed in the complex unless they're serving us, so the fixed-grin waiters, our boys on the private beach and the kids' entertainers in orange shorts are the only North Africans I've met in nearly two months of 'travelling'. (Amanda thinks that's what I'm doing. I send her emails every few days so she doesn't worry about her old mum.) Also, we're miles from genuine life – the isolation is proudly advertised on the literature like a recent award. The closest thing to a village is the shopping centre, which is a ten mile taxi ride away, too far for most of the whales. They can hardly summon the strength to squeeze into their swimsuits after injecting the all-you-can-eat breakfast buffet, never mind actually brave the outside world. Another guest here told me, with great pride, as if she'd built it with her own sausagey hands, that the shopping centre is modelled on some upmarket Parisian suburb – I had to stop myself from giving her a lecture on globalisation. But but but. Never mind never mind never mind. Even if I don't like what I see on land, there's always the sky, and the sea. As Hassan tells me, his hands in mine and his mind on the future, *Certain things no regime can steal.*

I'm trying to explore my surroundings a little each day, even if that's a victory so small it seems like defeat. Last week I made it to the nearest shop without consulting the map. Five nights ago I reached the restaurant at the far end of the beach without asking for directions. (The website described this place as 'a stone's throw' from the sand, but the hotelier must have a ferocious throw or a good imagination. The internet is getting worse, Jonathan. It's home to a hundred million lies and barely a single truth.) I did something else that night too: logged on to the forum Beata told me about, using her password. Would you believe such things exist these days? Are there no police officers in the virtual world?

Well until there are, it's good to know that widows with half-beating hearts can surf for fresh meat online. Fresh meat that writes messages like, *I am looking for good woman with pure heart to be precious for all rest of my life.* Like, *I am good lover, v understanding.* Like, *I dream of London but would be happy in Norwich or other small England town.* These boys ignore the sea of tight shimmering virgins to focus on us, the second hand, every one hoping for things local girls can't provide. They're wise young owls, Hassan and his kind. They see their parents and don't want to become them. They see the glorious mountains behind this complex and know they might as well be a mirage. Three days ago, Hassan asked if he could kiss my hand and I damn near stuffed him in my beach bag.

Actually, in that moment, looking at the surrounding waiters and lifeguards, I thought about taking home a whole harem of them, a different boy for each day of the week. Does that mean I'm losing my mind, or finding it? I didn't think of such things while chatting with *FunBoy1985* at three a.m., glass of white wine in hand, but it occurs to me now that perhaps Hassan is on the forum too, under a different name. Maybe we're having the same conversation in two different places. In a universe with no God, or one too shy to interfere – not merciful enough to have let you survive what the judge called *the kind of senseless attack that leads one to wonder whether humanity is worth rescuing* – Hassan is right to pursue several options. My codename was *Rue de la Liberation*, the name of the road the complex is on. What names they have for things here, Jonathan! Liberation Street! Are they trying to make us laugh?

I've not told anyone about us, or what happened. You're mine only.

The other night I went swimming in the hotel pool, long after they turned off the heat. It was dark but for the occasional lamp lighting the palm trees and the hum from hotel rooms up above. I swam twenty lengths, thirty, then pressed on to fifty and beyond, till I lost count. I could feel the temperature dropping but didn't get out until I could hardly breathe. I staggered at the side of the pool, until Hassan appeared as if by magic, as if from under the pool, to steady me. He was dressed in a white short-sleeved shirt, shorts and sandals (not topless for once); he must have been on his way back to his room, or perhaps to the bus stop. (I don't know where the workers sleep. I realised then that I hadn't thought about where he lives at all.) He placed his hands on my forearms and led me to the door, then the lift by reception, then to the corridor on the nineteenth floor.

Once we were through the door into my room he insisted on putting me, still in my swimsuit, to bed like a baby. *Sshh, Christine*, said Hassan, rubbing a towel through my hair. *No troubles. Forget everything before.* Then he picked up a comb and stroked it through the strands of brown and silver, telling me a story about his childhood as I shivered, the lactic acid washing every part of me. The story Hassan told was something to do with his mother's hands. Or was I imagining that? He seemed to be in no rush. To have nowhere else to go. Either that or I was, for that moment anyway, his only care. As I began to feel myself slipping from consciousness he kissed my lips, tiptoed towards the exit and left, closing the door so softly that it hardly made any sound.

I slept without dreaming but the peace didn't last. In the morning I woke, joints throbbing, amazed to find myself alone. How could this be? How could it be happening? Again! Jonathan, I was overtaken by the urge to search under the bed to check you weren't hiding there. I lifted the pillows. Cast off the sheet. Slapped the bedside table with my hand, trying to strike away the image of you lying beside me, no longer breathing. This image was replaced in my mind by another, of Hassan in the en suite bathroom, shaving, a towel round his waist, singing loudly as if trying to prove how undeniably *alive* he was. But when I checked, no, he wasn't in my bathroom. Was he already on shift? Did he work all day and all night as well? Did he have days off? Sure only of my solitude, I stumbled over to the French windows, looked down onto the pool and watched the children splashing about in there. I can't continue like this much longer, Jonathan. Can you understand? Or would you rather me swan-dive from the veranda? Some women in my position make a sacrifice of themselves. Their funerals are steady affairs. The eulogies focus on their dedication to long-dead husbands. How these women didn't want to live without them. How that's what love is, and how it really is a beautiful thing and, despite the tragedy, we should all try to understand. I took one more look at the pool, then went inside.

An hour later I left the hotel room and headed towards the beach, texting Beata on the way. *How is your brave new world?* I asked her. *Mine not so brave.* For a woman with such a high-powered job, she always seems to have spare thumbs and time to reply. Her answer came through seconds later: *You are a predator. Grrrr. Now POUNCE!* I can't explain it, I shouldn't be expected to, but those capital letters made me feel so far away from my friend that, Jonathan, if you had risen up from the sand and explained right then and there that Beata and I were living on different planets, well, I would certainly have believed you. I turned off the phone and threw it into my handbag. I looked at my watch. Decided to put on a little make-up.

When I arrived at the beach I took out a paperback and settled down under a thatched umbrella for the afternoon, close to Hassan but not too close. It doesn't do to look desperate. I watched him at work, thinking how he smells of rich, thick Turkish coffee (strange given we're not in Turkey), and how he might look good propped up in our back garden, overlooking the pond like some kind of exotic gnome.

I took a spot between two others, both of these creatures, if you don't mind me saying so, making me look like an Oscar statuette by comparison. (At least I've made an effort. Some women have no shame.) Hassan is polite, of course, but he's not interested. Neither of those wear any rings on any of their fingers – and from the way Hassan stands, shoulders straight as a ruler, you can tell he likes a challenge. What male with an ounce of worth likes a door swinging open? Especially when that open door is a semi-retired Bed & Breakfast proprietor from Blackpool with dyed red hair, an accent like sawdust and a spare tyre the size of Marrakech? I summoned Hassan, ordered a mojito and threatened to sunbathe topless – if he behaved himself. He went to get my drink while heat raced from my lips to my toes then back up again. Yesterday was a good day.

Perhaps you'd have been proud of me, making this great not-quite-statement of what the young insist on calling *moving on*, as if love was something one picked up for a while, fingered then dropped, leaving no after-effects. Perhaps you'd have been appalled. But how long is it appropriate to wait? Exactly how miserable are you supposed to be before cracking? As Hassan served, I bundled my hair on top of my head, a chopstick through the centre and several strands of hair left to dangle, drawing his attention to that neck and shoulders he saw close-up in my hotel room, the same neck and shoulders you used to prefer me to put out on show. *Let them see what they can't touch*, you'd say, making me both a prize and a threat. As I am now. Briefly I considered kicking the mojito onto the sand. Isn't this exactly the sort of humiliation women like me spend lifetimes trying to avoid? Rather than overturning the glass, I drained it, and Hassan came soon after with a replacement. *On the house*, he said. *Please. A present. Welcome in Africa*. I protested but he said, *For most beautiful woman in all the beach*. Be fair to the boy, he's smart – he didn't specify outer or inner beauty. I accepted the drink without comment, then hardly moved for the next four hours.

The restaurant delivers food direct to the loungers, so I ordered from my seat and ate lunch horizontal, only rising every hour or so to paddle in the water or go to the Ladies. (Sometimes the same thing. One can only leave one's possessions unattended on a sun lounger so often without basically asking to be burgled.) In between conversing with Hassan, also one or two other waiters and lifeguards attracted like flies to the only lamp in the room, I read an entire book, one given to me by a snub-nosed woman in the complex who said I looked like I needed a thrill. (How could she tell?) Anyway, this book was about a disabled woman in 19th Century Germany who overcomes her own overpowering shyness and the prejudices of the society around her to become some sort of striptease or burlesque artist in Hungary (this is supposed to be a *happy* ending?). It's possible the main character was a lesbian. I don't know why I was compelled to continue reading, but at least that's one more book in the world I don't have to look at and wonder, *would I enjoy that?* And there are worse ways I could spend my remaining days: lying under the earth's life force reading mediocre filth. I would be doing less damage than most. Beata would approve. Though she'd like me to be more proactive.

As I read and read, only half concentrating, sun-bronzed boys in shorts fussed over the line of us, as if they were born to serve. I come back to this same spot every day, pretending I'm not watching them slink up and down the sand, sniffing the widows and divorcées, weighing up the least unsavoury option – no doubt trying not to think about what services they'd have to provide, for how long, and how it might feel, several years from now, to break for real freedom once the bedroom had simply become somewhere for sleeping and both sides were ready to trade in.

I think about these things sometimes.

When I have my eyes closed and the sun is doing the work of three, I imagine Hassan's future, the girl he'll meet in a bar, ten years from now. The Gayle or Patricia or Tracy-Ann he'll fall in love with. How he'll tell his shining young thing that although some find it difficult to understand, though some laugh, he really is grateful to the woman who liberated him from his past, the home that was really no home at all, and how without her he wouldn't now be the proud owner of a British passport, a chain of coffee shops and a 1969 Cadillac, the car his devout father always secretly wanted but was never able to buy. As Hassan will tell Patricia, at this point in the future, his father will be receiving letters every week, posted lovingly (along with generous contributions to the family finances) direct to the humble village shack less than fifty miles from this complex where I now lie, topping up my tan. *Papa*, the letters will say, *I made a life here.* They'll say, *Here are pictures of your grandchildren. And yes, I know Christine was rude to you but please, understand that without her I'd still be serving mojitos. Also, she taught me everything a good lover needs to know.* Hassan will be relating all this to Patricia. She'll clamp her hands round his cheeks, draw him close, wipe a tear away and whisper, I *get it, baby. Now shut up and show me what you learned.*

Every minute I spend thinking about this bullshit is a minute I don't spend missing you, which makes it time well spent: what are my other options? Reading about the voracious sexual appetites of German prostitutes, ordering cocktails from the local eye candy and trying not to bawl like a child. I won't let that happen, Jonathan. If I cry, even once, I won't survive it. Some things one feels one knows.

I look around this country you wanted to come to, and I'm frozen into wonder. You only said it once, a light comment in the middle of dinner three nights before you were murdered in our bed – *you know where I'd like to see?* – and maybe it was a fleeting interest. Maybe it was something you hardly even meant, or you meant somewhere different and got mixed up. Maybe you'd secretly wanted to visit here, researched the place for years in travel books and fallen in love with photographs – maybe you'd bought flights for our anniversary and never got the chance to tell me. That's death. You don't get to ask questions. You're left with a vague sense of the unknowable and a daughter guessing blindly at *what Daddy would have wanted*. I can't know what you wanted. I can only guess. So here I am, representing us both on this beach, wondering if we should jump into a new life. If you delay, others swoop. I'm not the only passport here.

This morning I woke to an email on my phone: Beata writing from some conference in Krakow where she's giving a paper on climate change. She's taken Youssef with her; they plan to see a few sights. She wants to see the Jewish Quarter (by which she means she wants to test-drive the bars in the Jewish Quarter.) She wants to show Youssef the Da Vinci in a museum with a name I can't pronounce. Beata's message is all short sentences and exclamation marks. Questions and answers. She says revolution is coming to this place, she's heard talk in the corridors. *Do you know?* she asks. *Are you safe? It's racing up the coast*, she says. *They want democracy.* Well, they might soon have it, who knows? They'd hardly report such things here. But it'll take more than a revolution to bring change to the resort, and by the time it arrives Hassan will have missed his chance. Democracy is all very well but the poor usually remain poor whoever is in charge. No wonder they fawn on the beaches.

Now I stand on my veranda once more, scrolling up and down Beata's message, rereading, not really reading at all, wondering if I should head down to the beach and thinking that really, now is the time. I sit down in the room, fan pushing cold air into the heat, and I start writing to Amanda, fingers clumsy on the touchscreen. *My darling girl*, my message begins. For a moment I think she'll understand. But I only get halfway through the first sentence – I have met – before Amanda's imagined reply stops me. I imagine her suggesting I come home, imagine her instructing me to *do so alone*. But I can't promise that, or anything. There's no telling what prisoners might do given a penknife and half a chance. I delete the message, consider starting another one, inviting her out here to join me, then I put the phone down and apply sun cream instead. Shoulders, arms, neck. Legs, face, feet. I sit up. I look around, twirling the loose ring on my wedding finger. Hassan is on the beach, surrounded by vultures.

'Liberation Street' is taken from *LoveSexTravelMusik*, Rodge Glass's new short story collection published by Freight Books in April 2013

Guga

John Jennett

IN THE PHOTOGRAPH my grandfather is a gangly calf of a man, wide eyes with round patches. Guga they called him, not rattling off his paternal line like they should: mac Alasdair Iain Callum. Just 'Guga', scratched onto a lichen-chewed headstone that's splattered with guano. He's buried shoulders to the sea, the wind breathing up kelp from the island dunes and tall skies reeling past in grey quilts.

He was eighteen the October Saturday they say he walked up the croft, the big white bird swaddled in his jacket. Said he'd found it dragging its wing along the beach where he'd been sent to rake for cockles in the sand.

Morus Bassanus,

Solan Goose,

Guga,

Booby,

Northern Gannet,

Sùlaire amongst the list of names I've unearthed for it.

When he'd come of age earlier that year, my grandfather had rowed out with the men on a two week trip to the offshore skerry; his first and last time there. He was game as any first-time fowler to winkle his bare toes into the cliff's black cracks and get scaling to the nests. Hands flexing eager for the hooking and snaring; fingers for the throttling and plucking. Final gutting and salting thickening his tongue before the homebound procession, gunwales pressed close to the cold August sea by stacked-high stinking barrels. Any man without an oar to work sitting stock-still beneath his bonnet, steadying the thwarts, the women restless on the jetty for the first returning bow to inch

around the point.

On the day my grandfather brought the bird home from the beach, his brothers joined a call for its slaughter. Other folk said it was a bogle, a shellycoat, fachan; perhaps a wirry-cow. One caileach diagnosed the spirit of a guga: an infant gannet, whose neck he had snapped at the skerry. A different old woman said it was a victim-bird's unforgiving mother, the 'broken' wing an easy trick to fall for. All agreed it would cause him bother, but with the gannet having been carried over the home threshold, his parents were wiser than to turn it out.

I've learned the facts.

How the long-lived gannet never flies over land, chooses just one mate for life. Parents raise a single chick before their ocean x-ray eyes reveal the fish are thronging south, calling to be dive-bomb plundered all the way to Africa and back.

It's said that when this girl-gannet stretched, its ink-dipped wings scythed wider than its lanky finder stood tall; its torso snowy as a swan, save the balaclava of its cold-custard cowl, its chill mackerel eyes. Grandfather fashioned a driftwood crate, at least that's how the story goes, stole herring for the bird. Stared at burrowing moles of the oily fish inching down its gullet, rippling the white velvet of its neck.

'Guga,' folk whispered to my grandfather's back. 'Guga guga guga,' until the name stuck to him, like salt splinters from a broken wave. His hands were scarred they say, his arms his face, from where the gannet swiped, the lilac dirk of its beak.

With the war, 'Guga' signed up to be a despatch-rider for the local navy bases. Dead before he was twenty, they found my grandfather with a crooked neck on the stretch where the track curves with the sweep of the bay; the motorcycle engine still running and seals watching shiny-headed from the shallows. After the funeral, my great-grandmother worried open the gannet's cage and watched the bird fly west until it faded into the wide horizon.

It wasn't long before a fair-haired woman dressed as a WREN tapped at the door. With her pale skin and her accent she announced they had planned to marry, that she carried his child.

Today we are at the hospital, my unsuspecting dad and I, amongst the smell of polish and rubber shoes. We are waiting for news on my mother: the Guga's daughter. Curling the corner of a magazine I admit hope to myself that her pale-purple lips will surrender something before she dies. Dressed by this landlocked city that I chose, I perch with Dad on the blue plastic chairs, trying not to preen at my straw-coloured hair.

There is a flash of white at the window but when I look up it's just a ratty gull. We are expecting a cousin of sorts to arrive from the Island, the only one who mentions the sùlaire. I think about the times when I can't avoid going 'home'. She takes me down the machair when it's all eyebright and plump orchids, humming with breeze-defying bees, the blown air buttery with clover and warm sand.

'Have you seen the sùlaire this year, Suzy?' she'll ask.

'I've not been near the coast,' my usual lie, reply. Thinking she is staring at my throat as I gulp a piece of scone. Me willing it to slip down without a bulge, scanning the sea. Beneath the waves I spot a school of silver herring. They are shoaling away from a lazy cod, its chin barbel curled like a piglet's tail.

'How about a man? Anyone suitable on the horizon? Mr Right?'

Over the Atlantic an invisible cirrus hatch has opened, letting sun through in sepia searchlight pillars. The wind must be gusting where the clouds have parted, the sea crumpling there in sharp white-horses crests. I see gannets then. Hundreds of gannets raining on the ocean, the same skew as the sunlight slants; peppered puffs of spray where they punch the swell like flak.

The cousin is saying something else, touching my shoulder, but my eyes are skinned sharp now with the sun-metal sea. I imagine myself diving. Diving the way I like to with my hands at my side, my hair pinned back, to split a cold loch's brackish skin. The way I can keep my eyes open, the silver flash of a fish and my ears hissing again, the foamy ribbon rush of every thrilling plunge.

THE HAIRDRESSER OF HARARE
TENDAI HUCHU

AN OBSERVER TOP TEN AFRICAN BOOK 2012

'This glorious book defies classification with its astute sociopolitical commentary nestling inside the appealing, often comic story of a young woman who will not accept defeat. With a light touch and real skill, Huchu takes us through the life-sapping economic realities of contemporary Harare...'
THE OBSERVER

RRP £8.99
Released: 18th March 2013
ISBN: 978-1-908754-11-0

FREIGHT
BOOKS

freightbooks.co.uk

Karaoke
Brian McCabe

IT WAS GOING to be his turn soon – he was on after Sinatra – and Les felt the nerves coming on like they always did beforehand, no matter how many pints of eighty shilling and spiced rum and cokes he downed while he waited. Butterflies, they called it, but it felt more like bees, a whole angry swarm of them buzzing around like crazy in the bulging hive of his gut. He was going to do *Fever*, a number he'd never done before. That would take Shanksy and Bert by surprise. They would remember it, and they'd spend half an hour trying to remember Peggy Lee's name. What they didn't know was that hers was just a cover version of the original song, and that Elvis also did a cover version. He'd be able to trot out the history of the song, because he'd looked it up on the internet, and that would shut them up.

What Peggy Lee and Elvis did wasn't so different from what he did on a Saturday night. The song was all there, the arrangement was all there. All you had to do was read the words and sing it. It wasn't so different from a famous singer doing a cover version. And he liked to think that he only chose songs that meant something to him personally, not just any old song he knew he could do.

He finished off his Morgan's. Time to get another round in and have a smoke out the back in the beer garden to steady the nerves, regardless of Doctor MacRae's orders. 'You're going to have to do something about your diet, as well,' MacRae had said, but already he was looking forward to that carry-out Lamb Tikka after the pub. He never felt much like eating before performing, because of the nerves. He drained his glass, heaved himself to his feet and nodded over to Shanksy and Bert, pointing to their glasses and saying 'Same again?' although they couldn't hear him because of the volume of the karaoke. That clown in the suit trying to do Sinatra, croaking his way through *Mack the Knife*. He'd show him how it was done soon enough. He'd show them all. Sure, he got up most Saturday nights, but he hadn't for the past three weeks because he'd had the throat problem, that and the pains in the chest whenever he tried to rehearse a song, hence the visits to the doc.

Shanksy was trying to protest that it was his round, making as if to get up off his seat and fumbling inside his jacket for his wallet, his usual anxious expression – drawn lips, creased brow – animated by his half-hearted appeal to Les to let him get this one. Bert shifted uncomfortably in his seat – he hadn't put his hand in his pocket so far tonight – and nodded along to *Mack the Knife.* Les held his hand up, closed his eyes as if he wouldn't hear of Shanksy getting it, pointed to his own chest and said 'My treat.'

He went to the bar. It was busy and, with the weight he was carrying, there was no way of shuffling around people, he had to more or less barge between them, although he always said 'Excuse me' as he did. This was the last round he was buying for them tonight, even if they were skint. It was hard with friends who were out of work who knew you'd come into a bit of money. He'd made the mistake of throwing a party right here in the function room when

➡

his premium bonds had come up six months ago. He'd even persuaded the Old Dear to let him bring her along the road in a taxi, although the pub wasn't more than a couple of hundred yards from the house. He wasn't going to have his mother staggering along the road at night with her zimmer frame. One of the first things he'd bought after the win was a motorized scooterette she could just stand on and press the button to move. It was just about as slow, but it saved her using her pins.

Everyone knew about the money and it was going fast. A good job he'd booked the flights to Memphis and the hotel when he did. It was going to be the experience of a lifetime and he was taking the Old Dear with him to see the Castle of the King.

'Same again, Les?' Julie the young barmaid was shouting over the bar to him just as the number finished and people applauded. He beamed at her.

'Thank you kindly miss, an have a li'l something for yo'self.' He was getting into the mood.

'Thanks, Les.'

It was worth it just to get the reward of that cute wee smile of hers. She was a looker all right. A student, he guessed, less than half his age – and weight – but you never knew how it took them. She liked him, that was for sure, but then everybody liked him. Of course, sometimes it was difficult to tell. That was the only thing about coming into the money. People treated you different, even your friends.

For a while there people kept asking him why he didn't spend some of the money on the gear and dress the part more, order the jumpsuit and the wig from the internet and go the whole hog. He kept on telling them why he wouldn't want to do that, but they just didn't get it. He wasn't trying to be a lookalike. Sometimes he did wear an open-neck shirt with the collar turned up, unbuttoned to show his chain and a bit of the old chest fur, but he drew the line there. Because apart from the fact that he didn't much fancy how he might look, all seventeen stone of him, crammed into a white spangled jumpsuit – even the King in his later years would look slim by comparison – it just

wasn't what he was trying to do. He wasn't an impersonator. It would be a kind of treason, a treason against the King. He just liked singing the songs, his voice maybe similar in pitch and timbre but he wasn't trying to mimic the King the way some of them did, shaking their legs and curling the top lip. He didn't have to mimic it, it came natural. As Bert had said to him one night after one of his best renditions of *Hound Dog*, there was a bit of the King in him. And maybe there was, in the way he moved, in the way he sang, in the way he combed his hair – what was left of it.

The clown in the suit was murdering *The Girl from Ipanima* by the time he got back to the table with the drinks – just the shorts, because Julie had volunteered to carry the pints over when they were poured. Shanksy and Bert barely nodded their thanks, seemingly caught up in *The Girl from Ipanima*, Shanksy tapping the heavily ringed fingers of one hand on the table, as if he was playing piano, Bert nodding his big, stupid, long-haired head in time, as if he was a seasoned aficionado of Latin American jazz. Les did the smoking gesture to them with a nod toward the beer garden and they got up to follow him out.

'It's a lovely evening, boys,' he heard himself say as he lit up, although the sun had gone and it was beginning to feel chilly.

'He's no bad, the Sinatra boy,' said Shanksy. 'He's getting better.'

'Aye,' Bert said, 'but he still murders *My Way* every time. He should leave that out.'

'Ach, it's one of those songs everybody murders,' he said, to show them he wasn't going to bad mouth the competition. He was big enough to be generous about it, and he was in a good mood. It would be easy to follow the guy, especially if he did finish off his set with *My Way*.

'What's it gonnae be the night then, Les – *Crying in the chapel*?' Shanksy asked.

'Naw, don't do ballads,' Bert said. 'Gie us *Blue Suede Shoes* or *Heartbreak Hotel*. That's the stuff.'

'And what is wrong with the ballads, I'd like to know?' he said, looking Bert meaningfully in the eye as if warning him not to get started.

'Nothing's *wrong* with the ballads, but you've not done *Hound Dog* for a long time.'

He didn't want to say that he'd been avoiding the up-tempo numbers because they took too much out of him these days. Plus he'd had the throat infection and he wasn't sure his voice would hold up.

MacRae had given him antibiotics for the throat, which is all he'd gone to him for in the first place, but he'd been more concerned about the chest pains and had insisted on doing all kinds of tests – he'd taken his blood pressure, taken blood and urine samples, and he'd interrogated him about his smoking, eating and drinking. When the tests had come back the doctor had called him back to the surgery to give him the bad news.

He'd pointed to a newspaper article he'd cut out and stuck up on a notice board on the surgery wall. The headline was: 'SCOTLAND – THE SICK MAN OF EUROPE'.

'That's you, Les. The Sick Man of Europe. I'm looking at him right now.'

The results were all bad. His cholesterol level was too high, the urine test indicated possible liver damage and the chest pains were caused by angina. His blood pressure was too high. The doctor went on to tell him he was going to have to give up smoking, cut down on the drinking, change his diet to cut out most of the meat and the dairy and the high-salt snacks and carry-outs and ready meals – the only pleasures he had in life apart from the singing – and there would be medication, pills he was going to have to take every day, and a spray for the angina.

He'd never really worried about his health – hadn't had a day in hospital in his life – although he knew he drank and smoked more than he should and over the years he'd piled on the pounds, but he'd never really thought he was in trouble because he'd never actually been ill.

'You do whatever you feel like,' Shanksy was saying. A blast of *My Way* blared out of the door as someone opened it.

'That'll be you on now,' Bert said.

They gave him the usual encouragements, but he wasn't really listening to them. The bees were getting angrier in his gut. As he went to down the last of his Morgan's, his arm spasmed and his right leg buckled at the same time. The glass flew out of his hand and smashed on the paving underfoot. He felt Shanksy and Bert steadying him with their hands.

'Fuck sake, Bert, get a grip!'

'You ok, man?'

He nodded and told them he was fine, it was just nerves, but he couldn't help noticing himself that the words were coming out slurred.

'You'll be ok. You'll be fine.'

And he was, once he was up on the raised dais in the corner of the pub that served as the stage. At least, the cheers and applause that greeted him made him feel fine, and as the opening bars of *Fever* came throbbing out of the PA he sensed the hush of anticipation around the bar – they'd never heard him do this number before. When it came to his cue and he started singing, the words were coming out wrong, slurred, but it didn't matter because they couldn't hear them, because he couldn't lift the mic to his mouth. His right leg was doing something strange now too, buckling and shaking, as if he was trying to jiggle it like Elvis, only this was a different kind of jiggle.

'On you go, Les!' someone shouted, but he couldn't. The mic slipped from his hand and hit the floor with a boom and a squeal of feedback, then there was confusion all around him and the barman was shouting 'Ok, Les?' in his ear and Shanksy and Bert were either side of him and manoeuvring him back to the table.

'What's the matter, Les?' Bert kept asking.

'He's had a turn,' he heard Shanksy say.

They sat him down but the leg wouldn't bend, and when he tried to pick up his pint and take a drink, his arm wouldn't do it. He was sweating, shaking, and when he tried to speak it came out all wrong. Then he threw up all over the table.

The paramedics injected him with something and he felt woozy but a lot better. In fact, he felt a whole lot better than he had for years. He felt like having a party. He tried to sit up, to move his arm and his leg, but the medics had strapped him down on the narrow bed and told him to relax. The doors were

➤➤

shut and the blue flashing light came on as the ambulance moved off, gaining speed, then the siren came on. He watched the streetlights flashing by through the windows in the roof of the ambulance. Tinted windows, like the windows of the black limousine he had already booked to take them from the hotel in Memphis to *Gracéland*. He began to sing: 'Fever in the morning, fever all through the night... Mmm hmm hmm hmm... Fever isn't such a new thing, fever started long time ago, everybody's got the fever, that is somethin you all know... Mmm hmm hmm hmm...What a lovely way to burn... Mmm hmm hmm hmm...what a lovely way to burn...'

Lilith
David Kinloch

Just a skelf, Dad said, just a chip off the...
But all I wanted to do was lie with Adam,
that big milk-toothed innocent;

yet when I got close, there was always a 'tut'
like a bone snapping, then Dad would appear.
He was always walking in the garden.

One night we lost the third leg and did it;
I gave as good as I got: good to be inside
him again, his utter equal.

Somehow Dad saw, up a tree;
or something. Said he'd try again.
I sit here now with owls,

with claws for feet, see nothing
in the blackness. But I hear her,
the new one, Eve, pottering about

on the other side. Adam doesn't seem to notice
how she is white while I am black;
but I can tell she's a curious bitch

and will do for them both.
Lilith can feel it in her bones.

Sarah
David Kinloch

Angels are good for a laugh; they come up
and they say: 'God will give you a child.'
I laugh and I say: 'I'm 90!'

They stand up indignant, unfold their wings:
'You can't laugh at God', they say,
I laugh and I say: 'I'm 90!'

They leave in a flap and I have a wee boy
called Isaac whose name means 'he laughs';
I laugh and I say: 'I'm 90,

but I'll be more for the lad needs a Mum.'
Life's been a laugh despite all the travel;
Abraham gave me to Pharaoh and then to Abimelech,

passing me off as his sister: even at 90
I'm pretty enough to tempt rulers to slit
my old husband's pendulous wattle.

At tea-time each night we laugh at our names:
'Mother and Father of multitudes';
I'm 90 and he's 99.

Ruth
David Kinloch

Ruth stands in the field and sees that it is hot and hard and dry,
feels she must not stop, say 'No' to Naomi,
who chafes her dead son's wife: 'Turn again,
go back; I've no more sons in my barren womb for you to marry'.

'No', Ruth says, and bends to gather up stray
barley heads that lie like individual bells,
notes lost as the harvest's hum is baled
in neighbours' barns. She works all day

careful of all that falls away,
then places her basket on the threshing floor:
at first she sees a simple glean of corn,
of grain, a glean of yellow thyme and wheat,

but as she stares a shoal of herring
weaves the wicker, dark glass glints,
brass shavings gleam, she sees
in part and finds her tongue.

'Where you go, I will go', she says to Naomi,
turns to the owner of the field,
proposes marriage, feels the kick of David
jump up the weir of generations,

the King who will love Jonathon
and the endless line of women who will give birth to God.

Orpah's Lament
Tracey S Rosenberg

Naomi told us: go home,
find new husbands in your own lands.
I have no more sons for you, only
a stranger's austere bowl.

I stretched into the sun; I laughed
once. Though the darkness streaked
behind us, I stood solid as the trees.
My hands were new pitchers
awaiting fresh water.
Naomi would need bear no burden
except the tiny blossoms I would bring her
every day, to remind her
that the joys of life
need not be eternal
so long as we bubble with praise.

Ruth crouched in darkness.
She cloaked her devotion in grief.
She pledged hard tears upon Naomi's neck.

When I kissed Naomi goodbye
flowers dropped from my hands.
On the barren ground
they drew their shamed petals
into closed, dry urns.

Bacchus and Ariadne

(After the painting by Titian)

Hugh McMillan

See Theseus is away then,
wis it the old
couldnae hélp it a Goddess télt me to routine?
Load o bull.
Better aff wi me,
weel kent roon here,
pimped ma own chariot,
bit showy but ken how tae party.
Dinnae be pit aff by wee Airchie,
goats' feet run in the family,
wee pun there.
Did you see my Uncle Davy
daein his snake dancing in the X-Factor?
Simon Cowell owes me, hen.
Stick wi me, see your name in lights,
make ye a star.

Diana and Actaeon

(After the painting by Titian)

Hugh McMillan

Whoa help, sorry wait a meenit there,
whit can I say
last thing ye expect in a wid
six lassies in the scud,
never mind hooseful o women at hame
used tae it, awfie scraps fur the hairdryer,
nice spot fur the alfresco noo the rain's gone hen,
cute wee chihuahua you've got there,
don't suppose you've seen ma dugs
looking fur them,
archery is it, yon's a sport,
Chinese were guid in the Olympics
but you look tasty,
didnae mean that the way it sounded,
what dye mean I've got the horn?
there's ma dugs noo.

Dionysian hangover
Stav Poleg

Let's shift some wine into water, turn the floor
into a paddling pool,
our living room
into a long night.
There's no moon left from last night's street-stargazing,
but we could fix something
tonight,
to press our dark sight into the glass,
manage our thoughts in night-water.
Come, lie next to me,
let's hold our own symposium.
*

The night's long as a foreign language,
the guests are filling up their plates,
and we're guests here too,
tonight,
where every glass is filled with last night's drunken moon
and makeshift light.
We start with Eros.
As if there would be any other way to start.
*

But there are all these stories.
How good we are with stories
or hanging on to them,
when we can't get drunk.
The half male-female bodies,
the lost equivalent of lust,
I like this one because it makes me think of
wooden toys, of a headless something,
that even when you glue it back together
it moves and cracks,
and falling still,
and still,
I'm not convinced
that this is it,
the way we've ended up with a half-shaped
something of a hole we may call
heart.
*

The flute-girl went away, the guests
are following her steps
behind the ice-glazed window glass.
It's getting late.
Let's gather all of our Socrates
of street-less stars,

the ones who stay awake like torches,
who even with their shoes on walking barefoot
on the icy road outside.
My dear husband, lover, holder
of my night-shift heart,
let's drink as if there's a Dionysian winter shaken in our glass,
until there's nothing shaken,
and winter is not winter it's the moon's deep breath
behind the thing we sometimes think
is glass.
*

Past midnight and I'm waiting sort-of sober
for Diotima to remind me
of the festivals the dancing the champagne,
how you could always find me trying
for your company or bed
or half-night something of a drunken sleep
instead.
*

If love is not beautiful but is the desire of beauty
If love is not wise but is the lover of wisdom
If love's lying in doorways, by roads, inside our rented-flat streets
If love dies and shoots into life and shoots into life
If love's a field and a hunter, a hunter
and a deer
Then I'll settle for love
tonight.

A Rough Guide To Grief
Anneliese Mackintosh

EVERYONE GRIEVES DIFFERENTLY. There is no right or wrong way to do it. Your grief is personal to you. It is unique.

However.

Unique is a very strong word, isn't it?

Actually, many people who grieve report remarkably similar experiences, and it can be really helpful to share such things.

What you'll find here are a few hints and tips on how to cope with your grief. A *rough guide* to grief, as it were. You may want to keep it somewhere handy over the coming weeks and months: on a bedside table, by the phone, or next to the kitchen knives, for instance, and refer to it when you are feeling bad.

You may also find it helpful to talk through the guide with your doctor, family and friends, or you may want to look at it in private, seething at its poor use of apostrophes and over-reliance on the passive voice. If the latter, try drawing moustaches on the people in the photographs to let off steam. Whatever works for you.

At First

To begin with, you may find you are in shock. Even though you cried when you saw the dead body, lying there so cold and yellow, with its downturned mouth and weary eyes, you may find it hard to believe that any of this has really happened.

You may surprise yourself by how strong you are as you walk away from the hospital, having kissed the corpse goodbye. As you cross the car park trying to remember where you left the bloody car, you may even find yourself joking about the fact that without your

loved one here to guide you, you could end up roaming this patch of concrete for all eternity, a ghost just like him.

When you try to eat that night, you may be astonished to discover how great your appetite is, and you may even try a glass of red wine, just a small one, and do a cheers in your loved one's honour, followed by an anecdote about the time he tried to warm up Frisky the lamb in the Aga when he was ill, and – oh, ho, the tears of laughter will stream down your face – how that poor little lamb jumped out of the scalding oven! You won't know where this anecdote came from. You haven't told that one for years. Everyone will laugh.

If you find you are not able to cry in the days following the death, make the most of this stoic strength, and spend your time:

- making funeral arrangements
- cancelling credit cards
- changing your loved one's Facebook status to 'dead'
- visiting the solicitor
- watching The Antiques Roadshow
- learning the implication of words like Estate and Beneficiary and Bequest
- using the 'F word' in public
- cleaning out the wardrobe of all your loved one's clothes, and setting fire to them at the bottom of the garden
- except for that one red shirt, you know the one, it still smells of him: that one you must keep forever

It is worth noting at this point how difficult the

funeral will be. But if you choose not to have one – well, good luck to you.

Once the shock of the person dying begins to subside, and this can take a very long time, you may find your emotions become stronger. You may feel 'up' one minute, and 'down' the next, as if you are on an emotional rollercoaster. You may start using a lot more metaphors and similes than you used to do. *I have a knot in the pit of my stomach. I'm drowning. It's as if someone has just ripped out my heart and is standing there in front of me, holding it up to my face, while the blood drips all over my feet.* Such phrases are not uncommon.

It is likely you will get ill shortly after your loved one has died. You tried to remain strong for so long, but now that your loved one is dead your immune system is at an all-time low. Though it may feel like something more serious, it will probably just be a cold or a prolonged bout of insomnia. It is not unheard of for the recently bereaved to shit themselves or get terrible acne or a verruca or two. If this happens, don't panic, just use the creams as your doctor advises.

Some of you may start to hallucinate. It may be the smell of his cigar smoke, or his hand brushing your cheek, or you may even see him sitting at the kitchen table, pulling faces behind your mother's back, trying to lighten the mood. Remember: people pay good money for visions such as this. So enjoy the trip.

Later
Grief takes time. That's worth repeating. Grief takes time.

In fact, you'll be amazed by how much of your time is taken by grief.

And just when you think you're almost done grieving, you'll find something sets you off again. The smell of Heinz tomato soup. Starman by David Bowie. Paper clips. The new series of Doctor Who. In such scenarios, don't despair. Your grief will come and go. You need to grieve, just as you need to live.

Do things that make you feel better. Go for a walk. See friends for tea. Make a scrapbook. Become completely obsessed with sex because it feels like 'the opposite of death'. Apply for bereavement counselling. Get very, very drunk and call the Samaritans and tell them you want to die. See friends for cake. Cut a cross into each of your thighs with a razor blade. Go swimming once the scars are healed.

You may find you need to talk about the person who has died over and over again. In truth, you may become a bit of a bore. At this point you will begin to discover who your real friends are. The real friends will come out to meet you when it's minus four degrees outside, and your eyes are bloodshot and hair a mess, and all you want to do is drink beer and talk about how much you wish your loved one had left you a message or a token of some sort to keep and remember him by.

Unfortunately, some of the people you thought were your friends will turn out to be your enemies. They will not forgive you when you forget to make a phone call, or when you get irritable over nothing, or when you have to cancel on them because you have just shit your pants but are too scared to admit it. Instead, they will write you nasty emails and call you rude names and block you on Twitter. Well let me tell you now: you don't need people like that. They can fuck right off.

Besides, if you want, you can make new friends. Make friends with people who have grieved. Make friends with people who are grieving. Make friends with people who are dying. Make friends with death. You will be very close in the end.

Eventually
Here's a phrase you'll hear a lot while you're grieving: it gets better.

Some of your 'friends who have grieved' will delight in telling you this as often as possible. The good news for you is that you will soon have earned the right to tell this to other people, those who are just starting out on their journey. It gets better, you will say, and you will pat them on the shoulder, and then go back to your flat and cut a swearword into your shin, which is a shame, because you thought you were over that, but never mind: it gets better.

Certain events are always going to be

➥

tricky. Birthdays, Christmas, Father's Day, the Anniversary Of His Death. This last one is a brand new date to add to your diary for the rest of time. On difficult days such as these, you may find it helps to be around family. You could even perform a ceremony to remember your loved one, perhaps lighting a candle or sending a Chinese lantern up into the sky, but try not to set fire to yourself, as this will make you feel worse.

Waking up will eventually become less painful, as will going to sleep. In due course, you may even find that you don't need to drink a whole bottle of wine or take two diazepams or have unprotected sex with a complete stranger to get you through such things. The world may start to feel a little more real again, and you may start to feel a little more like you.

One day you will realise that you haven't used a simile or a metaphor in over a week, and you will discover that you feel able to cope again. It is around this time that you will get a letter through from the bereavement counsellors saying you are finally at the top of the waiting list, and they are ready to schedule your initial consultation.

Go. I urge you. Even if you think you are done grieving. Even if the thought that you have been on that damn waiting list for the past eight months has you spitting feathers. Even if that is another metaphor, which makes you feel you are regressing. Go to that appointment.

When the old lady with the shawl asks you three A4 pages of difficult personal questions, be honest with her. How close were you to the person that died? Very. Have you finished grieving? No. Have you caused yourself any physical harm since the bereavement? Yes.

At the end of the consultation, with a face full of tears, ask to go to the toilet. The old lady will give you a key, which you must return to her in the busy reception area afterwards. 'I forgot to say,' she'll declare loudly as she takes the key, 'I hope you weren't cutting yourself in there.' Your cheeks will go red. 'Try to stop doing that, missy!' she'll call, waggling her finger as you dash towards the exit.

When you get home, put the letter from the bereavement counsellors in the bin. Call the Samaritans. Watch The Antiques Roadshow. Call the Samaritans.

As you lie in bed that night, unable to sleep, try as hard as you can to bring that nagging thought to the front of your mind. What is it? Almost got it. Ah yes, there it is: it happens to us all, sooner or later. And one day, if you ever allow anyone to love you enough, someone will grieve for you too. That's right. Even you.

Extract from the novel *Indecent Acts*

Nick Brooks

WE GET IN through the door home again and straight away sean comes up wanten a cuddel. He is sounden as though he has been greeten. Then he is of again like a maddy. Nothing bothers sean for too long it is all water of a ducks back to him. How was he i ask vincent and he says some thing effen nuisance he growls. Like always. I think that means his nephew was fine but i cant make out his expresshoun so im not sure. I am away out now he says and slings on his jacket. Him and bud give each other a wide berth. In fact they do not even speak any more at the moment. They just grunt. Wear are you away to vincent we have got chips i say. Do you not want any.

Bud is hoveren about in the kitchenet with sean. He is picken him up and slingen him backwards over his shoulder and is laughen. It gives me a mad feelen in my stomuck to see a blurry sean flyen up and down like that i worry bud will let him drop but he never does he is safe even if he dosent look it. The pokes of chips are all rapped up together on the work top and you can smell them all through the hall. I know vincent he will definitely be smellen them too.

Vincent i say.

What he says.

Chips i say. From the shop.

Vincent dosent say any thing but he comes in to the kitchenet after me. I know him the smell of the chips and the vin agar have reeled him in. He is not a great talker these days mind you was he ever i have to ask my selve. No.

Bud and vincent say nothing to each other but its like you can feel them pacen. There is a big wall of space between them. Even sean can feel it. I can tell be cause he is suddenly all quite when before he was laughen his head of.

Did any one call for me i ask vincent.

Effs sake he says its my mobile. Get your own.

I knew he would be like this about it but he has got a point. It is his phone. Even though i got him it for his christmas it was still a present. He is right to be fed up with me usen it. I should get one for my selve. Bud even says he will show me how to use it.

Effs sake vincent huffs.

I have given up tellen him of for his langwidge be cause its just to ask for bother. I can not say if hes been picken it up from bud or if he gets it of his pals but they are all talken like that these days.

Vincent i say im waiten for marie my sister to ring. Has she left any message.

He says no. He is acten like a fart would be too much trouble although i know for a fact that this is not the case. He can fart with the best of them. The best is bud of course. Well. At the very least they have got that in common.

Bud says hows the job hunten goen.

Vincent just grunts again.

Not found any thing yet bud says.

There is eff all round here unless your polish man vincent says.

Sean looks up at them both with big brown eyes and curly brown hair. I can see his face upturned in the kitchen light. He is eaten a chip that bud gave him as long as his head. I can make out him mashen it up his mouth openen

➡

and closen. It is so mad if you think about it.

Bud unwraps the chips properly and says weve got two special fish suppers and a special sosidge supper and a bag of special magic chips. Is that not right sean.

Sean laughs but it is a cagey one. He is obviously not sure about buds special magic.

What are you wanten vincent i say. We dident know if youd be wanten any thing so we got the sosidge just in case.

Aw bit of fish would be magic man vincent says. He has forgot to stay in a huff for now. Well that is okay there are two fillets in each bag so we have got plenty and plenty chips too.

Sosidge sean laughs.

Aw look bud says you have dropped your magic chip sean. There it is on the floor. No dont eat it. It is goen to be manky now. Here have a bit of sosidge wee man.

I say why dont we all sit at the table well the counter and eat. No body is much taken with this idea of mine although there isent any thing wrong with it that i can tell. Vincent says he will grab his and take of he has to see his pal so and so who ive never heard of before now. Bud says can we not have a seat in the liven room my leg is pure murder so it is. My toe. Only sean wants to sit here at the counter and that is mainly be cause he likes the high stool even though it isent safe for him hes inclined to fall of it frequently. He jigs about on it and then slides of back wards. Bud is always usually there to catch him though. The wee maddy does it deliberate. Of course my eyes bein what they are i ament any use to catch him. I am old for a grand mother round here it would seem. He would get kilt if he was left alone with you bud says. Of course its tiresome him and vincent thinken its a game. Even sean thinks its a game but it is no joke. They arent the one whos his grandmother. That is my job to worry about.

I hear vincent shout seeya then close the door behind him. He will be away half the night no doubt. I dont like to think what he might get up to but hes young theres no point in tryen to find out. They will never tell you the truth anyway why would they. I never did at their age.

When he was a boy well smaller than he is now vincent went of wanderen for a whole day until night and i can never get that day out of my head. He went up to the garscadden woods with his sister francis and they got lost. They were tryen to get lost deliberate and well they pretty much sucseeded. They dident come home for dinner like usual i had to go round all their pals houses and i got a lift of bobby in the street. It was a hot day june or july maybe. They were just playen they said when we caught up with them. They were comen down out of the woods with some older weans who run of. Bobby clouted the pair of them vincent and francis for worryen me and then i clouted them to. What were you up to i sayed but it was just to have some thing to get the fright of it out of me. What do you think you are playen at. Your tea is cold now there is nothing else.

I dident want to let bobby run us back. I dragged them up the road in front of me shouten. You should of let me know wear you were goen i told them. Your not to play in the woods francis you knew that. Vincent you knew that. He was greeten but francis kept still and quite as always. Maybe thats wear vincent gets it from.

We walked and walked and then i know i dont know wear we were even though it was right through the middel of drumchapel. Which way is it francis i asked which way is it vincent but they wouldent tell. They wouldent say any thing to me. They were leaden me round and round on a wild goose chase. I remember them gigglen. What are you gigglen for i sayed to them. It is not funny. I have been worried sick. Your mother has been worried sick.

Eventually bobby drives up in his car again. Eh you sure you dont want a lift gracie. Your away the wrong road. Have you not got your specs.

I wouldent get in though. I wanted them francis and vincent to take me back i wanted them to realise what they had done.

The kids are away on a head gracie. Get in. Come on get in the car. Come on gracie they will be all right now. You showed them.

So i did. I showed them.

I got in the car with bobby. Why havent you got your glasses on gracie bobby says. You need to start wearen them. This is not a good situashion getten lost in your own neighbour hood.

Bobby i sayed. Just take me home.

I want to lift sean up on the big stool but he might fall. Bud is away to put the telly on. He will play neil youngs powder finger on the guitar or ole dan tucker trad arr on the banjo and his food will get cold. He isent a great eater even though he thinks he is. He will only pick at his food and then forget about it. Probably he will roll up a joint for after when the kettle is on. Like i say he is of the heavy medicashoun for now. But he has been of before and gone back on again. He does not even need any encouradgement from any one least of all yours truly.

Bud is good on the banjo but better on the guitar. I can hear him pick it up and play with it then put it down again. Rememberen his dinner i would think.

I have a look in the fridge for some juice for sean and there are cans in it.

Whose are these cans i shout bud. Whose are they.

What bud shouts back. There not mine he says.

I take a can out and hold it up close to my eyes and try to see what it says but i dont recognise that word.

I show it to sean. What does this say sean. Whats this your grans got.

Moo juice he says laughen moo cow juice. But hes only copyen bud be cause he is at that stage.

So theres only one thing to do i open the can and take a sniff. It is definitely cider it is very appley smellen and i know bud will not drink that. It is vincents drink and i am mad hes put them in the fridge he knows better besides of him underage still. I pour the can down the sink but i leave the others. I want to keep on vincents good side. Plus now i will have to listen to buds i told you sos.

I take sean by the hand and lead him through to the telly room. I have got his poke of chips and sosidge but no fish be cause of the bones. Sure enough the telly is on just a big diferent coloured blur with a lot of shouten and yellen and cheeren. Some game show or other.

Bud is sayen will you look at these effen eejits what are they up to.

Grace what are they up to.

I dont know i tell bud ive no idea at all what there up to. You will have to tell me what there up to. Good i think. He has forgot about the cans debacle already. I sit sean down next to the coffee table and put his chips in front of him. Then i plump down in the arm chair too.

Your not eaten your chips grace bud says. They will get cold.

I can get some in a minute i say.

The gods honest truth is that i want my slippers.

Can you see them bud i ask.

He says hell look for them in a minute when he has finished rollen this wee number. He knows fine hes not to smoke it in here but sean is too wee to care just now. Mind you i said that about francis and look what happened with her. Vincent as well.

Sean honey i say. Sean can you see grans slippers.

He turns round and says some thing.

Grans slippers can you see them. There in here some wear.

Sean giggles and burbles and eats chips or maybe sosidge how would i know.

I guess i will have to find my own slippers.

It is a mad thing about this house that when you put some thing down it just dis apears never to be seen again. I am always the one putten things down in places wear they go so that i will know thats wear they have been put. It is totally logical. So how come i am the only one that ever seems to lose any thing i ask you. Why is that. Well. You know the answer to that one gracie. It is be cause you are blind as a bat. You can put things wear they go as much as you like they will still not be wear you put them be cause you cant see them even when theyre right in front of you. So why dont you put your glasses on grace. Why dont you wear them silly. Well maybe be cause then i would be abel to see all this mess about me. It would be plane as the nose on my face.

Besides my glasses are in port adventurer goen round and round the carousel with the lugidge. Its best not to think about canary isles and marie. It will only put me in a mood be cause i have got to go and dig out an old pear. The ones with the taped arm.

Lets put this telly rubbish of will we wee man bud says. He has the lights on dim but thats okay. I like it dim at home at night. I pick at my chips but have not got any appetite really. Sean is gigglen at buds antics. Silly wee man he calls him. Silly wee man and leans over to put the telly of. There is a big purpley blue ghost in my eyes from the light goen out.

Silly wee man sean says laughen.

Is the body away out bud says. That is his new name for vincent. Vincent has worked laboren now and again and is a big lad. He has mussels all over him. Some times his pals call him the body and bud laughs at that. He is jealous i think. His own body is in some state. He dosent have any mussels at all but just roles of podge on his belly.

He picks up the guitar and plays a few notes then starts tunen it. I hate tunen. Nobody who can play guitar is listenen to a word you say either when they play but even more when there tunen. The sound of the notes benden like that would drive you mad as well. It is never right for them bud especially. Flat he will say. Flat. Flat. Flat. Flat. Sharp now would you believe. Now flat again. Sharp. Effen sharp or flat on this effen lump of wood. If you have said any thing to him at all duren this time he wont take in any of it not one word. Did you hear what i just said you can ask him. What he will say.

Flat bud says. Flat. Flat. Flat. Sharp. Sharp. Flat. Jesus effen christ this thing is ready for the bucket. Or some new strings anyway. Life less so they are.

I think they sound okay i tell him. We could of got some if we dident bet today.

Bud is okay about it though. Its not your fault doll he says. There just old strings. I can boil them in the mean time.

Bud some times does this with old strings. They can last a bit longer that way for some reason.

Flat sean says. He is bangen his hand on the coffee table top. Flatflat he says all one word.

Bud starts playen a tune neil youngs powder finger like i told you. Lookout momma theres a white sail comen up the river and after that i cant remember the words. Our song he says isent that right wee man. Mummy and daddys special song. I ament so sure about that though. I like blondie sunday girl.

You shoulent say mummy and daddy around him it isent true i say.

I know i know bud says. Sorry. I dident mean it he says.

Its not fair to mix him up.

Aye well he is just a wee lad bud says. Hes not goen to remember it is he.

Its not worth arguwen about i say. Play us a tune.

Okay. What do you want to here.

What will we get bud to play i say to sean. He laughs and burbles.

Two littel boys sean. Lets get bud to play two littel boys. I sing two littel boys had two littel toys each had a wooden horse i wave my hands from side to side. Bud joins in singen and picken on the guitar then sean too. Then we are all singen me and bud and sean.

Sweet Tooth
Kirsten McKenzie

FOR A START, they'd turned the ice cream shop into the toilets. You could smell them as you walked down the old stone steps to the beach. The ice cream was being sold from a stall now, and it was Walls, which Lena hated. Maybe it had always been Walls. If it's got sugar in it, children will eat it, she supposed.

Lena wasn't a child anymore. Her sweet tooth had disappeared with age.

Her grandmother walked briskly in front of her, always two steps ahead, her wicker basket over her arm. She must have been the only person on the beach with a wicker basket. Everyone else had coolbags or coolboxes or plastic bags from Tesco. They had windbreaks and colourful towels and some even had little tents you could get changed in. But her grandmother always carried the same old wicker basket. She'd probably had it since the war.

Lena scanned the beach. It seemed stonier than before. She remembered a stony section and a sandy section, and looked for the sandy bit, but it had disappeared. The little river that ran down the middle of the beach and into the sea had a seaweed encrusted sewage pipe running its length. She couldn't remember that either.

'How about this, darling,' said her grandmother.

Lena looked around. They had only walked a few yards. In the distance she could see patches of white sand at the start of the coastal path, sheltered from the rocks at the side of the bay. The water there seemed more tranquil, greenish blue. She could see a large group of boys in bare chests and long shorts playing volleyball near the edge of the water.

'We could walk over there...' she began to say but then stopped herself. Her grandmother had put down the basket, and the colour had drained from her face. The energy that had brought her from the bus down the long suburban road to the beach had vanished.

'Those houses were never there before,' she had said, as though someone had carelessly abandoned them, like litter.

She helped her grandmother spread out the towel, an orange beach towel with a 1960s design of brown flowers, which they had sat on many times before, and then helped her to sit down on the ground.

'I've no stomach muscles since the operation,' her grandmother said.

Lena looked over to the rocks, where a small girl was looking into rockpools for crabs.

'That girl must be about the same age as you, last time you were here,' said her grandmother.

'I was a bit older than that I think,' she said. It was too fresh in her memory to be otherwise, surely.

'No, you were about that age,' her grandmother said, and she began to rustle in the plastic bags she had brought the food in.

Lena bit the papery loose skin of her lip as she looked out over the ocean. A group of older children ran past, laughing loudly. Their feet clipped the edge of the beach towel. Her grandmother straightened it.

'You'd think people would be more

➡➡

careful,' she said.

'They're just kids Grandma.'

'I'd like to know where their parents are.'

'Come here you little bastards,' a man shouted. He ran past them in his shorts, liquid fat rippling around his middle. She noticed now that the children were carrying a pair of trousers and running towards the sea.

'I think that might be the parent,' Lena said.

Her grandmother stared after him for a moment. 'People these days eat far too much,' she said.

There was a silence and Lena looked at the side of her grandmother's face, lips pursed tight, eyes narrowed against the stiffening wind coming in from the sea. Her matchstick legs stretched out from the thick sheepskin coat she wore, but she had slipped off her shoes, and her feet were bare and brown.

She smiled at Lena, and became young.

'Would you like to go for a paddle,' she said.

'Not just now, thank you,' said Lena.

'You used to paddle all day long.'

'It'll be cold,' Lena said.

'That's true,' said her grandmother. 'Look at those girls swimming there.'

Lena looked. The girls were in their early twenties. They were leaping in the shallows, splashing the water at their faces and screaming.

'They'll be blue when they come out,' said her grandmother.

Lena turned her head from the girls as a man in his late twenties walked past. He didn't even glance at her. She wished she had brought a bikini now. Maybe he would have looked at her if she had been wearing a bikini. She was the only young person on the beach still wearing jeans and t-shirt. But she was beginning to show. And not enough for it not to look like fat.

'You'll be missing Aaron, no doubt,' her grandmother said, watching her.

Lena looked away from the man, towards her swollen ankles. 'I can cope with being away from him for a few days.'

'Ah, but can he cope with being away from you? Nobody to wash his clothes or make his dinner.'

'Well, to be honest Grandma, he does that kind of thing himself.'

'He does?'

'I've got work to go to.' As though she needed a reason.

Her grandmother looked at her. 'Well, it's changed days. You count your blessings. Your grandfather wouldn't have washed a sock.'

'Well, I suppose he would have had to if nobody had done it for him.' Lena flicked the sand with her fingers.

'He would have just gone around in dirty socks.' Her grandmother's lips were pursed again.

Lena looked down at her phone. There was a message from Aaron. He would be asking if she'd got there OK, if she'd made the mammoth journey from the house to the bus to the beach. He liked to protect her more, now that she contained something of his. She clicked away from it. She would reply later. Nothing doing on Facebook. She flicked through her Twitter feed. There'd been an announcement about fines for dog fouling on beaches, someone was campaigning for an outdoor pool to be reopened, Sarah and Yacob were going for a boozy lunch. She scrolled further, then wondered what she was looking for. She put the phone back in her bag.

'Well then,' her grandmother said. 'We may as well eat. You need to keep your strength up.'

She took out the sandwiches and gave one to Lena. It had too much butter on it and the ham was watery. Lena did her best to eat it, but then buried it under the sand when her grandmother was busy rummaging in the basket for something else.

Her grandmother produced a fairy cake.

'These used to be your favourite,' she said. 'Do you remember?'

Lena remembered. She took it, smiling, still remembering. But it tasted like fish; she couldn't work out why. She stuffed it into her mouth and swallowed.

'Is there any water?' she asked.

Her grandmother shook her head. She didn't drink water. 'There's tea,' she said. 'Good idea, that'll warm us up.'

It was a mild day, but her grandmother still had her coat on, buttoned up to the neck. Her hand shook a little as she drank the tea. Lena drank hers too. She hadn't had any caffeine for six months, and it was good and hot. She watched the boys play volleyball in the distance. She watched the movement of the muscles beneath their shoulders. They looked fit, tanned. She decided that when she got home she would go to the gym. It was still safe, she thought. Better to start now than to leave it until afterwards, 'til she had no time left.

No time left. In her mind she began to plan a routine. 6am – get up. Quick breakfast, 6.30 leave for gym... she'd combine it with a diet... But then when the baby needed feeding, when would she fit that in? She'd have to rethink the whole thing. There was no time left.

'I know,' said her grandmother, and Lena turned to her. 'I know what will cheer us up. An ice cream.' She was struggling to her feet.

'No, really I...'

'I insist,' said her grandmother. 'My treat.'

So she watched the old lady hobble over the round cobbled stones of the beach, clutching her purse. Nothing wrong with the muscles of your fingers, Lena thought, like a baby gripping a rattle. She noticed how tiny her grandmother's body was now, the bones frail and receding. She thought about this as she fingered a strand of hair, and it came out in her hands. Her hair had been doing that. It was the hormones, apparently.

But her grandmother hobbled fast, and her white hair was freshly done, set so solid it didn't even move in the wind. When she came back her smile was bright, and Lena noticed with satisfaction that her lipstick was still intact, perfectly outlining the thin lips.

'Mmm,' said her grandmother, licking the ice cream. 'This is damn fine splendid, is it not?'

Lena watched her grandmother, completely absorbed in the ice cream. Your sweet tooth increased as you got older, she'd heard. She looked at her own ice cream, its pale plastic gleam. She wondered if she could get away with burying it in the sand, but her grandmother

was watching her, smiling, anticipating Lena's enjoyment of her gift.

She would have to do it, Lena thought, for her grandmother.

And she remembered her mother's words to her, when she found out. 'When you become a mother, Lena, life is full of sacrifices.'

There was no getting away from it, and so she took a tentative lick, and it didn't taste as much like plastic as she had expected it to. In fact, it was sweet and good, and so she gave herself up to it.

It was starting to rain. The people were leaving the beach. Lena made to get up.

'Sit down,' her grandmother said.

Lena sat down. Her grandmother reached into the bottom of her basket and pulled out two perfectly compressed raincoats. She handed one to Lena.

'Cagoules,' she said. Lena wondered if her grandmother was the last person in Britain to call them that.

'There,' said her grandmother. 'Spot of rain won't bother us.'

Lena put on her cagoule and finished her ice cream. It lay in her stomach with the baby and congealed into the gentle sickness that had become part of her.

The beach quietly emptied. The air had cooled, and smelled like leftover chips, with a vagueness of toilet. The children had gone, and the volleyball playing boys had gone, taking their muscles with them, and Lena listened as the rain pattered on her hood. Her grandmother poured her a second cup of tea, and she breathed in the steam. Her grandmother took hold of her arm and squeezed it tight.

'Might as well enjoy the peace while it lasts,' she said. 'One day you'll wake up and you'll be a grandmother.'

Lena closed her eyes and wondered if she should ever open them again.

'I'm not even a mother yet,' she said.

She felt her grandmother's hand on the rise of her stomach. 'It's not going to get any smaller, Lena.'

Lena's teeth ached from the cold ice cream;

➤➤

the pregnancy had made them more sensitive. She licked the granules of sugar from them and they dissolved in little sweet explosions on her tongue. She opened her eyes and leaned a little closer to her grandmother, as the waves grew louder on the rocks, and the tide crept stealthily up the beach towards them.

Making Chinstraps for Sombreros

Elaine Reid

DANA RESTS THE soles of her bare feet on the glove compartment. I take my right hand off the wheel and swat at her knees. She screws up her face. My eyes, Jan's nose, her own mouth. Her toes have left sweaty imprints on the leather. When she was born, she came out feet first, her heels tearing down my wife's insides. First thing I saw was those toes, bloody and blue. The midwife had joked that Dana was born thinking she was landing on solid ground. I couldn't go down on Jan for months without imagining those toes creeping into my mouth. Little kicks to the face that asked what the fuck was I doing to her mother. I told this to Jan once. She laughed and spread her legs and began prodding around down there. Fishing for toenail clippings was what she said.

Dana pulls at one of the corks sewn into the brim of the sombrero.

'Why have you still got that thing on?' Jan asks Dana from the back seat.

'I like it,' Dana says, winding the cork string around her finger.

'You'll get your hair all messed up under that thing if you keep it on the whole way back.'

'Why was Gramma so pissed about it?'

'Don't say pisssed, sweetie.'

'But I'm right, it really pissed her off. She said, don't be buying anything off that spic cart and spat on the ground right in front of Rosita.'

'Don't say spic, either. And her name wasn't Rosita.'

'But that's what Gramma called her.'

Jan raises her arms, upturning her palms but doesn't say anything. She turns to face the spread of food on the empty passenger seat. She's had it laid out since we left Pittsburgh. Plastic tubs with chicken legs, sweet potato wrapped in foil, dry matzo balls, bags of salted potato chips and thick slices of watermelon in saran wrap. All the windows are rolled down but the car still has that deli stink. Jan peels the skin off a chicken leg and chews it slowly. She wipes the grease on one of the paper napkins from the stack beside her. A little while back, just after the West Penn Turnpike, we stopped at a diner. The waitress stood with her mouth open as Jan filled her purse with the things. We left before she could clock the basket of condiment packets.

'You want any of this?' Jan asks me, looking down at the food.

'I'm good for now, maybe in a little while.'

Dana shifts around in the seat and crosses her legs. Pale and bare. Jan bought her a razor a couple of months back, taught her how to use it, but she always misses bits. At the tops of her knees, there are dark patches of black hair.

Dana bats at the corks, leaning backwards then forwards to avoid them hitting her forehead. The sombrero slips down her face, over her eyes.

'Stupid thing,' she says, pushing it back onto her head and pushing her hair behind her shoulders.

At a distance, the sandbags in the middle of the freeway look like roadkill. Cars pass by us like rushing water. If I could, I would pull Jersey closer. The backs of my legs are damp. I wipe a clean strip of sweat off my forehead. The windows let in a lazy stream of cool air. It doesn't help much.

'How long has Harry been Gramma's boyfriend?' Dana asks, sucking on a piece of watermelon.

I catch my wife's eyes in the rear view mirror. I'm trying to say, she's your mother, you take this one.

'Your Gramma's too old for boyfriends, Dana. Mr Bernolz is just a friend.'

'I'm not stupid, Mom. You don't need to treat me like I'm this dumb kid who doesn't know what's going on. Why else would he be there for Pesach? You don't call up all your friends. It's a time for family. Even Dad could tell you that.'

'Don't get smart,' I say.

'I'm not. I asked a real easy question. I just wanted to know how long Harry's been around since Gramp only died like, what, six months ago? Now here's fat Harry at Gramma's dinner table, stuffing his face with shitty Seder food.'

'I'm warning you,' Jan says.

'Rosita was right. Gramma is a nasty, old kike.'

'You shut your mouth,' I say.

Jan takes the chicken bones off the napkin covering her lap and places them into an empty tub. She presses hard on the corners of the lid, her head down for each of the four plastic clicks.

Nobody speaks for a little while after that. Dana puts her feet back on the glove compartment. I let her keep them there.

We're a few miles outside of Bethlehem when the low fuel light starts flashing. Albany County spits out gas stations so I don't worry. Jan offers to drive the rest of the way home but I tell her it's fine. I'd rather watch her in the back gnawing on sweet potatoes, sucking on her fingers. Dana's fallen asleep. Every so often her legs jerk and twitch. I tease her because she sleeps just like the dog. Mouth open, restless limbs.

There's a bite to the early evening air so I roll my window up. It clicks as the glass meets the rubber. Dana stirs and blinks. The sombrero's covering her face from forehead to nose. She pushes it back, balancing it on her crown.

'Welcome back, Bear,' I say to her.

She blinks again, swallows and lets out a soft bark.

'I'm gonna pull in at the next gas station. Another quarter tank should do us the rest of the way.'

Jan sits forward and brushes the crumbs off the front of her dress.

'Good idea,' she says, 'I could do with stretching my legs. Half of my body's fallen asleep.'

Dana reads the roads signs as they pass.

'Wait till we get a little further up, Dad,' she says.

'Why's that, kid?'

'I wanna go to the gas station opposite Salma's Dollar Mart so I can get yarn.'

'What are you wanting yarn for?' Jan asks her.

'For this,' Dana says, tapping on the sombrero, 'stupid thing won't sit right. I wanna make a strap for it so it stops falling off.'

Jan smiles and shakes her head.

'Why not,' I say, 'I could go a coffee and maybe something sweet to eat.'

'Gramma had doughnuts hidden in the back of the cupboard,' Dana says.

'Oh, she did not. Please stop talking like that about your Grandmother, Dana,' my wife replies. 'She spent a whole day clearing the place of chametz and you run around telling everyone she's hiding doughnuts. Gramma doesn't think you're too old for a spanking, you know.'

'Big round, glazed ones,' Dana laughs, 'and sugar ones and cream ones and chocolate ones all in a big box behind the spice jars. I bet they were fat Harry's.'

Jan rubs at her temples, pursing her lips.

'Watch your mouth,' I say, flicking Dana's knee.

'Why is this night different from all other nights?' Dana chants, 'because tonight we eat bitter herbs and behind the bitter herbs are Harry's stash of doughnuts.'

Jan reaches over and knocks the sombrero off Dana's head. The hair underneath is damp with sweat and sticking out at the ends. Dana scrapes it away from her face and picks the hat up. She pats around the brim, straightening the corks, before placing it back on her head.

'You've had that piece of shit on for too long,' Jan says.

Dana goes quiet. She's not used to hearing her mother curse.

I turn my blinker on right as we're coming into Plainfield. The front of the Dollar Mart is lit up by flashing, neon signs. Food. Liquor. Photocopying. Passport pictures. Dana sits forward and drums her fingernails on the dashboard. She's only just stopped biting them and calls that sound her pat on the back. I park by an empty pump at the gas station and shut the engine off. The three car doors open and close in quick succession.

'I'll do this,' Jan says, 'you two get your coffee and your yarn and whatever else.'

I nod and squeeze her elbow as she reaches for the pump. Dana walks beside me as we cross the parking lot.

'You're really keeping that thing on when we go in?' I ask her.

'Of course,' she says and pats the sombrero with an open palm.

It's almost wide as her shoulders. Dana walks a few paces in front of me. The corks bounce up and down as she moves.

'Those things make you look like you're out to hunt crocodiles not cook quesadillas,' I say, knocking one of the strings as I catch up with her at the entrance.

'I think Rosita knows how to make hats, Dad,' Dana says, scrunching up her face.

The signs hanging from the ceiling of the Dollar Mart sway back and forth in the manufactured breeze. Dana wanders off in search of yarn. I make my way over to the coffee machine. The cups and stirrers and packets of sugar lay next to it in a plastic tray. I fill a cup three quarters of the way up. Then a couple glugs of milk from the metal jug. I wonder how long it's been sitting out. I rip open two packets of brown sugar and mix them in. Across from the coffee machine is a display case of pastries, cakes and doughnuts. Glazed ones, cream ones, chocolate ones. All plucked

right out of Dana's head.

I catch up with her at the cash register with the coffee and two jam doughnuts. The cashier is looking her up and down, thin lips curling. Dana pays $2.20 for a ball of red yarn and a pack of safety pins.

'You think this'll work?' she asks me.

'I don't see why not.'

The badge pinned to the chest of the cashier tells me her name is Marlene. She has dyed blonde hair and her gut pops out from the gaps in between the buttons of her blouse. Dana pockets the change in her shorts.

'Buenos noches, Marlene,' I say as I hand her a dollar for the coffee and doughnuts.

Dana elbows me lightly in the stomach as we exit the store. I spill a bit of coffee on the ground.

The night air is calm and mild. Back at the car, Jan is sitting on the raised strip of concrete next to the pump. Her legs are stretched out, only crossing at the feet. I pass her my half drunk cup of coffee and she drains it. Dana walks to the opposite pump and sits down. She removes the plastic cover from the yarn.

Jan notices the doughnuts and smiles. She nods before I make the offer. I sit down next to her and pass over the biggest one, the one with most powdered sugar and a jam crust at the other end. With closed eyes, she bites down.

'Much better than fat Harry's,' she says quietly, her mouth full.

I put my arm around her.

Dana fusses with the yarn, tearing a long wind off with her teeth. From the pack of safety pins, she picks two big ones and fixes them to either side of the sombrero. Her tongue pokes out from the corner of her mouth. She pierces each end of the yarn and closes the fasteners around it. Jan watches Dana as she puts the sombrero back on, pulling the strap under her chin. It cuts a little tight. Dana dips her head forwards. Backwards. Tipped to the left. Then tipped to the right. It doesn't move.

Dana stands up slowly, taking big strides and walks towards us. The sombrero keeps still. She sits down next to her mother on the concrete. Jan tears a corner of doughnut and

➤

pops it straight into Dana's open mouth. She chews and laughs, spraying wet flecks of dough onto the ground.

'You ready to get going?' I ask.

Jan and Dana shake their heads. I take off my jacket and spread it across our legs like a blanket.

'We can sit here for a little while then.'

Hornet Eat Cicada
Simon Sylvester

THE MOMENTS OF waking are the strangest of the day. Breath hot on the pillow, dark shapes crawling in the corners of the room, and a little girl is somewhere shrieking. Opening eyes a breath of air, great clean lungfuls after days spent underwater. The smell of chlorine, leaves, a thousand drowning insects. In the back of my throat there are lemons, mandarins, pollen, dust. Sunlight filters through shutters into morning. Wake up. Get up.

The apartment in half-light, tiles of glossy terracotta, glass for a door. On the other side, children in swimming costumes yell and run, all their sounds and colours muted in the bubbled glass. A parent shrills at them to pipe down, Keeley, for christ's sake.

We've slept in. What day is it. Thursday. Tuesday. We're supposed to be touring the castle today. Or was it the ruins? I stretch out in bed, and decide I really don't care. I'm on holiday. We can do whatever we want.

I look across at the lunk of my husband. He always rises early, but he came to bed hours after me. Must have been blind drunk to still be sleeping. He'll have a reeking hangover. Serves him right for trying to keep up with the fat man who owned the taverna. He kept calling us his friends, his good friends, and fetching trays of sticky things to drink. I think he offered us a job. John was laughing and laughing, flirting with the waitresses. I laughed too, it was so funny.

I roll over to poke John's arm. It lolls, but doesn't move. He's clammy, the single sheet wound about him. He always kicks in his sleep. I always kick him back.

'McAffie, you lunk. Are you awake?'
My voice is a strange thing in the room.
'I suppose not. I'll make the coffee, then?'
John McAffie is asleep.
'Alright. I'll make the coffee.'

At the sink in the apartment, I rinse the mugs and fill the kettle. I change into my bikini costume, hopping one-footed on the floor. The kettle boils a tiny fury because the switch is broken. Pour two mugs and place one beside the bed for husband dearest, and take the other outside with my paperback. The day is warm already, the resort quietly busy. The pages crease. Slightly hungover, I finish a chapter in which the hard-drinking detective gets his first inklings of whodunit, then decide upon a swim.

'I'll be by the pool, husband.'

John is still unconscious. I think I hear him grunt, but he'll be out for hours. He gets crippled by his hangovers. He'll be sorry to miss such a lovely day, but every day is lovely out here. Children wearing water wings chase each other through the pool bar, splash yelling in the deep end, doggy paddle to the edge. The water is grand, warm enough to tarry, but cool enough for clearing cobwebs, and the bottom of the pool shines back a perfect blue. I climb out and rearrange my bikini, order an omelette and a salad, thick with feta cheese, order a gin and tonic, and settle in for a hard afternoon of sleuthing and sunbathing.

I don't remember sleeping, but I wake up just the same. Hot spots dance in my eyes in black and brown and orange, shifting wherever I look, and all Cyprus is in monochrome. I take

➤➤

off my sunglasses, squinting in the sun. Sweat films me. The pool bar is deserted. A wheeling hawk, sepia hills, the pine trees all husky and roasted. I've a headache pounding at me.

Dehydration.

A tiny crunching noise, a buzzing. Look around and see nothing, head reeling with heat. Crunching, sucking. The maddening noise John makes with boiled sweeties. There, there it is again. Crunch crunch crunch. It's close. I roll onto my front to investigate.

Beneath the lounger, a hornet dismembers a cicada. It's as thick as my finger, the upper body furred and red, the lower body shiny and stripy. It functions, it functions obscenely. The cicada is a shambles of membranes and wings and exoskeleton turned inside out. The hornet chews nonstop, gnaws the cicada into chunks. It pauses in a bustle, takes a piece all staggered and lurches upwards at me

up at me

at me and I shriek and cower as it sways up in a drunken loop, circles my head and gone, gone, skimming the rolled and watered lawn of the holiday apartments. Feeling slow and stupid, foolish, I look around to see who heard me scream. The resort is a ghost town. I look down at what's left of the cicada, sick to see a leg still twitch. Ants scatter and scurry on the patio. I will one towards the carcass. A scooter beeping somewhere, pulse thrumming, something kicking deep inside my hangover. My bikini is a clammy drape, damp and sticking to the skin. I pluck it from my chest, my groin.

I hear the hornet before I see it, buzzing and biting. It flies unerring back to the cicada, ducks in beneath the lounger. What a radar, red tinted in the eyes. It tears free another piece and hauls it away, and now I know it's coming back. I wait and watch it make another sortie. The head so alien, the mouth parts moving independently, antennae crooked and always hungry. Its awful body groping and flexing, the red fuzz pulsing. As it starts work on the next piece of the cicada, I lift my glass, sloshing with the melted ice. And carefully, slowly, deliberately, I lower it down and crush the hornet. As the glass touches the insect, there is a frantic buzz that vibrates up into my

palm. I can feel it in my wrist, but keep pushing downwards. There is resistance, but not much, and the hornet crunches flat. I push the glass until it clinks and grinds against the tiles, then lift it up. The hornet is completely squished on one side. The other is damaged, legs still flailing. The carapace is split wide, a brown smudge on the tile below. There are mechanical pieces falling out. It doesn't buzz, but moves in a stupor, a slow and smeary half-circle.

The first ant discovers the hornet. It scurries off, returns. More ants come. The hornet has stopped moving by the time the column arrives. They cover it entirely. They tear it into tiny chunks. They take it to their nest. I think of pieces of cicada festering in the hornet's den. Maybe there are eggs there, larvae, itching and grubbing in the dark. The ants are frantic, a twitching line like handwriting, stretching from my lounger to the lawn. Where the tiles meet the grass, they disappear. Eventually, they even take the wings, the whole wing held by three or four ants and taken like a sail. Tributaries traced within, bubbled glass, sunlight on the surface of a pool. The last ants sweep for crumbs. Fewer come back, and then they're gone. After an hour, the tiles are clear. I've watched the whole grim thing. The sun bakes. I'm raw and stupid.

I feel a little sick inside, but that's because I'm dehydrated. I've a headache. And where's my John, the slugabed. He's slept the whole day through. He'll have a stinker of a head. He'll be fuming to have missed a whole day. He wanted to see the castle. Or was it the ruins? It doesn't matter. We're on holiday. I walk back to our apartment. Passing the top end of the pool, there's a bright blue sticking plaster suspended in the water. There's a smell of chlorine, of pollen. Over the hedge, between pomegranate trees, a large woman dressed in black hangs sheets out to dry, scowls at me. They are blinding in late afternoon sun. It would be a good photo, but I'd never dare to take it.

It's almost evening. What a wasted day. The maid has been in, the sheets on my side primly smoothed and straightened, new neat towels in squares across the foot of the bed. The sheets over John are still caught wrinkled in his legs, his coffee untouched. Water from the fridge swigs like snow melt on Schiehallion. I plonk down beside him on the bed, crumple the nice clean sheets.

'Hello, husband dearest,' I tell him, then have to clear my throat and start again. 'You won't believe what I've just seen.'

Not a peep from him.

'I watched this hornet eat a cicada. Proper took it to pieces. It was gruesome.'

Not a dickie bird.

'C'mon, wake up, you. You've slept the whole day. I'll get you a sandwich. Are you not starving?'

I push him again, and he slumps, his arm slithers to the floor, knocks hard upon the terracotta tiles. I flinch at the sound of it, stupid seconds to see that John is colder than his coffee, cold as snow melt. In moments I might come to remember like photographs, his chest seems shrunken, hollow, smashed. The limbs are disconnected from his torso. I think of the fat man, the waitresses.

I saw a hornet eat a cicada, saw it function. I saw a line of ants. And somewhere in the resort, a little girl starts shrieking.

Mechanics' Arms
Audrey Henderson

The smell of beer and cigarette smoke poured
onto the pavement through a stained extractor fan
with waves of laughter from the Mechanics' Arms.
Wet fluorescent squares lit the macadam, two stops
before the terminus where a slag heap once stood
behind some un-explained donkeys. To the south
lay industrial countryside, streets without trees among
pit heads and turnip fields, northwards down the spur
lies Edinburgh, its monuments, spires, crags, alleys
and rivulets of puke. No one else will tell you about
the Mechanics' Arms, loud and smoky by the Kirk yard.

On the cusp of greatness
Mark Waddell

one evening
I was standing
at the bar
and blurted out
how I was
on the cusp of greatness

everyone
raised their drinks
and shouted
me too.

The State of Scottish Football

Graham Fulton

In the pub with everyone talking about
the state of Scottish football
and the state of Glasgow Rangers
and the state of everything
that's ever been
in the illustrious history of mankind,
and this bloke
who used to work
in the same place we used to work
comes up
and gets a bit demented
about the state of Scottish football
and the state of the election in Libya
and the state of the greenhouse effect
and how
he's not going to renew
the season ticket he's renewed
for the past five hundred years
when John Knox had just been signed
as the new centre forward for Rangers.
And sweeps his arm
to amplify his commitment, topples
my handy-size-slightly-
effeminate bottle of tonic water for one
which empties onto the table
and spills onto the floor
and sparkles onto
the cabernet sauvignon-coloured cushion
between my legs
but doesn't stain me at all
because of my lightning-fast reflexes
which is a miraculous outcome
in this cynical age of disbelief
and doesn't even say he's sorry.

Landlocked
Simon Jackson

They measure their evening's progress
by the high tide lines around their pints,
talking of unmapped oceans they'll never know

till shaking like dinghies caught in a tempest,
above them the moon a port-hole to clear skies,
they map out their rolling passage home,

unaware that these streets they know so well
are the only straits where monsters still dwell.

Halloween Skite

William Bonar

Through coal stour
smirr and smoor
particulate
in heidlicht beams
a sleekit

manta ray
man-car jouks
the deil's elbow,
sooks kist-cauld braith
hauds the road.

Trail

Theresa Muñoz

maybe there is a way to see you always

not only in the rooms we enter
linger   breathe in silent sync   and exit

but as a way of tracking   sensing

your location: your feet along Princes St
past the blocks of art galleries stamping up the Playfair steps

and mine in the library
on George Forth Bridge
                        tapping the same beats

maybe we could use that shirt   the one I bought you
a map of Edinburgh on burgundy cloth

I'd slip it on while you were out   you'd be the red dot
running down my shoulders

                  my inside elbow
                                    to my pulse

I'm sending you a letter
Stav Poleg

Inside, I put a full-size blue guitar, a slice of sea (so you
could shake it in a glass over the Mediterranean coast),
a saxophone I borrowed from a local busker because
I know you'd like her work, all my air-miles, so you could
come and visit me, a crow, crushed ice, a glass
of pink champagne, just open carefully, mid-August
Edinburgh (a bunch of slightly boozed-up actors, a box
of unpredicted rain). I marked: fragile, FRAGILE, all over
it. Let me know when it lands or crashes into your hands.

Outer Circle
Claire Quigley

I'm your foreign correspondent from the one place
that you cannot go, for all your fearless travelling.
A city where the angels stand, their faces worn

from looking up into the rain. Where redstone walls
become illuminated manuscripts, alight with crumpled
symbols from an empty Book of Hours. You want me

to explain the customs to you, but the words
can't be translated into any living tongue.
The citizens have felt the shell-fire of desire

to leave this place, the myriad of ways that it can
take you. Yet the tickets out you send come back
untouched. Each building rots around a room

where someone waits, the door nailed shut;
the streets spin out without a destination;
this is a city under an empty sky.

To a train ticket
A C Clarke

Orange and cream
vade mecum
no bigger than a Garibaldi biscuit
mere card
not even the dignity
of plastic
you open doors
to a future
miles from the present.

Pointless
like all forgotten currencies
when your time's up
until then potent
as once were
cowrie shells
feathers
a signature
on a letter of conduct.

I've often pondered
the weight of your meaning
as I delve
for your three-inch reassurance
in the depths
of bag or pocket
proffer you
to be clipped or scrawled
holding five hundred miles
pinched between finger and thumb.

the refreshment trolley is now closed

Iain Matheson

a man entices a child
to look at the sea
there is no sea

a girl shows a duck to
an empty seat and takes
its photograph

the girl's name is Holly
she is on the train
cows race past

a second man rattles a newspaper
a second girl reading
aloud from Puzzles Compendium

people repeat in their own
voice *there is a délay due*
to a train on the line

the child bellows Sea! Sea!
there is no sea
a tannoy confides

that sandwiches handcrafted
by the on-train chef will shortly
pass through the carriage

a third man struggling with zips
a family playing snap
a nun sending texts

The Heart of a Pig
Vicki Jarrett

HAMID HAD ONE of the big knives and was holding it out towards me. 'Come here,' he said.

His face, as usual, was unreadable. My boss has a sour set to his mouth and narrow eyes that glitter with suppressed emotion. That's his normal, everyday look. I do my best to avoid finding out exactly which emotions he's suppressing. Behind him there was something frying on the griddle, strips of something dark sending up twisted spouts of metallic-smelling smoke.

'Try this.' He made a gesture with the knife which I realised was supposed to be reassuring. There was a sliver of cooked meat balanced on the flat of the blade.

I breathed out. 'What is it?'

Hamid often cooks up a little something private on the back grill. Eats it through the back with some watery yoghurt drink he keeps in the fridge. He'd never touch a donner; says he doesn't like Scottish food.

'Just try it.' He held the knife out towards me, nodding.

'No. Thanks. You're alright.' I didn't move.

He almost smiled, and tilted his head. 'Come on. I'm not trying to poison you.'

The meat behind him on the griddle shrank and hissed. The shop was empty. I looked at the door and wished for a customer, or for Ali to come back from his break but the door stayed closed. I walked towards Hamid. I'm no longer vegetarian but that doesn't make me keen to experiment with unidentified bits of animal. But on balance I reckoned it'd be more dangerous to refuse. I asked myself, how bad could it be?

Col snorts with laughter when I get to this point in the story. So far he's hardly been listening. It's 2am and he's stretched out flat on the sofa, watching something on cable that involves a lot of pink flesh and squealing. I try not to focus on it.

'Worst case scenario?' he says.

I shrug. Typical Col to think it's up to him to supply the ending to my story.

'It's dog, or cat or something,' he says. 'No, hang on, that's the Chinese, isn't it? What are that pair you work with?'

'They're from Iran.'

Ali and Hamid are brothers, although you'd never guess it to look at them. Ali came over when he was a kid, went to school here, calls me *hen* and *pêt* and laughs easily. Apart from his silky black hair and dark eyes, he's hardly exotic. Hamid was already middle-aged when he arrived a year or so ago. Since then a wiry white tuft has appeared at his hairline and the lines around his mouth have deepened. He describes himself as Persian, doesn't talk much but when he does, his English though accented is faultless.

'Well then.'

'Well what?'

'You've no idea what he might be cooking up for you.'

'I do know.'

Col acts like I haven't spoken, distracted by a more interesting thought of his own. 'Oh! No. *Worst* case is it's human flesh.' He grins and nods, leans forward and puts on a pantomime scary whisper. 'He's killed someone and has the body stashed in the cellar and is using you to dispose of the evidence. Piece. By. Piece.'

'Don't be ridiculous.' Col watches too much telly. He thinks everything's some kind of show.

'It's not just anyone, either.' He stares at me and widens his eyes in a meaningful look, 'it's his brother.'

I sigh. Why did I even bother trying to tell Col about this? Why do I bother trying to tell him anything? 'Ali was on his break. He came back after.'

'Oh right.' Col is deflated but that lasts about a second till he comes up with another theory. 'Okay then. Even better. It's his wife.'

'He's not married.'

Col grins at me like we're playing some kind of a game and I'm giving him clues to solve. Listening is not one of his strong points.

'His mother!' He bounces on the sofa, sitting up now, pleased with himself. 'Yeah. Like Omar Bates or something. Iranian Psycho.' He sniggers and swills a mouthful of beer from the bottle in his hand.

'You're being childish.' Col isn't insulted, isn't listening anyway. I realise that being childish *is* one of his strong points and wonder if it could really be described as such. I used to see it as playful and imaginative, liked his sense of fun. Now that feeling is being pushed out and something else is rushing in to fill up the empty space. I look at him, still in the same place I left him when I went to work, one hand down the front of his stained tracky bottoms scratching his balls. I'm tired. My feet ache and I smell like kebabs. Maybe I'm hungry too. There's a half-eaten sausage roll on the table but I don't fancy it although I've been eating meat again for some months, having slipped out of vegetarianism like an inconvenient skin. One of many I seem to have shed along the way.

'Oh god. No.' He slams the bottle down on the cluttered coffee table, wipes some foam from his lips. 'I've got it! It's his own flesh. He's cut it out of his thigh or his chest or something and he's bleeding under his clothes the whole time he's talking to you. Yeah.' Col lies back down and sighs, pleased he's solved my story to everyone's satisfaction. It's like I'm not even in the room any more. I'm starting to wish I wasn't and am just getting up to leave when Col starts laughing and chokes on his beer, waving the bottle at the TV. Eventually he spits out, 'It's the only way he can get his meat into your mouth!' before dissolving into helpless snorting giggles. I close my eyes and listen to the sound he's making merge with the muffled grunts from the television.

So weighing it all up, I took the piece of meat off the edge of the knife with my fingers.

'Careful. Very sharp knife.'

It was about the size and shape of a strip of gum and that's what I focused on as I popped it into my mouth and chewed. It was rich and dense but not fibrous, like superconcentrated pate. It wasn't so bad. Just meat. I swallowed and tried a smile.

'You going to tell me what it is now?'

'Did you like it?' Hamid was staring at me, his eyes greedy, looking me up and down like he expected something to happen, some kind of transformation.

I shrug. 'It was okay. What was it?'

'Heart.'

Generally I try not to guess at what's going on behind Hamid's eyes but right then I'd say it was a type of triumph, mixed with disgust.

'Really?' I ran my tongue over my teeth, picking up grains of ferric meaty residue.

'Yes.' He poked the remaining pieces on the griddle, scooped another up with the knife and offered it to me.

'From what? What animal?'

He was looking at the meat, avoiding eye contact now. 'Pig,' he said, spitting out the single syllable like it might contaminate his mouth if he let it linger.

We don't sell anything with pork in it. The kebabs are lamb or chicken, sometimes beef. Donner meat, a complete mystery to me before this job, is minced lamb, threaded in fat rounds over a metal rod and shaped into a tower of packed meat, cooked by rotating it in front of an upright grill. The absence of pork isn't a religious thing. Hamid and Ali aren't Muslim, although most people assume they are. Not being Muslim was the main reason their family left Iran in the first place, their choice of religion not being popular with the authorities. Technically, they could eat pork if they wanted, they just prefer not to. It's complicated. Ali explained it to me once but I didn't take in all the details.

'No thanks.' I try to keep my tone light, wondering all the same where Hamid got a pig's heart from. And why. 'I'm not really hungry. Why don't you have it?'

'I can't eat that.'

'Why not?' I thought that as long as we concentrated on the reasons he wasn't eating it then maybe we could avoid discussing why he wanted me to.

'If I eat this meat,' he hesitated, put the knife down. 'If a *man* puts this meat into *his* body, the blood from it will mix with his own blood and when it travels to his heart it will transform his heart to the heart of a pig.'

'What about a woman?'

He looked at me, his eyes glassy.

'You said if a man puts this meat into his body. What happens to a woman?'

He shrugged, dismissive, like it hardly mattered in that case.

'Where did you get it from?'

'Kevin. The butcher. When I buy the shop meat from him, sometimes he gives me things he has spare. Today it was this. I can't eat it. But I thought, maybe you...' He trailed off as if unsure himself what he thought, as if the urge to take and cook this thing for me, to have me consume it, was something beyond his conscious control.

At that moment a customer pushed through the door, making the bell ring. Hamid flicked the remaining blackened scraps of meat from the grill into a paper wrapper and dropped it into the bin.

The rest of the evening went by with a constant stream of customers. Ali came back from his break and the three of us worked steadily, the column of donner meat reducing as slice after slice was shaved off and deposited in dozens of pitta breads, topped with salad and chilli sauce. By the end of the night it was shaved down to the metal spit.

Tidying up in the cellar after closing time with Hamid, the small space felt claustrophobic.

He asked when me and Col were getting married.

'Not right now.'

'But you plan to marry?'

I glanced over at him. He was standing gazing upwards, longingly through the hatch of the cellar, back into the bright light of the shop as if looking at sunshine from behind prison bars.

He sighed and shook his head. 'Women here...' His face was sad and he looked at me with disappointment, his eyes asking how I could have let him down so badly.

'People live together. It's normal,' I told him, bristling a little despite myself. 'Gives them a chance to find out if they get on before having kids and all that. Even then, some couples never get married. It's no big deal.'

Hamid looked at me pityingly like I'd just told him I believed the earth was flat and he was about to put me right. He reached one hand up towards the light. 'In my country, a woman is like a flower.'

I concentrated on gathering up some onions that had spilled out of a torn sack. I cast around for something, maybe some tape, to repair the rip and realised Hamid was looking at me, expecting a response.

'Oh?' The cellar walls contracted and I strained to hear the sound of Ali moving around upstairs, cleaning down the grills and mopping the floor.

'Once she is plucked,' Hamid made a mid-air snatching motion with his outstretched hand and stared into my eyes, 'she dies.' He shrugged and turned away sorrowfully, started moving boxes around.

I wanted to ask him what he meant by that, to tell him to go and pluck himself, but I know enough to be sure it's never a good idea to provoke a man you can't get away from. My face grew hot. I felt my blood spewing through my veins, the pig blood working its way deeper in toward my centre, changing me, pushing fast in and out of my heart, the muscle swelling, coarsening, becoming an animal thing.

I undress and look at myself in the bedroom mirror. White flesh, raw on my bones. I drag an old t-shirt over my head and slide under the sheets. The sweaty soundtrack from the living room oozes through the crack in the door, punctuated by the tight pop of released air when Col opens another beer. The creak of the couch as he settles back down.

I can't sleep. The clock says 3.30am. I've been lying in bed for an hour, listening to the roar of blood in my ears. The blind pumping machinery of my heart, dense and dark, convulsing, the blood forced this way then that, under pressure from both sides.

I need to be moving. I throw off the sheets and pull my clothes back on, deciding to go for a walk. It's summer so there's only an hour or so before dawn. In the living room, Col is sprawled with his mouth open, snoring.

Outside the sky is already lightening to the colour of a fading bruise, the air hanging cool and still, passive in the path of the coming day. I walk for maybe an hour through deserted streets, silent but for the drum of a thousand beating muscles behind stone walls, on and on, working while their owners sleep. I keep walking, my steps falling into rhythm with them, the world throbbing hypnotically under my feet.

There's an angry squeal of rubber on tarmac, followed by the blast of a car horn and I realise I'm in the middle of the road. I raise my hands in apology to the driver. He's right up against his windscreen shouting, spit spraying from his mouth onto the glass. I back away, keeping an eye on him just in case he's thinking about getting out of his car. And that's when I make the same mistake again, jumping back onto the traffic island just in time. The truck stops right next to me, blocking my path and lets out a furious hiss like a red hot pan dropped into water.

The truck is huge with slatted sides. It smells of shit and something worse. The driver leans out of his window. 'Wake up doll. I nearly had you there!'

I mutter my apologies and he disappears back inside.

From the body of the truck comes the scrape of shuffling feet. Through a gap in the side I see movement in the dark and suddenly a snout is pressed to the gap, wet and trembling, desperately snuffling the free air. Asking: *are we here? Is this the place?* It's so close I could touch it, this breathing, questioning thing, this life. The truck rumbles and shakes as the driver throws it back into gear. The snout disappears back into the gloom but in its place comes an eye the colour of blood, framed by white eyelashes and creased pink skin. The pig looks right at me. It sees me and it knows. It knows I don't have the answer either.

The truck moves away, huffing exhaust fumes into the early morning air.

I know the slaughterhouse is nearby. Before long that heart will be silenced. The taste of it rises to my mouth like betrayal. I walk in the opposite direction, cross the road and sink down onto the low wall outside a supermarket. Delivery vans trundle into the car park, past a trough of parched geraniums and round to the back doors. The weight in my chest grows heavier and I think of the pig, freed from the truck, skidding unsteadily down the ramp to the holding pens, blinded by the sudden light that lies between.

A Promise
Philip Miller

I SLEPT WITH my sister that night.

She kicked me and said I was breathing too loudly. Emma wore socks in bed too, because it was cold. That's why I joined her: the sofa was cold. Even with the fire still burning. She slept after a while. But I lay there, staring at the ceiling, at the dark wooden beams set in the white ceiling. It was a big bedroom. It was too quiet there. I was not used to such quiet. Or trees shaking, the letter box slapping in the wind, cars away over the hill, the sea roaring by the beach.

Auntie Margaret gave us hot milk. Its skin was thick. As Auntie stoked the fire, I ran my finger around the inside of the mug. The milk came off in my hand, and hung from my finger, pale and thin. Like I was melting.

Auntie Margaret told me to drink the milk and get my head down. She sat on the sofa and stroked my hair. I think she thought this would help get me to sleep. She bent over and kissed my head and said everything would be OK. She turned off the lights and she walked up the stairs to bed. I heard her checking on my sister.

'Everything will be OK,' she said.

Dad was missing for a day before they found him.

I was stacking shelves in the supermarket. I didn't know he was gone. I was putting dog food up on the shelves. Wiping the shelves clean, then putting the cans on top of each other. They fitted perfectly. Auntie came into the store. I could hear her shoes. She spoke to Sandra on the checkout. She came over and told me.

'Your father is missing,' she said.

I said: 'What do you mean.'

She opened her mouth.

'He's at home,' I said.

No, she said. 'He is missing. I could do with some help.'

A few minutes later, as I slashed open a new cardboard box with my Stanley knife, the manager came up to me. Dracula, we called her. She had a pale face and severe black hair.

She said: 'James, I hear you might need to get away early tonight.'

'No it's fine, it will wait,' I said, slashing at the box. I didn't look at her.

'No, it's OK James, finish this section and you can go,' she said.

I left early and went to a pay phone and called my sister. She answered straight away. The telephone ate up my coins.

She didn't know where Dad was. She had tried The Golden Lion. They hadn't seen him. He wasn't at the Green Bridge, or the County Bridge. She had gone to Old John's house but he was not there. Old John was drunk anyway.

Auntie was looking for him all over town, she said. Auntie was frantic, she said.

Shall we call Mum? my sister said.

I said no.

They found his body downstream, hung up in low branches. The river had been high with heavy rain from the hills. It had flooded in parts: farmers had lost sheep in the storm. Dad was hung over a branch. He was fully clothed, they said, when they found him.

There was a funeral. We sat in the front

row, me and Emma. The vicar said something but I didn't hear. Auntie and her friends had done the flowers: lilacs and lilies.

People sat in their black clothes and me and Emma faced the empty coffin: they couldn't fit Dad's body in. It was too bloated.

As we left the church, people shook my hand. Like congratulations. At the wake, Old John gave me a brandy. I fell asleep on the stairs.

Auntie said we needed a holiday.

She owned a place on the coast, a quiet place.

I said: 'I know, you took Dad there a few times.'

She said yes and looked away and started crying again. She just cried, and made no noise. But she cried more than Emma or I did.

She cried far too much. Emma held her hand.

'Its going to be OK,' Emma said to Auntie.

The first day there we walked down to the beach. She and Emma walked arm in arm and I walked behind. Auntie was wearing a furry black hat. My sister had borrowed her black scarf. Rain clouds covered the sky. The sea did not move.

We stopped at the jetty and looked out at the dead sea and the grey sky.

'I'm glad he found peace at last,' Auntie said.

Oh fuck off I thought.

'Oh fuck off,' I said.

Emma looked at me and Auntie sighed and said nothing. I thought she was going to cry again: she did that thing with her mouth. But she didn't. She tried to ruffle my hair. But I walked up the jetty.

At the end, a rope was wrapped around a large metal stud. I sat down on the wet wooden jetty and felt the rain seep into my jeans. I heard footsteps behind me and it was Emma. She sat down too.

'Why do you have to be like that, Jim,' Emma said.

'You can fuck off too,' I said.

She sat there for a while and then stood up.

'We're going to go back and make some bacon and some waffles.'

I shrugged and looked out at the grey solid sea. It didn't seem to move. It wasn't even water. It was all mud, from coast to coast.

I looked at the solid sea for a while. And when I turned around I could see them walking back up the hill to the cottage.

I got cold. Light was fading. I walked back after them.

As I got to the cottage I began to feel sick.

I went to the ditch beside the road and vomit suddenly poured from my throat. My body shook. Sick came from my nose, and burned my throat. I felt lumps slide over my tongue and through my teeth. My stomach ached and my back hurt. That sick smell covered me. Like fire. I was just standing there, bent over. The vomit steamed.

It began to rain.

I walked into the kitchen of the cottage and Emma and Auntie were eating waffles and listening to the rain on the windows.

Auntie looked at me and sat there for a while. Then she stood up and told me to change out of my clothes.

I came down from the bedroom and she had made me tea.

As I drank it Emma stared at me.

'You can fuck off too,' she mouthed at me, silently.

We had sat on the bridge and watched the river flow underneath us. Dad smoked and asked me how school was going. I said fine. He said that I needed to knuckle down.

He said I should knuckle down and go to college, leave the town behind and find a proper life.

'There's life out there,' he said.

I looked at him. His nose was red in the cold.

He was a good looking old guy. Auntie had said that to me once.

I sat beside him on the bridge.

'Don't do what I did,' he said to me.

I said nothing.

'Do you still want to be a writer?' he said and I said uh-huh and shrugged my shoulders.

'It's a lonely life,' he said and looked at me.

➣➙

I shrugged again.

Later, I got my coat and went out the back door.

It was a clear night. Stars were out.

We sat by the river and drank cider and talked.

Me and Martin, Paul and Jen. Jen was shivering.

'There's a witch in this water,' I said, watching the black tide glide by.

Everyone laughed.

'Oh fuck off, Jim,' Martin said, and pushed at my head.

'You and your stories,' Jen said.

But I had read about it: there was even an old song about it, the music teacher had said.

This woman had been drowned as a witch hundreds of years ago. And her spirit haunted the whole river. She would suck people in. She was a tempter: a beautiful girl. She would sit beside the river. She would sit there, and look like she was up for some fun.

Then you would go up to her and she would wrap you in her long green hair. Her black eyes. Her red nails. You could hear her singing in the waterfalls, her laughter in the thunder of the rapids downstream. The whole river was her home, the water was her window, the reeds her hair, the shuffling sands her voice: the souls of men her food and drink.

I told this to Martin and Paul and Jen and they drank more cider.

'It's true,' I said. 'There's even a song about it.'

The teacher even showed me the song about the witch in an old songbook.

I saw it there in black and white. I believed him.

'Do you want to live with your mother,' Auntie said to me as I watched the football. It was still raining. Emma was having a bath with Auntie's bath salts.

'Do I fuck,' I said.

I stared at the TV.

Auntie said she would make more tea. I said I didn't want to live with anyone.

She came over with two cups and then touched my hand.

'We will have to sort something out,' she said to me. She lowered her voice. Like she was my pal. Like when she tried to convince my Dad to do something. I stared at the TV and wondered what it was like to kiss her.

'We'll talk about this tomorrow,' she said. 'You relax and watch the football. I'll go and see how Emma is.'

Emma was upset again. She had been talking about the note.

They found the note when they were going through his bedroom.

Emma found it. On the floor under his desk.

We were in the back of the car, under blankets and duvets, driving to the cottage, when she told me about it.

We could see Auntie's head, dark in the night. The dashboard of the car glowed orange. The car noise filled our ears. Trees and telegraph poles went past, black slits in the night.

I asked her what the note had said.

'Too much pain,' she said.

I said: was that it?

She nodded.

Too much pain.

I was lying on the sofa and staring at the fire as it crumbled and died.

Little blue flames of gas burst from the cheap coke. I saw the heat and the ash and I moved to the fire and warmed my hands.

I heard the gas escaping from the coal, it squeaked.

Outside the wind rose and I could hear the breakers on the beach.

I was cold. I got my duvet and slowly walked up the stairs. I opened the door to the bedroom and saw Emma lying awake in the bed. Her eyes glinted.

'Get in,' she said quietly.

I got in to the bed and we held each other for a long time. She smelled of soap.

She said I was breathing too heavily. I said, 'fuck off.'

She giggled.

She held me. Then she said, 'be nice to Auntie Margaret tomorrow, do you promise?'

I said, 'Why should I?'

'Just be,' she said.

I said nothing.

'Just for me, Jim, do you promise?' she said.

I said, 'I promise.'

She said 'good', and turned over. And, after a while, she fell asleep.

And I stared at the wooden beams on the ceiling until the night faded into light.

And it was morning.

Orpheus
Maria Sinclair

THE TREES ARE comforting in a way, encircling him in the darkness. The fire throws out sparks. He takes a drink, stares into the flames, the white-hot centre. People think they're alone out here, but they're wrong. This is where the soul is: in the forest, under branches and stars. Between the trees, he sees the glimmer of the loch, translucent and ghostly, like a thought spreading out towards the corners of his mind. He thinks of it closing over his face, a cool veil, lulling him to sleep.

A branch crackles and he looks up. The boy is sitting on the other side of the fire. He's so quiet you'd hardly know he was there. But the boy never stops watching him, as though he's afraid of him disappearing. 'You should never be afraid,' he tells the boy. 'The darkness has its own special music. You have to live through it, open your eyes to it, embrace it. It's the only way you'll understand. Do you know what I mean?'

The boy says nothing. He's so young. How is it possible to be so young with eyes so old? Sometimes it's like the boy has always been here, beside the loch, the trees; like he knows them better than anything. Maybe if he tried to explain, got him to understand. 'Come on.' He stands up, reaches out his hand. The boy doesn't take it but follows him through the line of trees. A strip of pebbly sand stretches between them and the water. 'Look,' he says, 'how clear everything is.' He points up towards the constellations, the splash of the Milky Way, tells the boy that in Heaven the water tastes like sweet milk. 'First there was Chaos. No stars, no light, only the darkness, like the hard shell of an egg, covering everything. But inside the egg, something began to happen; dividing the finite from the infinite, sky from earth and then, out of the egg, came light.' He points towards a static brightness, a planet, shinier than all the stars. 'Up there is the brightest light of all: your mother.'

The boy nods but says nothing. He tries to take his hand. The boy shakes it off, like an untruth. Instead, he kneels and pokes with a stick in the sand, his body small and snail-like. Wind blows smoke from the fire, clouding the distance between them, making small comets over their heads. He leaves the boy, goes to fetch another beer from the cool bag. He returns and sits at the edge of the wood, splaying his legs in the sand. 'Why is she up there?' the boy says, his eyes wide and dark.

Froth spurts from the can and he swallows, wipes, looks down at his knees. 'Because from up there she can see you best.'

'Like the moon?' says the boy.

'Like the moon, yes.'

'I could go there,' says the boy. 'People go to the moon, don't they?'

'Sometimes. But she's further than the moon, further away.' He feels annoyed. How much of an explanation does he have to give? He wishes he could say it without words. If the boy listens long enough without speaking, he'll know. The darkness will whisper it, the trees will shake it from their leaves and the knowledge will seep into him like light.

The boy sighs. He has that look, like she did: of being somewhere else, a far distant place he could never hope to reach, couldn't touch.

Except sometimes, way back in the beginning. They'd be sitting on the doorstep, back in those early summers when he couldn't take his eyes off her. He'd be whistling some tune, didn't know he was doing it most of the time, and she'd say, 'Don't stop.' Other times he'd be polishing his shoes in the kitchen, newspaper underneath, getting ready for another long haul contract to some distant port, already smelling the sea, hearing the clang of metal, the smells and shouts of the harbours. It took months to build those big ocean liners; seventy decks some of them, like building a floating city. 'Sing to me,' she'd say. 'Before you go.'

He'd make a big show of it, taking her hand and trying to get her to dance, *'Though I've sailed all the oceans wide, there is no place I'd rather bide, than by your side, by your side.'* But she never danced. She'd close her eyes and drift away, further than the ocean. Maybe that's what did it; if he'd been home more, paid more attention, then...

How to explain it to the boy, though; the two of them practically strangers. He tips the contents of the can down his throat, down to the dregs. 'Back in a second.' He gets up and turns back through the trees, the light of the fire becoming larger, spreading its heat. He stops a moment, staring into the flames; the warm red glow of moss, the way the thin branches ignite like flares. He pokes a stick into the fire, breaking up the logs, rearranging matter.

'Dad.' The boy's voice, strange out there in the darkness.

He watches the ashes sink. If there is no light, everything is chaos. 'Coming,' he says, and, grabbing a beer, turns towards the shimmer of water, so quiet it is almost soundless. It reminds him of when he'd lie awake in bed with her beside him, her breath like the slow ripple of waves. They were interchangeable, her and the sea; the sea and her. Only when she'd gone did he realise, it was like someone had rolled back the ocean.

Maybe he was wrong to bring the boy here, all this way. It's strange to him; the trees, the fire, the water, the cold stars. A cloud extinguishes the moon, and the hills on the far shore look like they're encroaching, closing in. The boy is pointing. 'Dad.' Tugging at his sleeve. 'Dad. Dad. What's that?'

He tastes the beer. It's warm, has been too close to the fire. It doesn't matter. The boy is by the edge of the loch now, crouching down. There's something dark and wide, floating like a shadow, a black shape rocking gently. The boy is reaching towards it, trying to pull it forward.

In the darkness, chaos.

He feels his feet crunching slowly across the sand; the thought of the water like a thick hand over his mouth, his body sinking down, flesh and silt. The cloud shifts and the moon returns. The shape in the water is flat, almost square; the wood sleek and wet, all shimmering star-flecks. The planks are close together, but broken at one end, as though part of an old landing platform, a jetty, has fallen into the loch. There's a rope attached. Another mouthful of beer. 'Stay back,' he says and wades into the water, his trousers ankle-wet. He grabs the edge of the platform and drags it in. 'Hold the rope,' he tells the boy, then runs across the pebbly sand and returns with a heavy boulder, enough to secure the rope, weight it down.

The boy's eyes glimmer with excitement. 'You could make it into a boat, couldn't you? It'll float, won't it?'

The effort of lifting has made him dizzy. He takes another drink to settle the blood.

The boy sticks his finger in the loch, tastes it. 'Salt. That means the sea's not far. Can we, Dad? Can we?'

'No. It won't float. It's useless. It's fucking useless.' He doesn't mean to shout.

The boy is looking at him, scared, as though one of them might take off; disappear through the trees. It's wrong, all wrong. A boy needs a mother. But the thought of someone else. He couldn't stand it, not her breath and not her voice. He sinks down to boy-height, making himself small, compact like a shell. 'It's just that a boat needs to be caulked, waterproof. You can't go on any old thing that floats, no way to steer. A man needs direction. He has to know where he's going.'

'Why?'

The boy's questions are not leaving him any time to think, making his head throb. He needs another beer, can feel himself sliding, dropping. He has to bring himself up, get back on an even plane. 'I'm going to check on the fire,' he says.

The familiar crunch of his feet through the trees. He tosses another branch on the pile, grabs the last of the beers and carries them back to the shore. The boy is sitting on the boulder, pushing the edge of the platform with his toe. He looks sullen.

The click of the ring pull. The can fizzes and he sits down, his feet still wet, the damp sand under his trousers. He gulps, wipes his mouth. 'You see that water out there?'

The boy nods.

'Flows right into the Atlantic ocean. Do you know how big the ocean is?'

'It's big.'

'It's big like the sky, so big you can never see the edge. For miles and miles, there's nothing but water.'

'But if you kept on floating, eventually you'd get somewhere, right?'

'Or you might just keep floating forever, drifting on and on.'

'Not if you used the stars. You can tell where you are by the stars. Then you'd know which way you were going.'

He feels surprised at the boy's knowledge; a pleasant feeling, his muscles creasing in a smile. Though he doesn't know why; the boy isn't stupid. Maybe he learned it at school, navigation techniques. Didn't he do a project once, about the Vikings?'

Another swig. 'Right you are. All the best sailors know how to read the stars. None of your GPS nonsense, not like the ships you get now. Back then, all you needed was a clear sky then you'd track your way using the pole star and the constellations.'

'Are you a good sailor, Dad?'

'I build ships, I don't sail them.' That distant look again, as though the boy is disappointed. 'But I suppose that means I've as good a chance as any, better in fact.' He starts to sing, hoping for a smile. '*There's many a man been lost at sea that never did return. But all*

you need's the bright pole star and the light of the morning sun. By the light of the sun I'll sail south west and off to distant lands. And there I'll meet my one true love and ask for her fair hand.' But the boy doesn't look like he's in the mood. That feeling of slipping again, sinking. He takes another drink.

'Maybe if we went on the raft, if Mum could see us she'd guide us, like the pole star.'

The metal rim of the can on his lips, growing cold. He's trying to think. Too hard. He'd hoped it wouldn't be like this; that somehow he could explain without saying it out loud. But there's no getting away. 'It doesn't work like that. You know she's not coming back, don't you? She's, gone. Gone forever.'

The boy says nothing. The quietness is awful. He throws a stone just to hear the plop as it sinks into the water, then he looks at the boy. There's a tear on his cheek, just sitting there, suspended, not moving. Maybe he should wipe it. No, that would be like saying he's noticed. Maybe the boy doesn't want him to notice. Still, he has to do something before the tear drips, falls, is followed by another, and another. 'Ok, let's do it,' he says. 'Let's see if this thing floats.'

He tells the boy to stay where he is; Daddy will do it first. His feet are already wet. It won't matter if he slips. He finishes the beer, takes the last one with him, still in its plastic ring, hooked onto his pinkie. He lifts one foot onto the raft. It tips with his weight, rocks downwards as he lifts his other foot out of the water then leaps onto to the centre, bending his knees, stretching out his arms to get the balance. The raft sways. He feels the buoyancy of the water beneath him. The raft rocks then steadies itself. He's floating. 'Hey, look at Daddy.' He jumps up and down, starts to sing. '*I was a sailor in the navy. Her skin was smooth; her hair was wavy. And I'd give anything to have her here, have her here.*' He's singing and dancing, one arm in the air. He turns round, the words bouncing back to him from the far shore, echoing through the emptiness. Tired, he sits down, his heart drum-thudding in his ears. He'd no idea he was so tired. Takes it out of you at his age, this clowning around. He opens the last can, gulps it down fast, throws the empty ashore. 'She liked that one, your mother.' The boy looks at him, not smiling.

'She killed herself, didn't she?' says the boy.

'Yes.'

The glow of the fire is visible between the trees. The boy turns, walks back across the sand. He watches his son; his small silhouette receding. He'll be alright, best leave him alone. It's hard news, hard to take in. Best give him time. A cloud of smoke and then sparks. The boy's thrown another branch on the fire. He's learning now, how to make order out of the darkness, things you need to do to survive. A lot of it comes down to instinct. And he's getting it alright, getting the hang of it.

Christ, he never realised he was so tired. She liked that song, liked the songs with sad endings. If he lies back he'll see the brightest star of all. He closes his eyes, hears the water, the slow breath of it near his ears. 'Sing to me.' His voice mumbling at first, then expanding, filling the vacuum, *'her skin was smooth; her hair was wavy. And I'd give anything to have her here, have her here.'* The raft bumps, the water under him rocking. 'Is that you?' He opens his eyes, sits up on his elbows. The boy is pushing the boulder with his foot. It rolls once then stops. He waves. The boy doesn't wave back. 'Hey,' he says, but the word drifts across the water. The boy stands watching him from the shore. The sky is moving. Everything is moving: the trees, the shore, the dark shoulders of the hills. Then the boy is gone; the fire, a small floating light extinguished by the bank of trees. He tries to think but his head feels heavy, empty. He lies back. *'There's many a man been lost at sea that never did return. But all you need's the bright pôle star and the light of the morning sun. By the light of the sun I'll sail south west and off to distant lands. And there I'll meet my one true love and ask for her fair hand.'*

He closes his eyes. Nothing to do but keep floating.

Extract from the novel *The First Day*
Simon Biggam

Eight

Gleich nach Sonnenaufgang hoeren wir die Schuesse.

We hear the shots not long after dawn.

We spent most of last night hardly progressing at all. The foothills, dense with trees, kept us to a crawl. When we realised it was getting close to sun up we changed our route and climbed higher into the forest to find a safe place to hide for the day. We dug in quickly and found enough forest debris to camouflage our foxholes. Erich took first watch.

As the sky was beginning to lighten I found it difficult to sleep. The sound of shelling to the north and the west a constant reminder the full force of the war is only kilometres away and here were we, hiding in the hills.

After what seemed like an hour I found myself, at last, begin to drop off. Then the shots.

My sleep dulled senses make me think we have been discovered and I fumble for my rifle, realising I have left it too far for easy reach. I curse silently as I stretch to retrieve it, then curse myself again for being sloppy over such a basic necessity.

I cradle the rifle to my body and can now tell the shots are not as close as I had first thought.

I crawl through the undergrowth towards Erich, who seems to have a better idea of what's happening. Carl appears beside me wide-eyed with concern, as though he was awoken from a deeper sleep than mine.

As we reach Erich we hear more shots and now the sounds of shouting. The voices are German.

Erich points down into the gorge below us. Half a dozen German soldiers are scrambling over rocks and through brush. Less than fifty metres behind them are fifteen or so American soldiers. Some kneel to shoot while others try to get closer to the fleeing figures.

As the Americans advance I see them checking the bodies of four of our comrades already fallen. Satisfied they are dead the Americans continue their pursuit.

The leading enemy tops a rise and fires a full clip at our retreating brothers. I watch as four of the shots find the back of a soldier. He lets out a cry as he falls. The crack as his head hits a boulder snaps through the three of us, even at this distance.

Two of the Germans return fire and the American leaps behind a rock but the shots are fired in haste and don't find their target.

More Americans crest the rise and open fire and another soldier drops.

Only four left now.

They are shouting to each other. *Keep moving. Keep to cover when you can. Don't stop.*

I feel Carl tensing at my side. He pulls his rifle forward and sights one of the Americans. Before he can squeeze the trigger Erich reaches over and pulls the gun aside. Carl snatches it back. *I had him in my sights*, he hisses through clenched teeth.

You'd give away our position.

It's our soldiers being chased. We've got to help them. He looks to me for support.

I shake my head. *The Americans could*

radio for reinforcements and we'd be trapped.

Carl gives a defiant stare and deliberately takes aim. Erich puts his hand on the rifle again and pulls it to the side, this time keeping a firm hold. *Don't be stupid.*

We must help them.

We can't. We're outnumbered.

But we're in a superior position. We could give suppressing fire and force the Americans into cover. It'd give our comrades a chance.

Erich shakes his head firmly. *It's too much of a risk.* I can see the strain on Erich's face and I know he agrees with Carl. It's ingrained in us to support comrades in need. The brotherhood bond. But Erich knows what we would lose if we try to help.

I look back at the gorge. Three German soldiers are still standing. They know the end is near and that terrible knowledge has given them a desperate burst of speed. They're almost directly below us and beginning to climb out of the gorge towards our position.

In a few minutes, if they are lucky, they will reach us. I signal we should move back to our camp and get ready to leave quickly. Erich gives a sharp shake of his head and I immediately stop. He's right, moving now could signal to the Americans there are more enemy soldiers nearby. I feel foolish for making such a mistake.

With a sickness in my stomach I watch events in the gorge. In their panic to escape our comrades have left themselves exposed to enemy rifles.

The Americans are spaced out in a rough arc, all converging on the slope out of the gorge. More than half of them stop and fire volley after volley. In less than ten seconds only one German soldier is still alive. He's crouching behind a rock frantically looking around for a safe escape.

Fuck, whispers Erich as the Americans begin to flank the lone soldier's position.

Carl looks to both of us. He mumbles something then turns away not wanting to witness the inevitable end of the chase.

A few of the Americans reach their flanking positions and fire on the now exposed soldier. His only choice is to break cover and move in the opposite direction. He must see the trap as he stumbles directly into the line of fire of the second group of flanking Americans.

His body jerks for a moment as multiple bullets rip into him, then he crumples to the ground.

The Americans converge on him and the two other soldiers that fell only moments before. They talk and laugh as they search the bodies. I see one of them take a Luger then lean down again to rip off insignia patches. War souvenirs. Trophies.

Erich and I keep watch on the soldiers until they move away back down the gorge. Our comrades lie where they fell. More German bodies left to rot.

Carl finally lifts his head and looks down into the gorge. *They were German soldiers. And we didn't help.* He grabs his rifle and crawls back to his foxhole. *What does that make us?*

Nine
Der Vormittag nach dem Ueberfall.

The morning following the ambush.

We've settled in to hide for the day, adopting the now familiar routine of stopping before dawn at a spot we think will be suitably secure and digging in.

After what we witnessed yesterday we were determined to put as much distance as possible between ourselves and the gorge. Our advance was hampered again by the thick forest and overcast sky. We stumbled through the dark as best we could but I'm sure we have only managed a handful of kilometres.

Throughout the night we saw flashes in the distance. We've already heard planes this morning. We're still too close to enemy lines to rest easy.

The tension between the brothers is palpable today and in a way I'm relieved Carl seems to blame Erich solely for stopping him from helping our comrades. Little comfort though, I'm carrying enough guilt already. It has meant hardly a word has passed between us since yesterday morning.

We've chosen a good hiding place today. In

➤➤

front of us we have an excellent view across the forest for a couple of hundred metres before the trees become too tightly packed again and obscure our view. Behind us is a sheltered dell, only easily accessible from our position. Perfect place for uninterrupted ablutions.

Now I'm waiting patiently for Erich to go for a shit.

I've had hardly any time alone with Carl since we left the other night and a question has been burning in my mind each day since our journey began. Not a question I risk asking again in earshot of Erich. His earlier response was enough to convince me that some old wounds had not healed nearly enough.

Erich finally moves and I think I'll get my chance. However, he comes over to our foxholes and crouches down beside us, his voice barely more than a whisper. *I've been thinking*, he says. *After yesterday, staying here is too dangerous. It's only going to get worse. We need to leave.*

And go where? Carl manages to make it sound as if Erich's suggestion is the stupidest thing he's ever heard.

Erich tries to be patient. *Out of the forest and away from the foothills for a start.*

You mean leave the best cover we have?

Any pretence of tolerance vanishes and Erich turns sharply to Carl, his voice still low but lacking none of his anger. *Yes. It's too dangerous here. We're going to go west then south.*

West? Are you mad? We'd be walking right into enemy held territory?

Erich ignores the protest. *Once we've passed through the frontline I don't think we'll have much trouble. The Allies will be more interested in pressing our army back through these mountains to the Rhineland, three soldiers should be able to go through easily enough, if we are careful.*

Easily? Carl shakes his head. *You're insane.*

Erich moves close to him. *That's what we're doing whether you like it or not. If we stay in here a whole platoon could creep up on us before we'd know it. These mountains are the last barrier before Germany. They'll be overrun soon with troops from both sides. So stop moaning like an old woman and do as you're told.* With that he

grabs his rifle and moves out of camp. *I'll be back soon.*

Carl stares at the ground, the fire of his defiance dwindled to embers. I feel a pang of annoyance at Erich for speaking this way to his brother. He might be younger than us but he's a man, his opinions should count

I crawl out of my foxhole, check the terrain surrounding us then sit beside Carl. *I'm sorry he spoke you that way. The more you let him the more he'll think he can get away with it.* I know it would be easier to tell him just to agree with his brother, we would all have a more comfortable time if he did so, but it's difficult to see him being bullied.

Carl smiles at me. *You've got a short memory. He's been doing this all my life.*

I return the smile, recognising the truth of his words. *I suppose he has.*

Thanks for saying it though. I don't think I could take both of you ganging up on me again.

I wonder if I should attempt some sort of belated apology but it seems inappropriate. Erich will be back soon so instead I seize this chance to speak privately. I try to be nonchalant, not give my game away. *So Carl, how's life been back home?*

He gives me a puzzled look. *Like I said, I haven't been there for a while, but fine. Fine.*

And your mother and Giséla?

They're good.

Here it comes. Got to be subtle, dare not risk Carl mentioning it to Erich. *And... Sophie. How is she?*

Carl looks at me directly. *Three lovely children, Bernie. Two boys and a girl. You should see them. Gorgeous.*

My head begins to spin at his words. They come at me like blows. I mumble, *children?*

Carl beams at me. *Yes. Three, two and one. The girls as beautiful as their mother and the boy as handsome as his father.*

I shake my head, unable to fully understand the full meaning of what he's telling me. Sophie married. *Married?*

Carl continues excitedly. *Yes. You don't know the man. Not local. Nice though. Money, good looks. Swept her off her feet. It was all very romantic.*

Dazed, thoughts stillborn as they form. Resort to automatic platitudes to try and cover my shock, *I'm glad she's happy.* Words stick in my throat. Try not to think about her being married, try not to think of other arms around her. Even after all this time, I thought... I hoped. No. She is married. My heart begins to shrivel in my chest.

Carl continues. *Nice of you to say. I'll mention it. She'll be touched by your concern.* Carl laughs as if he's been trying hard to hold it back. *Bernie, your face.*

What? Mind still numb. *What's funny?*

He reaches over and puts his hand on my arm. *She's not married.*

Not? I shake my head, bewildered by this sudden change.

He squeezes my arm. *I was teasing you, that's all.*

Teasing?

You've got to stop repeating what I say Bernie.

She's not married?

He laughs harder. *No.*

Hope buds. *You bastard Carl.*

He smiles wickedly. *Sweet revenge for all the teasing you used to inflict on me.*

I reach for a stick and throw it at him. *You bastard.*

He dodges the half-hearted throw easily. *Had you there.*

I move towards him, intent on throttling him for his mischievous joke. We hear Erich coming back and I whisper, *I don't think we should mention our chat to your brother.* Carl shakes his head and laughs and I can't stop myself from joining in.

Erich sits. *What's so funny?*

We answer in the same breath. *Nothing.*

Ten

Regen in der Luft noch mal.

Rain in the air again. I can feel it coming. Still a little way off, but it will be here soon enough. Maybe thirty minutes of cursing the threat of it then cursing it again once it arrives.

I'm sick of the rain. Sick of feet squelching in boots. Sick of being soaked. Sick of slowly drying out just in time for another drenching. The ever-present damp smell clings to my uniform and mixes with the pungent scents of sweat and mud. I must stink.

Shifting to a more comfortable position in my foxhole I pull my tent quarter in close, glad of the protection it will provide when the rain finally arrives.

Carl is on watch.

When we stopped this morning we found good cover was scarce so decided to separate to use the best of what was available. Sensible. Lonelier.

As I watch Carl it occurs to me I'm now feeling much more comfortable having the brothers as my travelling companions. Could almost say it's like old times, though in all our adventures back home we wouldn't have dreamed of facing anything close to what we are experiencing now.

Carl must feel my stare. He turns and nods before resuming his vigil.

I can barely see Erich from here at ground level but I know he'll be deep in slumber. No matter where we are he seems to sleep the moment he puts his head down, and wakes to take over watch more refreshed than I've ever managed. The sleep of the just.

I close my eyes and try to doze again. Like the last few days it does not come easily.

My mind wanders back to the brothers again. Might go as far as saying I'm enjoying being with them given the circumstances. For all Erich's abruptness and reluctance to say more than a sentence at a time, I feel we're becoming close again. Past misdemeanours put aside for the time being.

When we were growing up Carl was a nuisance. Always following us around like a needy puppy. We wanted so much to tell him to leave us alone but Erich had promised his mother we would look after him and play with him once chores were done. The death of her eldest son made her adamant the remaining two should look out for each other.

Erich didn't like it and neither did I. So Carl was always at our heels. Running and stumbling and trying to keep up with us though we didn't

➤➤

slow our pace.

If he had to be with us then he had to do things our way.

He would do anything to please us despite our efforts to ignore him. He was too young for boys our age to be saddled with. The seven years between him and Erich were a gulf, almost impossible to bridge, even the five between Carl and me were just as huge.

How we must have tormented him, but still he stayed with us and occasionally managed to keep up. We would never have told him how impressed we were when he did so.

I watch him as he grips his rifle and scans the countryside for signs of troops and I get a strong feeling there's something about the young man he has become I really admire. A passion in him he keeps well hidden but can't help to let out now and again.

However I have the feeling my thoughts of friendship might not be returned. Less for childhood teasing than the situation we're in. If the decision had been his alone, he wouldn't have come with us. Only the force of his brother's determination made him follow.

Once again he's at our heels, this time reluctantly.

I feel guilt at forcing this on him. Being younger than Erich and I he was at just the right age still to have the patriotic fervour, fired by the promise of a new Germany, burn brightly in him. No, that's not accurate. I'm revising my own feelings because of where we are now. The truth is we all felt the zeal of the promises made. We all wanted something better than we had inherited after the last war. Most were happy to take arms to ensure we got it. But the long years of the war have tempered my views, to some extent. Carl still had some of that fire. Only months in the army, still raw and eager for the lessons only real combat can teach you. Only fighting reveals what strengths you have within. In his eyes he must think I stole it from him. I made him a deserter. I gave him shame.

Perhaps by the time we get home he'll come to see I did it for the best reasons. Perhaps then he can forgive me.

Maybe I'm letting my own fears distort my perception. His manner when we talked about Sophie the other day surely suggests the problem is more in my mind than in reality. I hope so.

My own fears and self-doubts try to resurface. I force them deep into the hole I've made for them.

If I'm honest I didn't think I would ever see the brothers again. I thought the war would take at least one of us, and even if not, in the early days I had little intention to return home, only the rare visit to see my parents, but not to catch up with old neighbours and childhood friends.

Early on I knew the life of a farmer was not for me. Duty made me stick at it for as long as I was able. Farming was the family way and everything would pass to me. But I had always been one for books, few though we had, and escape into the wider world became my only dream. An education, a future of possibilities, new choices and decisions at every turn. If I stayed, my life was mapped. Every moment known to me. So I left. With no regrets.

With one regret.

Sophie.

Even the pull she brought was not strong enough to keep me there. If I stayed I would've married her, I'm sure of it. Then over the years I would have been ground down by the promise of dreams I'd given up. My love for Sophie would sour over time and then even the joy of being close to her would wither. I would blame her for keeping me back.

Not wanting to face that pain and unable to imagine a way to sweeten the bitterness that would eventually take me, I ran. To explore the world in all its splendour I told myself.

Well that was my plan.

It didn't quite work out that way.

I thought I was being courageous, that I had greater imagination than my friends, had deeper needs. But over the years I began to suspect I was a coward. Running from problems. Not knowing my place. Searching the world for answers that can only be found within.

I watch the rain come up the valley towards us. After a few minutes the leading edge arrives and I burrow deeper in my foxhole.

Hours left until nightfall. Hours of waiting to move again.

Tomorrow we will find a better hiding place.

Tomorrow we should risk a fire.

Eleven

Erich hat sein Ritual.

Erich has his rituals.

Each morning once we have chosen our hiding place for the day and made ourselves comfortable, Erich takes the first watch. My turn comes next.

When I take over from him I surreptitiously peek as he carefully removes his boots and inspects inside them, first with his eyes then with his fingertips, exploring for holes or stones he might have picked up. He then ties the boots to a nearby branch close enough to the ground to be within reach when he's lying down.

He then, with the same care, removes his socks and inspects them too. If they are wet he'll wring them out and hang them on the branch next to his boots. He takes an old shirt from his pack and meticulously dries his feet, taking care over each toe, then takes a container marked *Vasenól* and sparingly rubs the powder onto his feet.

From inside his shirt he pulls another pair of socks, like the ones hanging beside him these have aired for a few hours and have then been kept in the layers of his clothes where the warmth of his body has helped dry them a little more.

He catches sight of me watching him as he pulls on a sock. *Best to look after your feet. When it's wet like this it's even more important.* He pulls on the other sock. *Started doing this in Russia. I've done it ever since.*

He finishes and immediately moves to his next ritual. Cleaning his rifle. Every day he does it. It must be his way of relaxing.

I slide across my tent quarter until I'm close to him. *Tell me about Russia.*

He stops and stares at his rifle. Then he gives a little double nod and says, *it was cold.*

I wait for him to continue but he's silent and after a moment he begins on his gun again.

Then tell me about the Russians.

There were a lot of them.

I sigh loudly, showing my dissatisfaction at the lack of detail in his answers. *I mean, what were they like?*

He continues with his gun and doesn't look up. *Just like people.*

I stare at him until I cannot take his silence any more. *Anything else you'd like to tell me?*

He pauses, thinking. A faint smile. *No.*

So, you sum up your entire time on the Russian front with 'it was cold'?

He looks at me again, this time with a frown. *No... It was* very *cold.*

I'll keep on asking until you tell me, I say somewhat petulantly. Erich shrugs and keeps on at his task.

What about your war Bernie? Carl's still awake.

I stay staring at Erich but I think I have got all I can from him today. My own little ritual. I'll try again tomorrow.

I cross over to Carl and settle down beside him. *It's been easier than many I'm sure.* I say it loudly enough for Erich to hear, his words from the first day together still in the back of my mind. *But there's been a lot of fighting since the Allies invaded southern France.*

What about before that?

Not much to tell. I stayed in Saint Armand, a town a bit further south from here.

With a girl? Erich told me you had a girl there.

I look over my shoulder at Erich. *And how did Erich know that?*

Lucky guess, he says then mutters, *girl in every port.*

I get annoyed at his tone. It's not as if it is any business of his who I see. I think about challenging him when I get a picture of Sophie in my mind and it stops the words in my throat. Of course he's annoyed with me.

What's her name? Carl continues.

I don't want to say more in front of Erich, too many old wounds just waiting to be opened.

Bernie what's her name?

I glare at Carl's persistence and see it's genuine interest rather than trying to cause tension between Erich and me. The way he used to. Got to remember he's a man now. Those silly games far behind us all.

Before I can answer Erich says. *Tell him, don't mind me.*

He must have guessed I've already made the connection with Sophie so I quickly say, *Elise*. But it's not enough for Carl, he wants much more detail and I begin to describe her. *Blue eyes, light hair* – I hear Erich make a noise through his teeth and look at him again. He pretends to be busy with his gun but I know he's thinking my description of Elise sounds like I'm describing his sister.

Bernie –

Carl, enough questions now. You should be sleeping. It'll be your watch soon.

He throws me an annoyed look. *I'm not a child anymore*, he says lying back down and pulling his tent quarter up too his chin.

I begin to tell him I didn't mean it that way but my words trail off to silence. Erich has finished with his rifle and he too lies down. He gives me a smile, sweet as ersatz sugar, and closes his eyes.

RUNNER-UP IN THE DUNDEE INTERNATIONAL BOOK PRIZE

'A delicate and fascinating study of a life in which intellect
and external microscopic and cosmic fields of force interact'
STEPHEN FRY
DUNDEE INTERNATIONAL BOOK PRIZE JUDGE

RRP £8.99
RELEASED: 8TH APRIL 2013   ISBN: 978-1-908754-14-1

**FREIGHT
BOOKS**

freightbooks.co.uk

Granny Island
Ruth Mainland

The ocean was buttered with seafroth
The day she died. I didn't see it, of course,
Being inland, but felt it, *on the rocks*,
The next day when I arrived.
I had hoped to skim over the top of the sea
Like cream, but when I arrived
The sea's foam was seasick, its clots had gummed
themselves to stones, a yellowed skin
That looked like the whisky-plaque
Which used to eddy in your gums.

We used water to weaken your drinks
Just as each wave here now breaks
Into bile, leaves a taste I don't want.
I pick up a shard of a bird's wing.
Brittle bones, they said, and
her lungs didn't work.
This sea is now coagulate,
Reeks of adhesive for false teeth;
It is the new cartilage between
The bones of you and me.

Beached
Mairi Wilson

We splashed in the shallows of a tide-stretched beach
washed-up on Gili Trewangan.
I played with urchins learning language in the sand
until foaming tides wiped out their pictures.
You sprawled aloof on a salt-bleached log
dangling bottles you emptied then dropped
until dusk bruised the shingle of the shrinking shore
and the first thrum of insects threatened.

I danced *sevillanas* in a tin-roofed shack
high in Andalusian mountains.
Lo cojó lo comó lo tiró I sang
And stamped my feet in fiery rhythms.
Hissing at shadows in the lengthening night
you coiled in a dim corner drinking
until dawn spread its fingers under the loose-hanging door
and doused the guttering candle.

Short crimson curtains wave in your wake
on a dreich day in Greenock crematorium.
Marooned in a pew I watch you gliding away
with my passport tucked in your pocket.

Beachcomber
Ruth Mainland

I am breathing in rounds of cumulus clouds
Gasping into old tissues from my coat.
Pocket each memory which I am allowed.
Remember Edinburgh, September
breathes unfamiliar. I am home-poorly, not sick, just under
The weather as my bones overgrow tarpaulins of skin.
But I have let the gales in, giving space
To the heather-hills and lochs.
I'm hollowing here. To fill each exposed crevice
With the land I left. I can conceive my gum-ripped teeth
as ragged limpet rocks, see sand flow down femurs
Making hourglasses of my bones,
Home's fragile sleet-stones
Slender in my hands, turn to water
As old memory skins itself upon my sea
Like seafoam, rancid slurring suds
lathering the shore. Now I pick debris
from clean sands in Portobello, salvage
the new air, my lungs snatching the palpable grey.
My needy lips taint the very way I breathe -
I'm becoming new smoke from a cigarette, or
The dark grey of a newborn. Slowly,
I exhale me. As the new wind catches
My breath I remember the wonder on my face when
I realized I could breathe new worlds in the face of you.

Sky
Jenny Paine

Sky! – What are you saying? So red and big
I bump into you and set you quivering.
You're like a dead whale standing on fluked feet,
filling space and puffing out your ribbing.
The wind brushes through the wood with a brush
and the leaves won't sit straight or still; it throws
the branches forward, they lurch like a cough,
arms curling as a clean sheet curves - billows
over the bed, and the branches, shaking
uncontrollably, try to catch the leaves
that they know will drop and go gambolling,
flat feet – without a body – down the street.
Sky! – What are you saying? So red and big
With your whale-blown clouds, violet, and distinct.

Aura
Claire Quigley

the sky is thinner here
stretched way past blue
a skinless world
that barely holds us

edges so sharp a glance
could slice the eye
the wind is salt
with sparks of glass

only the world reflected
comforts us, we see
reality revealed
in coffee cups

the rain-drunk gutters
can't run deep enough
for us: a dry Atlantis
waiting for the flood

Falling
William Bonar

Learn in this year of rain
its beauties   its whelmings:
whitebait winds   skies
deep-dyed indigo
starbursts on tarmac   streets
unlocked sluices
rinsed light   gold
beneath dripping trees.

The Unintelligible Conversation of Unpicked Rhubarb
Marion McCready

Silver rain flies through tumbleweed trees.
Black-eyed brambles are knocking at the door.
The babies lie, three, on the dining room floor.
One named Forty and one named Four
and the other, face-down, is no more.

In Glasgow
Paul Deaton

The north world wakes from the deep freeze,
feeling comes to fingers as it does to trees,
new leaves don't grow, but cut themselves free.
The crocus pipettes suck up the earth's stored bloods.
Why would we expect the sheer-sharpness of spring to be different for us?

Skunk Cabbage

Elspeth Brown

Whoever called you skunk cabbage?
What bitter jealous man, surely a man,
who saw your proud erection
and golden petals, large as hare's ears,
huge leaves spring glossed
thrusting from the winter mud.
Strange scent in the air –

but skunk?
Overblown lily or dying hyacinth perhaps.

You are a Swamp Lantern,
lighting the loch shore in early spring.

Big Stupid
Rob McClure Smith

MACPHERSON'S VOICE CAME pealing into the room, louder than the air-conditioner's whirr. 'So, after ah told the burd black underwear turns me oan,' he yelled, 'she goes and disnae wash mah fuckin boxers for a month.'

A cacophony of drunken laughter erupted, mostly female.

'Mac's a big hit,' Eileen whispered.

Looking across the Fosters' lawn, lake shimmering in the distance, Rich glimpsed Giselle. She drifted, wineglass in hand, pulling at the straps of her white dress, males cowering around her like bonobos in heat. Giselle was married to Callaway, a renowned dullard. They'd met in Barcelona on the exchange program. Eileen, who was in the same book club, said Giselle was shallow and stupid. Stupidity was fine by Rich, if it presaged susceptibility. He took a swig of crème de menthe and saw a blur of green sun through the wet dome of the glass then MacPherson flying through the screen door towards the liquor table.

'Nice party this. Whit youse call it?'

'An eating collective,' Eileen said.

'More of a drinking collective.' MacPherson inspected a Jack Daniels bottle. 'Two rules for drinking whisky, Eileen. First, never take it withoot water. Know the second?'

'No.'

'Never take water withoot whisky.' MacPherson drained his glass and refilled it. 'This is situational drinking tae get me through the night.'

Harmony Shadwell took MacPherson's hand, lifting it up and down. MacPherson watched his hand being lifted.

'Mac is helping us out while the Hislops are in Rome,' said Eileen.

'Doing what the Romans do,' Rich added.

'How's that?'

With the exception of her choice of spouse, Harmony never displayed any discernible sense of humor.

'Harmony teaches in French,' Eileen explained.

'Wid it no be better teaching in English?' asked MacPherson.

Harmony looked querulous. 'How is Illinois treating you then?' she offered.

'No much tae do. Ah usually blow mah cash oan burds, booze and horses.' MacPherson waited a beat. 'The rest ah spend foolishly.'

Harmony glanced at Rich, hopelessly.

'He's a terrible kidder,' Eileen explained.

'I was just going to show Mac the lake,' Rich said, tugging at his sleeve.

'Ah've seen it,' MacPherson said, slapping at his fingers. 'Big hole full of water?'

Rich maneuvered MacPherson hobblety-hoi across the lawn towards the jetty.

'Laugh a minute her,' said MacPherson. 'Face like a frying pan. Ah only drink tae make ither people interesting, but she wis a lost cause.'

They stared at a dilapidated rowing boat.

'That is wan ancient ship. Back then Long John Silver still had two legs and a fuckin egg oan his shoulder.'

MacPherson leapt into the boat and commenced unhitching the rope.

'What are you *doing?*'

'How's aboot a paddle?' MacPherson pushed off and the rowboat spun into the jetty. There was a splintering sound. 'Don't worry,' he cried. 'Ah can swim. Ah jist don't have much cause tae do so in the common course of things.'

The boat lurched when Rich jumped in, canting to the left.

'Get out!'

'Why? There's plenty room. We'll fish for fish. Eat like island chieftains.'

Eileen stood on the bank. 'How's about you bring Ed's boat back before he sees you?'

'Mac's drunk,' Rich shouted, clinging to the gunwale. The rowboat was twenty feet out, creating a vortex.

'Wheee,' MacPherson screamed.

A group of partygoers joined Eileen, lining up on the bank like bath-time figurines.

'How funny,' Jennifer Coombs said. 'Mac's gone for a ride in Ed's boat.'

Rich's shoes were sopping, a mossy green liquidity seeped through cracks.

'Sabotage!' MacPherson yelled. 'Man the fuckin lifeboats.'

'Calm down.'

'Abandon ship. Women and cowards first.'

'Sit down,' Rich shouted.

The splash MacPherson achieved drew a cheer from the onlookers. He commenced beating his arms on the water. 'Ah've forgot how tae swim again,' he screamed.

Eileen was experimenting with her waffle iron. The first batch looked like shoes. MacPherson, last seen sprawled on a basement couch, could be heard clumping up the steps, a heavy tread, a moaning. He emerged wearing Eileen's bathrobe with a white towel wrapped around his skull like a turban. Slumped in a chair, he propped his chin on the kitchen table.

'Mah heid.'

'What do you usually take?'

'A Suffering Bastard? That's gin, brandy, lime juice and ginger ale.'

Eileen shook her head.

'A Corpse Reviver? A Thomas Abercrombie? That's two alka seltzers in a double shot of tequila? Buttermilk? Buttermilk is excellent for a hangover. If drinking it disnae work, you jist pour it oan yir heid.'

Eileen handed him Tylenol. He tried to remove the childproof cap then gave it to Rich.

'Whit ah do this time?' Rich handed MacPherson three tablets, which he commenced chewing. 'Did ah jump in the water?'

'Yes.'

'Thank Christ. Ah thought ah'd pissed mah troosers.'

'I think we'll write it off as a stupid mistake,' Eileen suggested.

'You ever hear of a clever mistake Eileen? God, Ah had this horrible nightmare. Ah dreamt ah ate a sack of marshmallows.' MacPherson widened his eyes. 'Then, when ah woke, mah pillow wisnae there.'

Eileen stared at him.

'Ah'm jist kidding.' MacPherson turned at Rich. 'Had her going there. Thought ah'd ate mah fuckin pillow. Wis there a wumman wi' a weird hairdo?'

'Harmony Shadwell.'

'Rich!' said Eileen.

'The husband is worse. He's supervisor of the Educational Language Program.'

'ELP,' said Eileen, grimacing. 'Come to ELP and get ELP the posters say. We call him Big Stupid.'

'We're going to dinner next week,' said Rich, sadly. 'I'd rather chew my leg off.'

'It's a lack of moral fiber. The alcoholic is often a weak person.'

'Bob, you and Eileen will have to agree to differ on this,' Harmony twittered. The only sound the clink of cutlery on china. 'Did you hear about Jennifer and the Dean? Not that we're ones to gossip.'

'No way,' said Eileen.

'That drunken tart's been with everyone else, why not the Dean?'

'Bob!' tutted Harmony, smiling. 'It's shocking, though. She's not even tenured.'

'I can't believe it,' said Eileen.

'So, how's that little Scot working out?' Harmony asked. 'I see he's shaved his head.

He has quite a reputation. Not to speak ill of alcoholics.'

'My student tutors say he drinks like a fish,' noted Shadwell.

'He doesn't swim like one,' Rich offered. No one laughed.

'Shows up to teach half in the bag and tries to get the sophomores in the sack.' Shadwell mouthed a slice of desiccated chicken.

'He's settling down,' said Eileen. 'He discovered the English Department. Around them he just seems like a social drinker.'

'Well,' said Harmony, 'I hear *he* is involved with Jennifer *too*...'

'Simultaneously,' added Shadwell. 'Him and the Dean both. Kids say they 'hooked up' at the nature station. Everyone's talking.'

'I don't think who sleeps with who is anyone's business,' said Eileen.

'Who sleeps with *whom*,' said Shadwell, swiveling his head at her like a tank turret. 'Don't shoot the messenger, Eileen. A college should be a marketplace of ideas, not a marketplace of behaviors.'

'It behooves us,' Harmony declared, 'to set an example.'

Monday morning Rich walked briskly to campus, trying to beat a storm making in the east. But as Giselle came flitting out Barrett Hall, the sky seemed to clear. She was radiant, wispy bliss in a white-ribbon ponytail. Rich skipped up the worn marble steps two at a time. The first voicemail was not good though, Dean's secretary. Rich trudged to Old Main, sickly with trepidation.

The Dean sat scrunched behind his computer, a big man with a little pencil in his mouth.

'Grab a pew, Richard.'

The office was in disarray. Rich located a chair under a pack of light bulbs.

The Dean finger-smacked the 'send' key. 'I'm having quite the day,' he announced. 'Now the Wellness Coordinator is out sick. Anyway, I have a concern. I thought I might make you part of the conversation.'

'Amanda's tenure?'

'No.' The Dean looked irritated. 'That film person of yours.'

'He's not mine,' Rich said. Being made part of the conversation meant it was his fault.

'How can I put this?' said the Dean, frowning. 'A college is an ecosystem. Very fragile.' Prior to becoming Dean, he was Chair of Biology. 'The intrusion of a new species alien to the environment has ramifications. With me?'

'He only comes from Chicago twice a week. What's he done now?'

'Student Development suspects he is schlepping students under his supervision.'

'Oh dear.' Rich felt immensely relieved.

'That doesn't bother me,' the Dean added. 'If they don't complain, I'd rather not know. The amorous relations thing is a cross you bear when you employ artistic types. They're always tracking paint on carpets and banging like cats. No, he's involved with a colleague and...' The Dean looked thoughtful. 'How does he find the time?'

'I believe there was a rumor of some kind that he may have been seeing Jennifer on and off, yes.' Rich felt a ring of sweat pool in his shirt collar.

'Jennifer?' The Dean looked perturbed. 'No, it's this Giselle business.'

'Giselle?' The name came out like a batsqueak.

'The Callaways are integral, without them Barcelona's down the chute.' The Dean had a paperclip between his teeth and was making peculiar sucking sounds.

'Well, I'll try to have a word.'

'I don't want you to *try*, Richard.'

'I mean I will.'

'I hear you two are of an ilk.'

The bruise-blue street was shining with rain. A cloudburst had rearranged crisped leaves, gelatinous now in scummy puddles. The walls were yellowing with sun, blue mud with sky in it, jewelry of parked cars, sidewalk coated with dying worms, his reflection in everything.

Of an ilk? What the *hell* did that mean?

'You OK?' Eileen asked.

'Fine,' he snarled, wrenching open the fridge and extracting a pack of Corona.

'You've been swearing so much lately. It's like you're turning into...'

'Is *it* downstairs?'

MacPherson, finding the setup to his liking, had set up a mini-lab in their basement. Two afternoons a week he edited student films on his laptop. Eileen also fed him, waffles mostly. Lifting two Coronas out the pack, Rich viciously unlatched the basement door. MacPherson was crouched over his computer. Now bald as a brick, he had grown a narrow goatee, making him also rather goatish in appearance.

The Pogues' 'Auld Triangle' blasted from iTunes. Rich asked him to turn it down.

'Whit?' MacPherson yelled. 'Ah cannae hear you!' He examined the Corona suspiciously. 'Urine sample?'

'It's a beer.'

'Ah don't drink beer. It's full of female hormones.'

'What?'

'Yir beer drinker puts oan weight quicker, talks withoot making sense, gits emotional, cannae drive right... Fuckin obvious innit? Drinking beer turns men intae women.'

'Anyone ever told you you're a repugnant sexist pig?'

'Aye, women. Usually in bed.'

MacPherson froze the playback. Replayed it. His fingers on the keys had a nervous elegance.

'You wouldn't be boning Giselle Callaway would you?'

MacPherson tapped the screen. 'There's a lassie takes aff her clothes in this.'

The light came into the basement at odd angles, the sun brightening sharply on the wall and clarifying floating motes of dust like shadows of minnows.

'Giselle?'

'Ah'm no deaf. Ah'm no Vincent Van Fuckin Beethoven. You want details?'

Rich nodded, chugging viciously.

'Well, Ah don't think she gets whit she needs frae that man of hers. It's off-putting. Ah'm no that keen oan screamers. As well, the walls of the Ramada ur that...'

'Not those kind of details, you little shit.'

'Well, she isnae married tae you is she?'

Rich sat and pulled his knees under his chin. This conversation was like eating a knife.

'We used tae go tae that nature place. But a gnat bit me oan the buttocks. Ah'm worried ah've got Slime disease.' MacPherson returned to his screen. 'This is coming thegither. A psychological drama featuring a buttnaked 18 year old wi' legs like pipe-cleaners. Kids used a shopping cart for this dolly shot. Stole it frae the Hy-Vee parking lot.'

Rich stayed and watched it all.

His last night on campus, they accompanied him to the Marzonis' bash. MacPherson had been doing Irish carbombs and Jagermeisters with his class all afternoon.

'You've been in a foul mood forever,' Eileen was saying.

'Yes,' Rich agreed. 'I'm sorry. It's him. The stress of...'

Their conversation was drowned by MacPherson's voice. He had trapped Harmony Shadwell in a corner and was telling her a joke.

'This couple ur driving through Wales. Tourists. And stop in lanfairpwllgwyngyllogerychwyrndrobwllllantysiliogogogoch.'

'What?' Harmony had the plastic smile people make when trying not to scream.

'Lgogerychwyrndrobwllllantysiliogogogoch.'

'Eh?' squawked Harmony, looking for help.

'Anyway, they chew the rag aboot how you pronounce it. They stop at a restaurant and the guy says tae the blonde cashier, 'Could you settle an argument? Would you say the name of this place... very slowly?' So the lassie says, very slowly, "Burrrrrrrr, gerrrrrrr, Kiiiiing."'

MacPherson howled with laughter.

Harmony was confused. 'What?'

'You know whit Harmony, is it me, or ur you packing the pounds oan? Ah read aboot this slimming course where they operate and remove yir bones. After that, not only do you weigh less, you look more relaxed. Ah'm no saying yiv got a colossal arse, it's jist you give the impression there's a massive pole jammed in back there.'

MacPherson staggered off, leaving

Harmony's mouth to form a perfect O. You could have fitted a fist in there. Rich bolted after, to discover MacPherson sprawled in a driveway gutter. He looked at home lying under the whispering black trees, in the gutter.

'Did you fall down?'

'Naw,' MacPherson scowled. 'Ah've a bar of chocolate in mah back pocket and wis trying tae break it. Of course ah fell doon ya fucking retard. Some eegit put a road where the garden wis.'

'You're plastered.'

'No if ah can lie oan the grass like this withoot holding oan.'

A figure appeared silhouetted in the porch light. 'You,' a voice screamed. 'I want to talk to you, little man.'

'Who the fuck's this fat fuck?'

'Be quiet. I'll handle this.'

Shadwell's fingers were balled into fists. 'Stand aside, Rich.'

'Come on Bob. Let it go. You can see he can't defend himself...'

'That's neither here nor there.' Shadwell commenced rolling up his sleeves.

MacPherson scratched at Rich's pants. 'If something's neither here nor there, where the fuck is it?'

'You stay out of this, Rich. I'm going to teach this specimen a lesson.'

'Aye, and then yir gonnae hit a home run at Wrigley Field wi' a fuckin breadstick. Who is this bawbag? And how come he talks like a fuckin TV set?'

'Shut up, Mac,' Rich wailed.

MacPherson stood up instead. His pants pockets were turned out like elephant ears. 'Don't tell me. Yir father wis a simple man. Yir mither wis a simple wumman.' He leaned against Rich, whispered: 'And here we see the result afore us: a fucking simpleton.'

Shadwell took another step, purpling with rage.

'Hey,' said MacPherson, in joyous recognition. 'Ah ken who this is!' He pointed at Shadwell. 'Yir Big Stupid, right?' Saying this, he charged like a billy goat, ramming his head into Shadwell's groin. Both men went sprawling, Shadwell doubled over, unable to

catch his breath.

Rich helped him to his feet. 'You OK?'

'I'm not OK,' Shadwell wheezed, crouching red-faced.

MacPherson promptly head-butted him in the face. Shadwell dropped to his knees, feeling at his mouth, red leaking through his fingers.

'He broked my node,' Shadwell screamed. 'The little thit broked my node.'

MacPherson, evading Rich's half-hearted tackle, booted Shadwell hard on the temple. He now lay very still on the grass.

'Will you quit that? What are you doing?' Rich groped for a pulse. 'I think you've killed him. My God, MacPherson, he's dead!'

'Uuuuuurgh,' said Shadwell.

'My mistake,' Rich said, raising his hand. Others emerged to see what the fracas was. 'Bob fell over and has knocked himself out somehow,' Rich announced. 'Help?'

'Why?' said Jennifer Coombs, 'he's more interesting when he's unconscious.'

They sat on the Marzonis' front porch. Rich's face shone alternately red and blue in the shadows thrown by the ambulance. The night wind scudded leaves over the grass. A neighbor's dog, agitated, looped trees in a figure eight. There was blood on the black brick also.

'Well, ah've had a wonderful time,' slurred MacPherson. 'But this wisnae it.'

'I'm in trouble now,' Rich said.

'His word against oors.' MacPherson pointed. 'Whit if we say he tripped and smashed his gob oan that wee tree? The wan wi' nae leaves.'

'That's a basketball stand.'

'Even better,' said MacPherson. 'You know, it's time ah settled doon. Whit ah need is a lassie like Eileen.'

'EILEEN!'

'Well, no yir Eileen. Some ither Eileen oot there.' MacPherson pointed at the stars. 'There's a time when we huv tae grow the fuck up.' He hiccupped. 'A person cannae keep screwing thousands of women. It's exhausting. Even withoot chemical assistance.' A half moon of blood curved like a sickle on the little man's bald skull. 'Goes for you as well. Don't end up some Big Stupid.'

MacPherson levered himself to his feet, gripping the porch rail, staggered down the steps and across the lawn before throwing his arms in the air and collapsing. He lay with his head under a privet.

The houses along the street were illuminated, and the branches close by the windows, but the grass was dark. In windows the incessant blue snow of televisions. A big yellow moon rode a rim of clouds, stars a fine talcum. Junebugs banged into screens.

'Is that Mac? He'll get pneumonia.' Eileen was carrying a coke bottle full of roses. He had no idea why.

'I love you.'

'That's nice.' She sat down beside him. 'What happened to Big Stupid really?'

Looking at him more closely, she commenced wiping his tears away. 'Oh, for heaven's sakes.'

'No,' he kept saying, crying, 'I mean I really love you.'

'It is exasperating to be beaten
for a fault one has not committed.
At times, I regret not having written
something obscene; it seems to me
that I should delight in receiving a
merited castigation'

Émile Zola, preface to 2nd Edition of *Thérèse Raquin*

New Expectations

Havisham
Ronald Frame
Faber, RRP £16·99, 368pp

Dickens' Miss Havisham, his eternal bride from *Great Expectations*, has to be one of the most notorious female figures in literary fiction. Jilted by her lover on her wedding day, she spends the rest of her life entombed within the darkened Satis House, her wedding feast rotting on the dining-room table, the wedding dress she refuses to remove slowly disintegrating. Dickens has long been considered incapable of writing a rounded female character – children and monsters are largely what his women are, and there are few more monstrous than Miss Havisham. She is an interesting study in female masochism – her pain at her faithless lover is not turned outward against him, but inward against herself. True emotional complexity is hinted at in Dickens but without a proper back story, how do we compare what she was before with the monster she became? How can we truly understand her?

Ronald Frame, best known perhaps for his Booker-longlisted novel, *The Lantern Bearers*, has imagined that back story for her beautifully, and with both style and sensitivity. Eschewing any attempt to mimic Dickens' style, he opts for a contemporary voice with curtailed sentences, truncated dialogue, short paragraphs. Dickens' wordiness is pared back as if to let us see more clearly a young woman, brought up next to the brewery her father owns, the smell of hops forever in her nose and hair, the tint of 'trade' always about her.

Betrayal begins early in Catherine Havisham's life, and is naturally always committed by those closest to her. Her mother dies giving birth to her, which means a closeness to her father which he betrays when he secretly marries the cook, Mrs Bundy, and has a child by her, Arthur. He sends them both away, but eventually brings Arthur back into the house, a move that horrifies and shames Catherine. She has pride, and we all know what that leads to. As she grows up, her father conspires with Lady Chadwyck, to whom he sends his daughter to become accustomed to more genteel ways and manners. Catherine falls for William Chadwyck but her love for him is betrayed when she spies him making love to a married woman. But the greatest betrayal is one of female friendship. Early on, Catherine befriends Sally, the daughter of one of her father's workers. They are extremely close, Catherine gives her her clothes, teaches her the manners and lessons she learns, loves her. She cannot, however, make her equal, and in residence at the Chadwycks, she invites Sally to attend an important dance with her, but as her servant. The alluring Charles Compeyson has already made himself known to her, charming her and making her laugh. He is handsome and witty, and distracts her from her disappointment in William.

We know, from the Dickens novel, that Compeyson will be the man to jilt her. But Frame gives us a twist: certainly, Catherine is devastated when she receives a note on her wedding day from him, telling her he cannot marry her. She falls into a fever, but recovers – there are no darkened rooms, no decrepit wedding dresses. She refuses to let her servants remove the wedding feast – there is still hope, however faint, that he will return – but she carries on looking after her deceased father's brewery business. She is not the mad grotesque Dickens has painted.

At least, not yet. For a greater betrayal is to come, and one that will tip her over the edge. The tragedy of Dido runs through Frame's novel, as Catherine attempts to elevate her suffering to epic proportions. Catherine is a tricky character to like in many ways – she is self-centered, proud, blinkered. But she is also brave, vulnerable and deserving of love. Dickens' Miss Havisham will never be quite the same again.
Argos

Special Effects

Full Scottish Breakfast
Graham Fulton
Red Squirrel Press, RRP £6·99, 58pp

Upside Down Heart & Speed of Dark
Graham Fulton
Controlled Explosion Press

Graham Fulton is one of our most productive and inventive poets; the Dyson, you could call him, of contemporary lyric poetry: always experimenting and refining new ways of elegantly and stylishly sucking you in Fulton's poetry unfailingly sends you spinning round in a sort of transparent whirlpool: It might look as if nothing too clever is going on, but deep down, you know there is.

His latest full-length collection, *Full Scottish Breakfast*, is divided into three sections: Space Age, Rage Age and Middle Age. Wonderfully pin-pointing three characteristics of his poetry, these titles prepare the reader for Fulton's familiar combination of far-sighted exploration, committed energy, and self-deprecating wit respectively, all of which abound in the book. While he can rage against "an iPodded boy in a Road Hog shirt" who inadvertently damages a Renaissance masterpiece, Fulton is equally adept when sketching the loss and sadness at the heart of a Dunblane coffee morning, ten years on, in 2006: "Mothers chat, remember, together/ not to look at the clock and cry." The title poem, which falls into the last section, presents Fulton at his lyric best: a virtuoso of the mundane. His gift for immediacy, responsiveness and exquisite deflation recalls the great New York School poet Jimmy Schuyler: "On a useless morning/ pudding is cooking/ egg is scrambling/ nearby/ I think".

One of this work's most defining qualities is its seeming immunity to cloy, something, rather like Edwin Morgan, that makes him a sensational and original poet of love. The 30 pages of his pamphlet *Upside Down Heart* are a series of love poems, sex poems, or more exactly, both. They're breezy and humorous, but the default setting is, above all, tender. Disarmingly, bewitchingly tender. 'Biological', for example, is a deceptively simple pair of couplets that pushes all the buttons: "You dream on the left. I dream on the right./ We make love somewhere in between.// I tug the sheets from our shagged-out bed and stuff them into the Hotpoint". Becky Bolton's illustrations share and perfectly complement Fulton's erratic verve and candour. With robustness and a kind of delicate disarray, her watercolour and ink drawings seep and ardently leap across the paper.

His most recent pamphlet, *Speed of Dark*, has a hurtling, disintegrating energy, in poems such as 'A Bit Twitchy' and 'Pixellated', which literally pixelates, blurs and just about stays together through misspellings and typos: "make me wjole". This chapbook also introduces one of his most compelling recent formal inventions, a list poem where each line begins "you got your", like a Glaswegian Joe Brainard. So 'The Story of Human Afflictions Without Having to Catch Any of Them' is a grim and darkly comic catalogue of ailments. Similarly, 'The Story of Mulder and Scully Without Having to Watch the Entire Nine Seasons' delivers The X Files in capsule form: "you got your vicious baby aliens/ you got your old unhappy aliens/ you got your aliens trapped in the ice".

This makes enthralling and compelling poetry, its repetitions crackling with drama and humour, taking a leaf out of Frank O'Hara's tongue in cheek, personist handbook which famously claimed that only Whitman, Crane and Williams were "better than the movies." Truth is, though, there's more flickering excitement, emotion, ingenuity and other hard to pin down special effects in this poetry than in most movies I've seen recently. With its 'down to earth' but 'out of this world' energy, Fulton's lyrics are some of the true treasures of contemporary poetry in Scotland.
General Woundwort

Highland Gothic

The Healing of Luther Grove
Barry Gornell
Freight Books, RRP £8·99, 224pp

All books have a genealogy. Barry Gornell's debut novel *The Healing of Luther Grove* has a particularly strong parentage: the forest-set class struggle of Robin Jenkins' *The Cone Gatherers* mixed with the intense, grief-impassioned sexuality of DH Lawrence.

The eponymous Luther Grove lives alone in his simple Highlands home, hunting and growing everything that he eats. But this is no idyllic vision of country life – Grove is swiftly falling apart, and the arrival of a young family acts as a catalyst for his breakdown.

Laura Payne moves into the house next door with her husband John and their infant daughter. Their house is modern, custom-built, and makes Luther's cottage look like a shack. Luther and Laura have an immediate connection, though it takes a while for Laura to understand exactly why. Relations between Luther and John, though, are strained at best – and the arrival of John's irresponsible, alcoholic brother Frank adds a spark to the kindling. The novel switches between Luther's and Laura's point of view, building to a terrible but inevitable disaster. It's a short and fast-paced book, and to reveal any more might give away vital plot details – and it would be a shame to do that, as the gradual unveiling of Luther's and Laura's histories is one of the joys of the story.

The Healing of Luther Grove has been described as a thriller and a crime novel. Although it is thrilling and several crimes are committed, it feels restrictive to class it in this way. If anything, this is a wonderful example of Modern Gothic fiction. Many of the classic Gothic tropes are present: the uncanny doppelgänger, the Byronic antihero, the damsel in distress, the sexually violent tyrant, the angelic child, the implicit threat of nature, the dark secret in the attic (or in this case, the cellar), and the sense that ghosts from the past can never be escaped. Looking at that list, it may seem that the novel could tip over into melodrama – but the restraint in Gornell's style keeps this in check. There are a few moments which, if read alone, could be a little over-the-top, but every dramatic moment is earned by what comes before. And there's a reason that we keep coming back to these tropes: sex and violence and revenge have always been a part of human behaviour, and always will be. Like all the best Gothic fiction, this novel has a modern setting, but feels timeless.

In a publishing climate when some new writers are in a rush to get their first novel published, it is refreshing to read such a polished, carefully written debut. Gornell's prose is a joy to read: effortless, considered and atmospheric. The novel's incredibly tight focus – not just tight, but almost claustrophobically small – is the perfect way to examine the catastrophe that swiftly follows. Every word earns its place, and it feels like every sentence has been carefully honed.

The novel isn't perfect: brother Frank's villainy can slip into the cartoonish, and there's the odd overwrought metaphor (such as smoke described as "hell-born snow"). But these are minor quibbles in a piece of work that is enjoyable and admirable from beginning to end.
Velveteen Rabbit

Crime and Judgement

The Guilty One
Lisa Ballantyne
Piatkus, RRP £6·99, 480pp

London lawyer Daniel Hunter, still stinging from the guilty conviction of a teenager he defended the previous year, is drawn to defending a child accused of murder. Eleven-year-old Sebastian was the last person to see his younger school friend and playmate Ben Stokes before his gruesome, violent death. Ballantyne's debut is a thought provoking exploration of the impact of accusation and trial on a minor, for the very worst of crimes.

In his mid-thirties when he takes the case, the story of Daniel's childhood with his adoptive mother emerges in parallel to Sebastian's arrest, remand and trial. A theme of The Guilty One is what it is to be a troubled youngster. Having tried and tested those around him as a child through unruly behaviour, it is Daniel's turn to respond to the needs of a troubled young boy. Sebastian is keen to please, longs to be loved and is highly intelligent. The question is, how far removed is Sebastian from Daniel at his age?

Issues such as deciding when a child becomes criminally responsible and the state of juvenile rehabilitation in the UK can be raised but are not going to be resolved by a work of fiction. The focus in the novel is on individual accountability, knowing the difference between right and wrong and the effects that early-life choices and relationships can have in adulthood. No act undertaken in The Guilty One is clear cut or without implication. The story builds to the eventual judgement of guilty or not guilty for the accused, but the outcomes presented for Sebastian demonstrate that what appears to be a stark one way or the other decision will always be blurred in its actual outcome. The courtroom scenes are delivered with harrowing detail, overlooked by reporters taking notes, keen to print every gory detail. Ballantyne gives the obligatory nod to the moral panic outside the courtroom but this is a book about individuals and the implications of their behaviour.

The Guilty One is an engaging novel. It is not a quick read – the back and forth chapter by chapter transition between Daniel's past and present takes repeated adjustment that a reader may struggle to settle into. While it may lead to a tea-break in between chapters, it is the only choice for the narrative structure to work. References to high-profile real-life cases involving the murder of children by other children are used sparingly, known to most readers already through their notoriety. The detail about real-life locations, cultural and other events does not come without its glitches in this book however and that does niggle. In fitting with the genre, the characters' choices and responses act as evidence given in context for readers to drawn their conclusions, so that which could be questioned for accuracy undermines the narrative. But the impact of the story relates to the reader's own memories of being the ages of the characters and their ability to comprehend the world around them, and indeed the difference between right and wrong, truth and lies.

The Guilty One is a dark novel in which the essential lighter moments come from warm, human relationships. The book is divided into two main sections: Crimes and Judgement. Both sections are about circumstance and response, and the latter explores how judgement is more than a delivered verdict. There is no time for wallowing – emotion is merely a side effect of action and inaction. The book is about life and how, once one matter has resolved itself, the next challenge will be on its way. And you never know when that thing you thought you had completely boxed-off, years back, that thing you were so certain about, might not be as clear cut as you once thought. This story, like life, is part of a continuous process of change and re-evaluation.
Fantastic Mr Fox

A Changing Edinburgh

The Magicians of Edinburgh
Ron Butlin
Polygon, RRP £9·99, 112pp

Ron Butlin has come a long way from the relative obscurity that dogged his career as a novelist and poet in the 1980s and 1990s. After the rediscovery of his coruscating 1987 novel about alcoholism, 'The Sound of My Voice', Butlin has achieved something like elder-statesman status in Scottish letters. In 2008, he was appointed as Edinburgh's 'Makar', the poet laureate of the city, and this new volume comes out of his experience in the role.

Butlin deftly avoids the first trap for anyone writing about Edinburgh; that tired and boring trope about the city's supposed 'duality', it's Jekyll and Hyde/Deacon Brodie/ Old Town-New Town character. A seam that has been mined of all profitable ore, it's cleverly sidestepped by a focus instead on three thematic aspects that reveal as much about Butlin's interests as a writer as about the city's real character.

Split into 'Magic', 'Music' and 'Virtual' Edinburgh, the book moves confidently from humorous, absurdist poems such as 'Oor Tram's Plea tae the Cooncillors o Edinburgh', which, from the trams' perspective, vocalises the central failure of the city government in recent years, to unflinching depictions of the continuing scourge of homelessness like 'EH1 2AB' and 'Edinburgh is a Thousand Islands.' The title poem is unashamedly celebratory, cataloguing a change from the depression of the 1970s to the more vibrant present day that is so profound it seems almost magical. In the 'Virtual' section, Butlin concentrates on the illusory world of finance, connecting and contrasting it with the equally insubstantial ghosts of the Napoleonic Wars as they complete the unfinished memorial on Calton Hill, and the scepticism of Scotland's greatest philosopher, David Hume.

The 'Music' section is probably the most successful part of the book. In the sequence 'Three Composers Respond to the Politics of Perpetual War', which grew out of texts Butlin provided for the composer Edward Harper, he imagines the response of other major composers such as Schoenberg, Cage, and Stockhausen, to a situation where 'New York and Kabul are suburbs of the same world.' As well as being something almost material, music here is evocative of the distant past and the uncertain future, and a consolatory means of bridging the two.

There is a danger for artists appointed to any official position, in that the demands of their patrons can override the demands of their art. With a foreword by the Lord Provost, Butlin could have felt constrained in his criticism, and it's to his credit that he gives equal stress to the problems of the city as to its successes. In 'Dancing in Princess Street' for example, he uses Edinburgh's main shopping street to dramatise the contentious ground at the heart of the city and the ongoing struggle between the municipality and the people, and in 'Homecoming' the disparity between tourists' perceptions and locals' in the 2009 Year of Homecoming is quite bitter. Politically though, the book takes the line of least resistance, assuming a straightforward, sentimental nationalism that seems slightly at odds with the inclusiveness implied by the title of 'Makar', or laureate. Butlin deftly weaves the sense of co-existing historical spheres into his poems, the sense of a city in which all times are happening simultaneously, but occasionally his observations have little meat on them and come across as no more than a catalogue of chance detail. Compare Butlin's sense of history with a poet like Mick Imlah's, and you will see where the breadth of his vision thins out.

On the whole though this is a successful collection. Playful, plain, unafraid of sentiment or of honesty, for the most part it works as a record of a poet's changing ideas about his home city, as that city goes through significant changes of its own.
Montmorency

Important Questions

My Gun Was As Tall As Me
Toni Davidson
Freight Books, RRP £8·99, 272pp

In 2000, a collection of interviews with new writers was published called *Repetitive Beat Generation*. It featured Roddy Doyle, Alan Warner, Sarah Champion, Irvine Welsh and Duncan McLean amongst others. One of those was Toni Davidson whose debut novel *Scar Culture* had been published in 1999, but unlike many of the above Davidson seemed to disappear in the following years, which was equal parts shame and mystery.

Scar Culture was arguably one of the more enduring novels to come out of that time, introducing readers to a writer not afraid to tackle the most controversial and often disturbing of topics. His second novel is now with us, and from the horrific first page *My Gun Was As Tall As Me* is a devastating reminder that Davidson is a serious writer. In this case he starts with a chilling examination of the world of child soldiers in South East Asia before the novel opens up to ask wider questions about how we value life, both our own and that of others, and the relationship between so-called developed and developing nations.

Davidson never shies away from depicting the full horror of what he is writing about, and some may find that too much to take at times. If this novel doesn't evoke a visceral, emotional, response from you then I would despair. The anger felt is all the greater because it doesn't come from the writer, he leaves the reader to make their own conclusions.

The story centres on silent twins from a village under attack by a teenage, and even pre-teen, army. (The shocking argument is that children have not yet developed a full sense of moral value, are more pliable, and more able to commit atrocity after atrocity). The two, named Lynch and Leer, are born into this chaos and manage to survive. Their life is contrasted with that of a young man named Tuvol, half the world away, not only geographically, who wants to end his own life in the Alps.

There is a distinct and jarring contrast here as to how hard the villagers fight to live and Tuvol, and we have to consider what the value of an individual life really is, and who gives it such. After he is saved, Tuvol seeks to give his life meaning by travelling to Burma and as these two worlds collide questions are posed as to how International Human Rights and Development organisations provide aid, and if such intervention is really positive at all. Of course there are no easy answers, but it's the asking of those questions that is important.

There is an honesty and integrity in Davidson's prose which means he doesn't push emotional buttons to trigger response. It is the vigour of his research, and his use of descriptive language rather than overly emotive language, which does that job. That is not to say that this is reportage. This is a poetic writer who manages to capture big themes in few sentences. Consider this description of the modern city as a place where you'll find; "people staring at things in shop windows that they cannot afford while keeping their eyes away from a human rotting slowly in the gutter". As I walked to and from work this month it has been hard to disagree.

The best novels are those which challenge us and take us out of our comfort zones. They shouldn't be easy to read or to forget. With *My Gun Was As Tall As Me* Toni Davidson has written a book which focuses on individual tragic situations to make us ask what we are, could, and should be doing with our lives, and for others. Perhaps it is unsurprising that it has taken him all this time to follow *Scar Culture* because, tough as this book is to read, I can only imagine what it took to research and write. A serious book for serious readers.

Kes

Hammers & Nails

Bevel
William Letford
Carcanet, RRP £9·95, 80pp

William Letford's *Bevél* was one of the most talked about debut poetry collections of 2012. For the most part, it's easy to see why. Letford gives lively performances and his poems are assured, uncomplicated and earthy. Most of all, he is what the Scottish literary establishment has been waiting for – a truly working-class poet. To be more specific, a roofer who writes poems about his job. Never has a poet's occupation been so central to his identity, an association which could prove complicated for Letford in the future. That said, let's start with the roofer-inspired poems. They are indeed refreshing in their paradoxically elevated, but down-to-earth viewpoints. 'Waking for work in the winter' closes with a gruff warning from the narrator himself: "Get up/ Like the dog that hears a sound in the dark/ Get up". 'Be prepared' is a kind of masculine worker's manifesto which could be recited to a new recruit:

> have a healthy fear of heights
> when working from a ladder
> know which way to fall
> railings and slabs are unforgiving
> flower beds and fuschia bushes are better
> practice your scream
> if you strike your thumb with the hammer
> don't squeal
> roar like a lion

Letford's own introduction of his art to his work is also humorously depicted in 'It's aboot the labour' where the narrator confides in a workmate: "hey Casey did a tell ye a goat/ a couple a poems published". When Casey asks if there's money involved and the narrator admits there's not, the two go back to the day's work of "hammers   nails/ hammers nails/ hammers   nails". Though subtle, this work compares the value of poetry against what is perceptibly more useful, roofs. In this poem and in others, Letford plays with his spacing in order for the poem's oral qualities to become more evident. White gaps between words infers pace, breath, movement or the passing of time. Long lines of spaced-out words in 'T-shirt wrapped around my head' give a sense of the sheer toil of "chipping cement/ taking it back/ to the shape of each stone/ and the craft/ of the hand/ that placed it". There's a definite energy in Letford's construction poems, an energy which is derived from his specialist knowledge and his meaningful presentation of materials.

But in Letford's poems about relationships, there's less bravado. There's a sense of trepidation and of not quite knowing what to say. 'Let's just be' features a couple trying to find the words to break up peacefully. Letford writes in short bursts of 'aye' and 'okay' and 'keep in touch', and even lets slip a cliché: "the ghost of our relationship". The poem concludes on a rather staid conclusion: "better nothing said". Going further down this route, Letford's first of three 'Sex Poems' is a pointillistic, word-by-word depiction of an awkward fumble: "aye right okay rightright okay". Interesting, but more of the same.

A switch from the domestic into the foreign is also less comfortable for Letford, though he concludes with some observations. In 'Helsinki, Finland' the narrator realises that "when you're away even the mundane is novel". On a too-hot train in Italy where two companions seem to be getting annoyed with each other, Letford concludes with "It's the not the forever/ that makes life beautiful".

Several of the poems are energetic creations that vary their use of language and spacing in order to achieve different instances of voice and time. And there's a strong intimation of hard work, both in the content and construction of these poems. It will be intriguing to see what Letford produces next.
P.I. Boots

The Anti-Heroine

The Waiting
Regi Claire
Word Power Books, RRP £7·99, 240pp

Bitch. That's the word that comes to mind when reading *The Waiting*, and not only because the characters in this book, like the chorus of Meredith Brooks' hit, realise the bad as well as good facets of womanhood. Lizzie, the elderly anti-heroine, has been hanging out with bitches all her life, and now there's a new one on her doorstep, pushing into her home and stealing her secrets. Yet calling the women in Regi Claire's latest novel bitches isn't enough – as the song goes, women are saints, sinners, children, mothers and lovers or something in between, and it is in this multi-faceted, realistic portrait of women that the book achieves its version of female empowerment.

Claire toys with narratives of women in fiction to deliver this portrait. She includes stock characters: Tinker Jeanie, who makes menacing prophecies; saintly Isobel, class swot turned nice auld biddie; even Rachel, a schizophrenic villainess straight out of one of the crime novels Lizzie devours – long black coat tails and possible dog-poisoner cum mixed-up student. Claire draws a contrast with this to the ways the characters create fictions for themselves, before tearing the narratives to let you see the real personality below. The moment when the young Lizzie, dancing around her aunt's shop at night in one of the dresses for sale, discovers she is stuck in it, neatly punctures her imagined role, throws cold water on her emergent sensuality, raises shame and guilt and teenage body-image issues all at once, and reminds you that she isn't a romantic figurehead.

Motherhood, as with much else in this novel, can never be relied on. Lizzie plays the part of a mother but is not actually one, Marlene neglects and abuses her children, and Marlene's mother repeatedly says "I wish I'd never made her." It is typical of Claire's layered, concise prose that in this one phrase, she can convey an unusual acceptance of responsibility and an emotional distancing, as well as reminding us of the further female aspects of sex, conception and nurturing. Responsibility for other people and the associated guilt inform much of Lizzie's decision-making throughout the novel, with her unease as to where her duty to Rachel begins leaving her vulnerable, much as her guilt for awakening Marlene to her illegitimacy affects her decisions in their friendship. Although *The Waiting* succeeds brilliantly at revealing different concepts of the maiden, the mother and the crone once thought to represent women (to have an elderly heroine with this much bite is relatively unusual), it is in the aspect of female friendship that the novel wavers.

Lizzie's relationship with her step-daughters is deliberately subverted, but they still achieve a noticeably familiar maternal bond. However, Lizzie's friendship with Marlene is the heart of the book, and yet it is hard to see why anyone would put up with Marlene for long. She lies, steals from Lizzie, betrays her and abandons her on numerous occasions; she taunts her own husband to suicide and lets her children go hungry. Lizzie, likewise, resents Marlene, taunts her with her illegitimacy and envies her freedom from the constraints of morality, and lets her slide into alcoholism. Lizzie does not find a traditional redemption through Rachel – and nor should she, given the novel's attempts to challenge our assumptions of storytelling – so the most she achieves in her relationships with other women is a kind of scornful regard or a traditionalised motherliness. This is a clever, uncomfortable novel that can capture a hundred emotions in one deft phrase; but the bitches don't do sisterhood.
The Maltese Cat

Many Lives

If I Touched The Earth
Cynthia Rogerson
Black & White, RRP £7·99, 256pp

I wouldn't have picked this book up if I hadn't been reviewing it. The cover picture, a side view of a woman holding a rose, and the title, made me think that it was going to be a novel aimed at a particular women's market where something bad happens but through the love of family and friends all is right in the end. That would have been my loss.

Something bad does happen. A young man, Calum, from a small Highland town dies in a car crash. We never meet him but his death reverberates throughout the town, to his best friends from school, his girlfriend, his aunt, Neal (an old friend of his mother's) and to Alison, his mother herself. It is the last two whose stories we hear in detail.

After sleeping with Neal after the funeral, Alison runs away to Glasgow without telling anyone. She falls into a job in a café and looking after an old woman. She lives a half-life there, carrying out her work in a daze, constantly having conversations with her son; reliving memories of their lives as he grew up. Meanwhile Neal's relationship with his wife slowly falls apart as he realises that he has married her because she was the only woman who had agreed to sleep with him but that he has always been in love with Alison. He had shared a flat with Alison and Calum in their youth and, despite years without contact, had always thought of Calum as his son.

There is also a priest who starts to lose his faith at Calum's funeral, an aunt who starts to gain a faith of sorts, as she worries that Alison has killed herself, and Calum's girlfriend who plants flowers for him on the site of the crash and visits it when it is dark to talk to him, constantly reliving the moment of his death and wondering if it was because of her.

Such multiple narratives are challenging but the author handles them skillfully and confidently. Every character has their story, sometimes told briefly, at other times in depth, and we sometimes enter the room with one person but leave it with another. Despite this, there is never a moment where the switch of narrator confuses, and we are never puzzled about who we are with or whether we are in the past or the present. In this way it reminds me very much of *Even the Dogs* by Jon McGregor, another novel told through multiple narratives, where the death of a man affects all the people that he knew.

Sometimes the number of stories and the in-depth explorations of the characters' thoughts slow down the plot more than I would have liked. There are also moments of slight mysticism that jarred for me – a woman in a shop drops her bag when Calum dies, someone dances in the kitchen when something happy happens elsewhere – but these are rare and generally they attempt to show us how a young man who has never achieved much impacts on so many lives.

This is a quiet novel. The characters are ordinary people living in a small town, working in factories, hating their job, falling out with their families, losing touch and then coming back together again. They are not always particularly likeable but still we care about them and we want Alison to have her happy ending, in as much as there can be one. I'll be looking out for Cynthia Rogerson's books in the future.
Aslan

Impossible Vanishings

Rooster
Gerry McGrath
Carcanet, RRP £9·95, 72pp

If McGrath's first collection *A to B* (2008) suggested a journey, a sense of travelling between poems, Rooster is a more enigmatic title which one may enter at any given point. The title poem includes the hauntingly phrased:

> who loves the sound of the rooster
> tearing at the day
> > will be killed for his blood.

Noise and ritual violence come together in this emblem, perhaps as a warning against saying too much, at the ability for words to go wild and 'tear' at the day. Much of the collection can be read against this emblem and McGrath's exacting focus on language and image through his minimal style is evident throughout. In 'The Photographer' the poem opens with "We see things / you and I", in a tone reminiscent of Plath's 'garden-variety poems'. Here we glimpse "hills / the skin of a pool / a lighthouse beam / of frost." This delicate imagistic skin allows McGrath to circle themes of fragility and strength, sparseness and depth. In his sequence 'Suite No. 1', for the late Margareta Persson, a Swedish tempera artist with whom McGrath collaborated on the 2009 exhibition 'Breaking the Silence', the poet sees "with a painter's eye / the tea horizon, soot, cauliflower white, / the raw pigment of your rage -" ('Wordleft'). Words become delicate shells around an idea and in an elegiac twist become:

> ...a space for living,
> the paint-layered grain
> where silence speaks to break
> its wordleft divinity.

I pondered over 'wordleft' for some time. The via negativa of silence speaking, deeper, more profound, than the residual divinity which this speech punctures, perplexed me; like many of McGrath's poems, there is no simple punchline or payoff. I began to think that this 'wordleft' offered a way in to thinking about McGrath's style – that, as much as one might aim for it, in writing pure vanishing is impossible. There are always wordleft residues.

Throughout the collection, this white space is as important as the black type on the page, speech and silence in a constant cycle: "the heart limns / unwriteables: [...] the endless return of a wheel // to zero" ('Zero'). Rather than rhyme or strict structure there are the subtle cadences of breath, the punctuation of the blank white space.

But this white space is not always benign, uncreated. As with 'Rooster', McGrath does not avoid or simplify violence through an ersatz-Zen. In 'Foreign Travel', the poet muses on airport foyers, the departures and arrivals of loved ones, and yet, "how quietly the wolf." No verb is needed. The wolf stalks the centre point of the poem where, later, "darkness will fall / over the splintered roof / where a girl who prayed nightly / into clasped hands / died in her sleep."

There are questions of accessibility in some of the poems. I do not demand a take-home message from my poetry reading and with the vast majority of the poems here, I wanted to stay with their carefully crafted fragility. But in a poem such as 'Roses', the economy felt frustratingly tight. A poem that has become so light and transparent can evince a 'so-what?' from more than one reader. However, as with the final poem in 'Suite No. 1', McGrath's beautiful, arresting, and demanding collection teaches us "that outright vanishings are impossible" ('Silence Cut'). The poet helps us understand what is left behind, wordleft, when we try and speak.
Moley

Sunshine City

The Hairdresser of Harare
Tendai Huchu
Freight Books, RRP £8·99, 256pp

Harare, Zimbabwe's capital, is the country's largest, busiest metropolitan centre, home of The University of Zimbabwe and nicknamed the 'Sunshine City'. It is also a place of such political and economic upheaval that the Zimbabwean newspaper The Financial Gazette has referred to it as the "sunshine city-turned-sewage farm". It is in this modern, vibrant, troubled, violent city that we meet Vimbai, our narrator, single mother and 'queen bee' of the hairdressing salon where she works.

Vimbai is known as the best. Dressing the hair of the salon's most wealthy and influential customers, she's confident of her job and reputation. Until one day Dumisani walks in – handsome, charming, cocky – and is offered a job working along side her in the salon. Vimbai's belief, the source of her talent, that to make a woman feel good you should make her feel "like a white woman" is questioned again and again as Dumi's confident and unapologetic hairstyles prove that to be the best you just have to make a woman "feel like a woman". As more and more of her customers chose Dumi over her, it seems that they will become enemies, but of course that's not how the story pans out.

When Dumi tells her that he needs a place to stay, Vimbai finds herself offering to rent him a room, almost against her will, but also for selfish reasons – she's fallen out with her family, is struggling to pay the bills, and with hyperinflation so extreme her wages are worthless a few weeks after they've been earned. So Dumi moves in, and the two form an unlikely friendship, each with a very different future in mind. After accompanying Dumi to his brothers wedding, Vimbai is shocked to discover that he's from one of the wealthiest families in Harare, and there are times when the generosity of his family seems to be more of an attraction than the man himself. But Dumi has a secret, and it's not long before we realise that he's using her for reasons of his own.

The plot hinges on this secret, but for me it was so heavily signposted that I saw it coming a mile off. Nevertheless, I'll not reveal it here just in case. Suffice to say that by the time Vimbai realises what's really going on, the reader will be more astonished by her incredulity than by the secret itself. But that is, perhaps, the real point of the book. This is a novel about a society full of conflict, clashing religions, morals and ideals, where everyone has to be careful what they say and in front of whom. All of that is subtly hinted at between the lines, and it's more powerful for being understated. The casual way in which we learn about the widespread violence in the city, the 90% unemployment, and the brutal corruption, emphasizes how the shocking and terrifying can become everyday occurrences.

It's a short book, and taken on face value it's also funny and fast paced, but perhaps because of its brevity a few of the side characters are neglected. Vimbai's daughter is used mainly to illuminate Vimbai and Dumi's characters, and she never quite becomes a whole person in her own right. The same could perhaps be said of some of the other hairdressers in the salon. But Vimbai and Dumi are well drawn and complex. Vimbai is proud, cruel to her house-girl, materialistic; Dumi is arrogant, and he flashes his money around to impress. Nevertheless they are both likeable, compelling products of where and how they live. Underneath the slightly predictable plot twists, this is an intelligent portrayal of people's struggle to live everyday lives – helping their kids with homework, flirting with co-workers, falling in love, hairdressing – in a city, and country, in crisis.
Golden Monkey

Looking Back

An Exquisite Sense of What Is Beautiful
J David Simons
Saraband, RRP £8·99, 294pp

In J David Simons' third novel, *An Exquisite Sense of What Is Beautiful*, celebrated British writer Sir Edward Strathairn, now in his seventies, returns to Japan where, decades earlier, he wrote the novel that made his name. Strathairn's debut, *The Waterwheél*, with its criticism of America's wartime use of nuclear weapons and firebombing against Japan, proved to be as politically explosive as it was successful. Now, the publication of his ex-wife's autobiography threatens to generate similar controversy in his personal life.

Accompanied by his long suffering and underappreciated personal assistant Enid, Strathairn retreats from the public eye to the safety of the hotel in Hakone where he was resident writer while working on *The Waterwheél*. On this final trip back east, he encounters a series of old friends and acquaintances which sparks a recollection and reappraisal of his life and work.

The narrative is split into chronologically alternate chapters, switching between the actions of the elder Sir Edward and his younger self, charting his early life and development as a writer across Glasgow, Japan, London and New York, with particular focus on his tempestuous relationship with the now-famous American abstract painter, Macy Collingwood. Chapter headings noting place and time divide the sections and the segmentation of the story is well chosen and executed, with what feels like just the right amount of space allotted to both early and later Eddie.

Simons' prose is clean and uncluttered, and he displays a particular knack for using fragments to quickly develop the atmosphere of his scenes and keep his narrative moving at a satisfying, though never rushed, pace. Eddie's thoughts and impressions are presented to readers with a closeness that is difficult to do well, and Simons' direct, unfussy writing succeeds in this task. This is particularly evident in the chapters dealing with Eddie's later life as he begins to experience forgetfulness and the onset of senility, which is skillfully, and sympathetically, handled. Ultimately, Eddie is believable because of the value he places on his reputation over his own happiness. A significant degree of selfishness and careerism has been essential in establishing him as a serious writer. The hopes and happiness of himself and others have been sacrificed on the altar of his ambition, and we imagine that even with the hindsight of his later years, these are paths and turnings he would take again. Despite his protestations to the contrary, we suspect that he secretly enjoys the opportunity to talk about himself and his works at readings, events and interviews, and although claiming to never have reread his novels, he engages in a kind of self-obsessed reanalysis of his oeuvre and its meaning, diagnosing his "more important novels" as dealing with "injustice," "the dispossessed" and "spiritual void" respectively.

It is here we find the one real difficulty with *An Exquisite Sense of What Is Beautiful*. The fictional fictions reveal themselves too transparently as novels of ideas for us to take them truly seriously as the kind of acclaimed classics which would win their author a knighthood. The inclusion of an epilogue of extracts from *The Waterwheél* undermines and detracts from Simons' actual ending which is elegant and taut, a certain suggestion of deus ex machina notwithstanding. This is the only part of the book where the prose seems flabby, and spotting the references to Strathairn's own life in the extracts from his text feels like a shallow and unsatisfying way to end the novel.

What we can be thankful for is that Simons' abilities with the pen outstrip those of his protagonist and ensure that *An Exquisite Sense of What Is Beautiful* is a sure-handed and satisfying read.
Macavity the Mystery Cat

Life, and Other Fables

Fabulous Beast
Patricia Ace
Freight Books, RRP £8·99, 70pp

This reviewer has no doubt that at least one of his lazy, older, white male colleagues will attempt to ghettoise Ace's wonderful debut collection as "wimmen's poetry", but that would do grave injustice to a moving, enjoyable book that resonates with a universal humanity: covering themes of birth, ageing, love, lust, discord, fear, separation, death and renewal.

What the hell is women's poetry anyway? One imagines the vicar's widow, pondering a chintzy ten minutes of Radio 4, clutching a Jaffa Cake and a cuppa whilst awaiting the next hot flush... There is nothing mimsy or mumsy about Ace, who is one of the freshest new voices in UK poetry. Yes, here and there are a few poems containing stretchmarks, knickers, breastfeeding and young motherhood but they are written with such engaging vitality that the reader cannot help but be carried along in the current of image and wordplay. Any old tropes are neatly trimmed and while the voice is unapologetically a woman's voice, its gender is secondary to its artistry.

If anything this is family poetry, for if there is one central theme that runs through Ace's work in this collection, it is kin. The poems are about lovers, mothers, husbands, fathers, and particularly daughters – of whom she is clearly perplexed but proud, as in 'The women': "Nudged awake from the slumber of nurture, / I find the women living in my house. /.../ bragging that their breasts are bigger than mine," and 'Ruby turning Thirteen': "She comes home from school smelling of rubbers / and Tippex and, faintly, of sweat /.../ She's in a play about the seven deadly sins"

The poet is not one to avoid difficult topics such as dementia 'The Birches', paedophilia 'The Woods', marital strife 'Storm Damage' the senescence and death of parents 'Diary in Old Age' and its companion poems. At the desk of lesser poet, a treatment of these subjects might be cloying, heavy-handed and trite. Not so with Ace, her plain-spoken approach is matter-of-fact, deft and effectively unsettling.

Amongst these 'domestic' poems, secreted like hot coals in the sand, are more mythic, feisty and pleasingly abstruse ones like 'spring / everyday I wake to the massacre of birds', 'Lions of Guia', 'Little Octopus', 'Dido's Marriage' and the title poem. There is also a third strand, this time of landscape/ nature poetry, and it is in these that Ace shows her gifts for innovation in rhyme and form, as in 'Skye Lines' (Trotternish was just crying out to be in a poem...) and 'Settlement'. Again, this is subject matter (the Clearances) visited many times by other Scottish poets, and again Ace manages to be fresh and spare in her treatment of it, something she achieves by economy of language and the occasional startling intervention by a talking deer: "O there is something greater".

The only possible quibble with this book is a minor one – given the three diverse thematic strands already mentioned, it did at points feel that three slimmer collections had been made into one volume. But that may say more about the economics of poetry publishing than anything else, and the wide-ranging selection means that it contains something for most tastes.

Ace is a poet with talent in spades. Her wit and sense of life's absurdity are never far below the surface, but if any premise unites this collection it is the unflagging determination of the human spirit and of Mother Nature in the face of worldly trials. An indefatigable chimera of a book, it is aptly a Fabulous Beast.
Moby-Dick

A Family History

Fremont
Elizabeth Reeder
Kohl Publishing, RRP £8·99, 352pp

Fremont is the accomplished second book from Elizabeth Reeder, whose debut, *Ramshackle*, was met with wide acclaim. It is a bold, ambitious novel which charts the fortunes of the dysfunctional Fremont family, opening with the impulsive marriage of Rachel and Hal, who embark together on an epic, everyday quest; building a family. Within the crumbling walls of Hal's family home, they have children in dizzying succession.

The Fremonts are pioneers, exploring the landscape of family a little further with the birth of each new child, but Hal's ambition and Rachel's fecundity attract increasing envy and suspicion in their small community and we see their children grow up against a backdrop of small town gossip and prejudice. As Hal and Rachel's marriage begins to falter, territories shift, boundaries change and loyalties are divided within their large and clamorous brood.

Rachel and Hal's ill fated romance is beautifully written and moving without ever being sentimental. Their first date in a registry office has all the resonance of a creation myth, rooted in careful, elegant prose. Myth slowly becomes realism as the initial passion between them fades, eroded by tragedy, betrayal and unrealised expectations. "Us Fremonts have boys," Hal tells Rachel when she is pregnant with their first child. His disappointment with each successive daughter and the pressure he puts on Tex, the sole son, warps his character, but he never becomes two dimensional. Flashbacks are skilfully used to evoke his flawed relationship with his own father and moments of tenderness and doubt humanise him. His relationships with his daughters are fraught but always believable. Rachel is the centre of the dysfunctional family, struggling against Hal's whims and caprices, trying to build a safe place for her children and continuing with her dream of building a family, even when her relationship with Hal has completely broken down. Her motivation for this is revealed in flashbacks to the island community from which she was expelled for the crime of being born a girl.

The language is vivid and original, with recurring motifs that guide us through the rapidly expanding family. So many daughters might have become an indistinct mass for the reader, but each of the thirteen children is a dynamic individual, named after American states and drawn with a cartographer's precision. Their personal dreams, hopes and fears are developed and clearly delineated to ensure that the characters remain distinct from one another. The various sibling relationships – friendships, jealousies, rivalries and unlikely alliances – are portrayed with emotional insight and a dark humour.

The enormous family home, in particular the mythic entrance hall with its vaulted ceiling, is almost another character in the novel. It is a vast mansion with rooms which mysteriously appear and disappear, built by Hal's father and crumbling under the weight of the family's history and failed aspirations. After each child is born, Hal carves their name state and affixes it to the painted map on the wall of the hallway. This map is the central motif of the novel, a chart of the family's collective past in the heart of their house.

Reeder has a striking facility with language. The writing is subtle and deft, and the metaphorical resonance of the imagery, the repeated motifs of cartography, the allegorical descriptions of landscape and above all the emotional truths at the heart of the novel dispel any tension that might have existed between the mythic elements of the story and its literary realism. *Fremont* is a beautiful novel which unapologetically recognises the decision to create a family for what it is; a bold endeavour, a momentous undertaking, a leap of faith.
Hungry Tiger

Family
Bet McCallum

WE CALLED IT *Little Sakaka*. In character it was like many of the shops we'd seen on the edge of the Absolute Desert, but it was in South London. The shelves were crammed with foods from everywhere and it was there I'd discovered rose harissa. Massive catering packs of rice and five-gallon drums of cooking oil were piled up in the aisles and there was hardly any room to pass. Cassava roots and scotch bonnets rolled underfoot. The counter was far too high for anyone under 5′10″ and all the alcohol was locked up in cages. It stood next to *Leone Step Out*, an all night barbers and nose-hair clipping centre but you could also send money home to Africa from there.

It was a very busy minimarket; it was a neighbourhood hangout. Everyone living off the High Street used it and Nargis, an astonishingly beautiful woman from Peshawar – third generation – ran the place like a club. She nurtured us all. Every day there were free samples of Coconut Barfi or other cakes and sweets. Cardamom or cinnamon coffee was on offer in the back and there was always music, the radio permanently tuned to Buzz Asia. Nargis loved Bangra. Buying their Oyster cards, the clients jiggled.

For some the shop was a drop-in, for others a home-from-home. There were even chairs out front for the local worthies – Androula and Mr Tang with their sticks. (He was teaching her conversational Mandarin.) Nargis' cousin was forever in there pressed against the glassed-in post office section, either peeling an orange in one go – one long careful paring cut – or eating a KFC Boneless Banquet directly from the box.

Nargis' cousin stank, too many layers of acrylic, but I don't think anyone ever told her. She was intimidating, too brash and too argumentative and she often looked for trouble with other regulars. Like Burko. Burko was off the Ogan Estate – a scowling teenager and always bunking school. He hung around the shop pretending to choose sweets but really defacing some of the labels: Sweet Piccallili became Wet Lil; Chewing Liquorice, Chin Lice; Chilli Beans, ill Ben and so on. Childish humour. Nargis (in fact all of us) knew it was him but she thought it was quite funny and ignored the offence. She even gave him free crisps and sell-by chocolate. She would break into angry Urdu and tell her cousin to lay off. I think she was genuinely concerned for him. His family were often banged up. Their flat had broken windows and their balcony was a scrapyard. She told me once she would rather he hung round her shop than get involved in serious trouble. But I had seen him watching the B-Block Crew monopolising the baby-swings in the park and he'd laughed rather too loudly when a flaming wheelie bin went spinning past the sycamores.

Mr Metaxas, a Tourettes sufferer from childhood and loved by us all, came every morning for his *South London Press* and a Vimto. You could hear his involuntary bark of 'Archbishop Makarios!' from as far away as K.K.Caterers. Then he'd shuffle through the door in his slippers and spend ages ranting at Nargis, Posh Dave and LarryLarry about the infrequency of the 171 from Catford, with the odd blurted 'Alan Sugar!' mixed in. He would

➼

harangue Burko in a grandfatherly way about missing school ('Bertie Bassett!') but would always end up buying him milk, bread and ('Andy Warhol!') a tin of soup to take home. (Although I'm not sure he always went back to the flats; I once saw him in a sleeping bag in the underpass and dropped a two-pound coin into the empty soup tin.) We all had a soft spot for Burko. He was naïve for a thirteen year old but he talked street and tried to be gangsta. He had the wrong trainers. It was kind of sad.

It was the morning of Sunday August the 7th. Nargis opened up as normal, brewed the coffee and turned on Asian Network The usual crowd were in and out but I didn't see Burko. He hadn't been seen for days. The art students had just come out of the nightclub (raucous) and were buying up all the instant noodles; some primary school children were handling the Pick 'n' Mix and squabbled over Fizz Wiz and Midget Gems. Traffic noise from the street was drowned in the drone of a police helicopter. Nargis turned up the volume for the news and the broadcast carried across the road: '...all the unrest. There has been more trouble in Brixton. T Mobile and Halfords have been targeted and gangland rivalry has flared in Coldharbour Lane...'

The rest was drowned as Tunde from the barbers and the comb-over guy from the family jewellers came out and started banging in nails and boarding up the fronts of their shops. Coldharbour Lane wasn't far from the High Street and I said to Nargis, maybe she should close up and go home early. But she said 'No' – people always ran out of stuff on a Sunday and anyway she had to take the dahl to the outreach project.

Nargis was singing along with Abrar Ul Haq and stirring the huge pot of lentils when there was a great jangling sound from the front shop – all the bottles were rattling, a menacing crescendo. Voices were raised, whooping almost. There was a splattering sound then harsh laughter and running feet. Nargis came round from the back and looked very sad. Someone had sprayed I K A P across the whole of the front window and the door.

Later we all heard that two hundred youths had come rampaging down the High Street. Cars were pelted with bricks, the bar at Club Cambo had been ransacked and a mob had swarmed into the bookies. My nephew, Tavish, from the ACE pharmacy had been trampled when trying to pull down his metal shutters. Mr. Metaxas had been viciously rocked (Jesus Christ!) then trapped in his van.

But he saw it all.

Amid the chaos, the B-Block Crew danced about outside the minimarket in a frenzy. Passers-by were egged. A bike went hurtling through the plate glass window, then the shop was full of youths in hoods and scarves covering their mouths. One was wearing a rubber Batman mask. They barged in over the cubes of glass, kicking at cauliflowers and grabbing any stuff they fancied. Mr Metaxas said it was like a greed circle – the inferno (Dante Alighieri!). A family-sized tin of ackee went through the post-office screen and cash drawers were rifled. Bags of letters and official forms were tossed high. The barrels of oil were gashed and deliberately spilled.

Mr Metaxas made out a face he knew. Burko was being goaded by his new-found family. He had something in his hand. Nargis was standing in the wreckage of her shop. Beauty among ugliness. She was looking straight at him, shaking her head and opening her arms. But he threw the petrol bomb anyway.

Man Overboard

Dan Coxon

RICK FIRST FEELS the urge to tip himself into the bay as he sits swaying in the wake of a two-berth cruiser. The rented kayak bobs in the swell, his hands white on the paddle. In his mind he is already in the deep. Earlier he'd disturbed what he thought was a seal, a grey blur sliding from a private jetty into the water. It surprised him almost as much as the strength of this sudden compulsion to join it beneath the waves. Down in the deep, where there's no noise, no light, simply the darkness and the cold. It seems so easy just to tip and sink.

Later that day, after he's returned to the shore and collected his deposit from the girl in the floating cabin, he tries to convince himself that his mood was born of the lulling desolation out on the bay. But at home he finds his eyes drawn time after time to the view across the harbour, the tears swelling behind his eyes like a migraine. He dreams of salt water burning cold in his nostrils.

The chance to relocate had seemed like a gift. His visit to Seattle two years ago was still a cherished memory: five days spent drinking with Clare, his girlfriend of only four months, watching tattooed bands thrash their way through thirty-minute sets in tiny dive bars. The memories had gathered such a halcyon sheen that he was the first to put his name down for the relocation. Practicing his Americanisms, he told his friends that it was a win-win.

The phrase comes back to him as he sets up his home office the next day, making a cursory check of his emails while the coffee gurgles awake in the kitchen. What he's won isn't clear. The two-storey rental house comes complete with a view across Pines Bay and out to the mountains; two bedrooms on each level, a balcony large enough to accommodate its own barbecue. But in reality he spends most of his time curled up on the sofa in the open-plan living room, or hunched over his laptop in the office. He'd invited a cluster of the early hires back for drinks one evening, but when they left before seven o'clock he found himself wrapped in silence again. He hasn't extended another invitation. Neither have they.

He's about to pour a cup of coffee when his eyes snag. The email's subject line is occupied by a long reference number, but it's the opening words that cause his attention to stutter. Five words on the screen: In Response To Your Ad. He knows he shouldn't allow his hopes to run wild, but he can feel his pulse quickening as if the morning coffee has already hit his heart. He sits back down and clicks through.

She doesn't say much. Her name is Kirsten. She saw his personal ad online, had noted it because he said he was Scottish. She's a Scot too, it'd be a shame to have a fellow countryman so close and do nothing about it, wouldn't it? She's just up the road from Pines Bay, in Purcell. He should contact her if he wants to meet, or just to chat. She signs it Kirsten, with a single x on the same line, then a number.

It takes him three aborted attempts before he manages to dial. He half expects her to be an internet phantom, an unreal presence whose sole purpose is to taunt him over the ether. When she answers he's so shocked that

➤→

he forgets to breathe.

'Hello?'

'Is this Kirsten? I'm Richard, I... I got your email this morning. You sent me an email, right?'

The phone hisses into silence. He wonders if she's hung up.

'I remember you. The Scotch guy? I forgot I gave you this number, but yeah, that's me. Good to talk to you. How's things?'

He can't place his discomfort at first, but it's with the nausea of disappointment that he realises she has an American accent. Hadn't she said she was Scottish? His eyes roam across the screen. Maybe it had been too much to hope for.

'Are you okay sweetie? You've gone awful quiet, are you still there?'

'Sorry. Sorry. It's just that I was expecting a Scottish accent, that's all. You said in your message...'

Her laughter crackles from the phone's tiny speakers. 'I'm a second generation Scot. My Mom was Scotch, or part Scotch, on her father's side. I've lived here all my life, but I can dream of going back one day. How about you? You don't sound like you've been here long?'

'Just three months. It seems longer. I don't really know many people here, to tell you the truth. That's why I posted the ad. Not that I expected anything back, but... it seemed better than sitting here alone.'

Does that make him sound too needy? He suspects that it does, and as he wipes the back of his hand across his brow he finds that he's sweating like a schoolboy. So much of his work is conducted via email that it feels uncomfortably intimate to be talking with a stranger like this, her voice whispering close to his ear.

'You have a car, right? You should come up here to Purcell, it can't be more than thirty minutes. We can get a coffee, or a drink. If you want to, that is. But it'd sure beat us sitting here on our own. You can tell me about the old country, I always like that. That sound good? You want my address?'

Once he's written it and double-checked it they hang up. Kirsten secures a promise that

he'll ring her doorbell at least, not just disappear back into the internet. He stares at the address for a moment, the long stream of unfamiliar numbers and letters. It seems so alien to him that the waters of the bay return to his mind. The endless swirling grey as they swallow him whole. He leaves his coffee warming in the pot and fetches his coat and keys.

Kirsten's building leans precariously at the edge of the freeway, its unmatched angles and aura of decrepitude reminding Rick of a toppling house of cards. The chimney stack is constructed of flaking red bricks, their surface dusty and cracked. The rest is wood. A couple of boards have slipped, and all are coated in a thin green film that might be mildew, or rot. At one corner the green blossoms into a furred clump of moss. Since the moved Stateside he's grown used to seeing this outward neglect, the interiors of buildings often putting their scabrous exteriors to shame, but something tells him that won't be the case here. The air feels cold and damp as he steps out of the car, as if it's spent the last ten years at the bottom of a lake. There is the promise of more rain.

His ride out to Purcell was uneventful, TomTom calling out the turnings long before he came to them. It gave him a chance to ponder what he was doing, as he was propelled northwards through towering stands of trees that overshadowed the freeway on both sides. It's an unavoidable fact that he's lonely. He's been alone more often than not since his feet touched American soil, the days stretching like wastelands. In theory he should have packed his bags and booked a ticket on the next flight home. But he made a promise to the agency, and his professional pride resists all attempts to break the pact. He has to give it a year, minimum. Then he'll see. Until then, he'll learn to rely on the misery of solitude.

As for Kirsten, she is clouded in his thoughts, as if the thick Northern haar that sometimes sits on the bay has rolled into his ear while he was sleeping. He doesn't know exactly what he means to do when she opens that grimy wooden door. He isn't even certain that he believes she's real. For all his musings as the car carried him through the northwestern woods, he hasn't given more than a few seconds' thought to her appearance. She might be a blonde, a redhead, tall, short, young, old – she might be a man for all he knows. It wouldn't be a shock to find Sasquatch facing him from the doorway. But it doesn't keep him from stepping onto the peeling wood of her porch.

The wood gives a hollow knock as he raps it with his knuckles, the impact leaving two white spots on the mildewed surface. A minute later the door cracks open to reveal a slim young woman with short, dark hair. She clearly hasn't dressed for the occasion, but she's pretty, in a plain way. Her boyish body is cocooned in dark grey sweatpants and a green velour hoodie that reminds him of the felt-like outgrowths of moss on the side of the house. She doesn't smile, but her brow unknits a little when she sees him. She may be a kindred Scot after all.

'You're Richard, right? Wow. I wasn't sure I'd even see you, but you got here quick. I guess you're keen.'

He swallows, his tongue tackling a slick of saliva that has risen in his mouth like a flood. 'I figured we're both free now, so why not... no time like the present, right?'

There's a dropped beat between them, a pulse of silence. Then Kirsten shrugs and turns, walking up the short flight of steps to her apartment. The move brings her arse into his line of vision, and he surprises himself by not looking away.

'You might as well come on up then. I've not had time to tidy the place, but I'm sure you don't care about that. Just excuse the state of it if you can. And watch your feet, I have a cat in here somewhere.'

The cramped living room is cleaner than he expected, given her warning, but it's dark and airless, a man-made cave. Only a collection of candles stands out from the debris, an eruption of wax beside her small flatscreen TV. Some are half-burned, others are tall and perfectly formed; some stand on small plates and saucers, while a couple seem to be wrapped in lace-like white gauze. He thinks he even spots one in the shape of an erect phallus. He's so busy staring at this alien cityscape that he

doesn't notice Kirsten's return until her hand brushes his shoulder.

'It's Rick, right? Not Richard? Or Dick?'

She laughs again, the cackle he'd heard on the phone. Something chill runs through him. A ghost of the waters lapping up his spine.

'Rick's fine. It's what they called me back home. I was just admiring your candles. That's quite a collection. I hope you're not expecting the power to cut out any time soon.'

He'd intended it as a joke, but if she notices she gives no indication. Instead her eyes search for something within him, her pupils wide like two bullet holes. He finds himself wondering whether she's on drugs. Medication is easy to buy here, and he knows from his web searches that there's an ongoing meth problem in the region. He considers turning and leaving.

Kirsten smiles at him, a self-absorbed, cat-like grin that arouses him even as it hollows out his insides. She reaches out a hand. Her fingers are cold in his, and slight, like brittle twigs left out to die in the snow. He holds them, but only gently. It seems they might fracture beneath the slightest pressure.

'Well, would you like to see my bedroom, Rick? It's cosier in there, and we can sit and talk. Or more, if you'd like. How does that sound, honey? Would you like that?'

He feels himself nodding as humbly as a child, and then those pale fingers are leading him through another door. The room beyond is musty, the air heavy as it trickles into his lungs. He can just see the bed in a pool of pale light, but beyond it his vision recedes into blackness.

When Kristen speaks it is with a confidence that numbs his will. Her voice stays low, humming through his skin, and he knows at once that he will not say no.

'It's forty dollars for thirty minutes sweetie, or seventy for an hour. I'll take cash only, and in advance. Beyond that, anything goes. Just so you know, my boyfriend is downstairs, and if he hears me scream or shout he has a key. But otherwise he'll leave us alone. Okay? Are we good?' He nods. 'I'll go freshen up. Leave you to get ready alone. If you want to strip and slide between the sheets that's good for me. Then

➽

we can start having fun, honey. I'll be back in a few minutes.'

She walks out of the room, leaving him standing alone in the murk. He feels empty, and light, as if he's falling slowly backwards into the endless grey waters of the bay. His hands clench one last time at his sides, then Rick begins to undress, slowly, the cold, damp air spreading tiny shivers across his skin.

Apartment Number Eight

Izabela Ilowska

I WAS THEIR neighbour. They lived on the third floor in apartment number eight and I lived at six. People say that seven is a lucky number. Maybe they are right.

She was in her early twenties, short, a little stooped; she never looked anybody in the eye. He was red-haired and had a freckled face. He wore battered sneakers and a leather jacket; I had never seen him without it, even on hot summer days. And there was this little boy, Adam, almost like an angel: blond, curly hair, blue eyes and a cheerful smile. I believe he was three years old. Only three years old when they drowned him.

People said that her stepfather had been raping her ever since she turned seven. Of course the mother knew about it, but she was afraid of her husband. When someone reprimanded him, he became unpredictable and violent. He yelled, pushed, hit; frightened and threatened them or shut them in the cellar. Then the mother started drinking and she drank a lot. After some time she stopped noticing and hearing what was going on in the other room. Sometimes she even thought she had imagined it.

When she was sixteen, the girl ran away from the house with Tomek, her boyfriend, who had stolen some money from his father so they could survive for a few days. Then they stayed at his cousin's farmhouse and lived in a small room in the attic. Tomek often said that he loved her and that he wanted to marry her and that they would always be together and that it would be like in the movies. But as soon as he started drinking, he would yell that she was a

slut. Sometimes he hit her, but only when she really deserved it.

One day, the cousin came into their room and he was very angry and said that he did not want to let them use the attic for free any more. Since Tomek had no money, he suggested that the cousin could 'borrow' his girlfriend from him for a few nights. The cousin had greasy hair and spots all over his face, so she had to close her eyes whenever he approached her. Of course she could not say no because she had nowhere to go. Tomek was mad at her and said that she stopped loving him and that maybe she preferred the cousin. She tried to convince him that nothing had changed and that they needed a place to stay and that, after all, it had been his idea in the first place. She said she would never look at a man like the cousin and that it should have been obvious to Tomek who was taller, thinner, had no spots and she really loved him. So, at times, Tomek acted as if he had forgiven her. But after a few days new quarrels began.

'I am going to kill him,' he said once. 'I will just kill him and then we will live in his house and drive his car. He is only an obstacle.' She did not know what to say. Truly, the cousin was useless, but did they really have to kill him? Tomek would not listen to her; he had already worked out a perfect plan. There was rat poison in the cellar. She would prepare dinner and add it to his cousin's meal. Then they would take his body and bury it in the woods of the nearby village. No one would find out and they would say that the cousin left the country to work abroad, in Germany or even farther, and they

➤➤

were simply watching over his property. 'I'm sure we will succeed,' he assured her.

On Monday evening she made goulash, added the poison and they all sat down to dinner. Tomek was silent, drinking vodka. The cousin said he was not hungry and that he had a strange stomachache and that maybe he should see a doctor.

'Eat something,' she told him. 'Then you will definitely feel better. You have problems with your stomach because you don't eat.' Tomek remained completely quiet. Then he got up and went to the cellar to bring up another bottle of vodka. In the meantime, the cousin started to eat, very slowly, reluctantly. She was getting impatient. Perhaps she had pricks of conscience. She went out, took a deep breath and came back to the kitchen. 'Don't eat that,' she said to the cousin. 'There is something wrong with that meat. Maybe they sold me a piece that was not fresh. Please, don't eat that.' The cousin went to bed and Tomek was confused. Did he eat enough goulash? Would the poison kill him? Then he went upstairs and beat her because she thwarted his plans. Maybe she even lied that she didn't like the cousin, he thought. He beat her with his leather belt, then he hit her in the face, and afterwards he grabbed her hair and was pulling it violently. She did not scream; she was too afraid. She thought he would kill her. In the morning the cousin got up and went to work. Alive. Not dead. Tomek said that he would not support her any longer and told her to get out of the house. She, bruised all over, got dressed and left. She did not know what to do or where to go; she did not know the village, the roads, the surroundings. So she walked straight ahead, slowly, dragging her feet just to be away from that small, dark room in the attic, although it made her sad that he forgot that he had loved her and had said that they would always be together.

She was alone again. It was getting dark and she had nowhere to sleep, so she knocked on the door of the first house she saw. 'What do you want?' a man's voice yelled. The door, however, remained closed. She explained she did not have any money, no roof over her head,

no future and that she would really like to stay the night somewhere, just till tomorrow. The lights went out and the man inside the house did not even try to pretend that the girl's fate made any impression on him. So she decided to continue walking. Finally she was so exhausted that she did not have the strength to go on. She fell asleep on a bench and, as it was a hot summer night, she covered herself only with her jacket and even managed to feel comfortable and hopeful. 'Is there anything worse that could happen to me?' she thought. She truly believed she had suffered enough so she was certain that when she woke up the next day, her life would take a different course.

Early in the morning she reached an asphalt road and struck out her thumb. A car stopped. It was an old, red Fiat Polonez. Inside was a dark red-haired young man. He was red-haired in an ugly way and his entire face was covered with large freckles. He was wearing a black leather jacket and smoking a cigarette. 'Are you getting in or are you going to stare like that forever?' he snapped and she got in, without thinking twice, into that red car and vigorously slammed the door. 'Don't do it again! Don't slam it,' he yelled at her and then stepped on the gas. She did not dare to speak; she was afraid of this young man, so ugly and red-haired. In the back seat she saw various magazines of naked women. They were blond girls with huge breasts and very red lips. Quickly she turned away so he would not notice that she had been looking at them. But he must have noticed because he stopped near a remote parking lot and said: 'Give me a blow job, cutie!' And she thought it was all because of those magazines that she had been looking at, at all those women dressed in strange, latex bikinis. I was just asking for it, I deserve to be treated like this, she thought and so obediently she did what he had told her to do.

Afterwards he became extremely talkative, somehow more amusing, excited and friendly. He was talking about his job at his friend's garage, that he was just learning but had already made a considerable progress and maybe someday he would open his own garage or a body shop and would have loads of money.

And then he would buy some cool car, most probably a used BMW, and would drive it all over town and be so proud and happy. This car, this old, red Polonez, did not really belong to him; it was his friend's and he was just picking up batteries, tyres, and other stuff. 'And where are you going?' he wanted to know. 'I guess I am looking for a job,' she replied very quietly, timidly. And it came out that he had a female friend who was just about to give birth so there was, in fact, a job at a small greengrocer's shop, very close to his garage. She could even live with him, he suggested. 'We had such a nice time at the parking lot, eh?' he said smiling. She agreed, of course, because what could she possibly have said or done? Surely it was better than sleeping on a bench or wandering about unknown streets of squalid villages, always alone and with no money, she thought. And she did not need to look at him and, after all, he was not so bad, he cared for her and maybe even loved her.

She was working at the greengrocer's shop and sometimes, when there were no customers, she could listen to the radio or read some colour magazines. She particularly liked stories, real stories about women who had unfaithful or abusive husbands. She wanted to read about everything that was sad, depressing or terrifying because then she knew that others also had hard lives. Sometimes there were upsetting articles about people who were successful and lucky and she hated them. What was luck really and why did her life lack it? she wondered.

Every day in the morning he went out and came back home dirty, exhausted, and sweaty. She cooked dinner for him and afterwards sometimes they went to bed together and he made her do different, strange things. She suspected that he had read about them or had seen them in those magazines he was buying. Then he would fall asleep and she would sit by the bedroom window. She looked at the sky and the stars and wondered why they were so beautiful and so distant.

They had saved some money and moved to a cramped one-room apartment in one of the local ugly high-rise apartment houses. She got a job in a supermarket where she worked longer hours, but they paid more. He was still under the illusion that someday he would have his own garage and his dream car. But lately his friend's business had not been doing so well and the boss had even suggested that he should start looking for another job. He became irritated, drank more and started to bring his friends over to their apartment at number eight. She, completely exhausted after work, did not know how to stand up to him. Sometimes she really thought about leaving, but the money kept disappearing and she felt powerless. Finally she, too, began to drink. She drank to forget. She drank to stop thinking and feeling. Often he did not come home at all, but then Marek would drop in, and Marek really liked her. He told her frequently that she was very pretty and sexy, and that he desperately wanted to kiss her. And Artur promised that he would leave his wife and they would run away together somewhere. She believed him because he owned a video shop and he was quite well off. He always bought good alcohol and once he brought her a box of chocolates. But in the end he never left his wife.

And then, in the same apartment at number eight, a baby was born: so little, defenceless and unwanted. He hated the child because he was not sure if he really was the boy's father. The child had fair hair, not red so he treated him like a stranger. Who came up with the idea to drown the boy? Was it the mother, tired of constant questioning, insults and anger? Or was it the father, tormented by anxiety, jealousy and hatred?

There is silence in apartment number eight now. Nobody comes in or goes out, there are no screams; one cannot hear the baby crying or his rare laughter. Because he did laugh occasionally, I guess. I'm not sure any more. Perhaps I wanted him to so badly that I was deceiving myself. There is despair, pain, suffering, doubt in God, in people and self-doubt in apartment number six. I could have done something. After all, I was their neighbour. But I did nothing and now it is too

➡

late. My tears will not bring the child back to life, they will not help him. I am sitting here, in my armchair and I am inventing reasons for that horrible crime. I am inventing various scenarios. I am creating stories composed of atrocities because I desperately want to understand it, rationalize it. Evil breeds evil. It cannot be otherwise.

But the reality is different. She had a mother and a father. In fact, her father was a well-respected surgeon; the mother was a pianist. She lived in an impressive house with five bedrooms and three bathrooms in a good neighbourhood on the north side of town. There was nothing traumatic in her life. She had not been raped by her stepfather or abused by her boyfriend's cousin and the ugly red-haired young man had not taken advantage of her. She did not have to work in a supermarket or to roam through the woods and godforsaken villages. She was just bored: at school during maths and history lessons, at home when she was staring blankly at the TV screen. She did not have any hobbies or friends. One day she decided to go out and have fun, dance to the rhythm of mind-numbing music. There she met a ginger-haired young man whose entire face was covered with freckles and decided to move in with him. I already know how this story ends and I cannot change it.

All I can do now is to invent those various scenarios, make up stories more and more atrocious and inconceivable so that, for one brief moment, I can deceive myself or, if I'm lucky, fall asleep at night.

Origin 1
Alison Flett

vagina *noun*:
meaning 1. core; essence; source
>   2. the warm place beneath a bird's folded wing where, if a finger is gently inserted, the flutter of the heart can be felt.
>   3. *in mythólogy*, a passage between two worlds; a channel where the tides of life and death collide.

or
vagina *verb*: to hold tight in the dark; *or* to hold and release, hold and release; *or* to emerge from darkness into sudden light and hear the frizzle of many struck matches; *or* to hold something sweet beneath the tongue and suck until it is dissolved.

Origin 2
Alison Flett

penis *noun*
meaning 1. strength; majesty; elevation.
>   2. the moment when, e.g. at a garden fete, a basket lid is thrown back and white doves flurry skyward.
>   3. Head of State (*cóll.*)

or
penis *verb:* to enter into uncertain dark; *or* to go forth and retreat, go forth and retreat; *or* to goosebump with pleasure on hearing an orchestral crescendo; *or* to use great strength to express tenderness.

Nursery Rhyme For Our Time
Anne B Murray

What are little girls made of?
Endometrial thickenings, fallopian tubes,
cervix, vagina, ovaries, boobs.
That's what little girls are made of.

What are little boys made of?
Seminal vesicles, deferrent ducts,
penis and prostate, scrotum and fucks.
That's what little boys are made of.

The Difference
Seth Crook

I'm a man in a chair thinking of you,
thinking of you and looking at you,
looking at you and undressing you,
undressing you as soon as the family leaves.
They'll be gone soon.

You are a woman in a chair thinking of me,
thinking of me and looking at me,
looking at me and looking at my nose hairs,
looking at my nose hairs as the door closes.
I'll be clipped soon.

Twa poems fae the Kalivala

Aila Juvenon / Liz Niven

Suid ye see a wean upon the flair
even if it's yer sister-in-law's wean
heize the bairn ontae a bench
dicht its een an smooth its herr
pit some breid intae its haun
spreid some butter oan the breid
if ther nae breid in the hoose
pit a wuid-chip in its haun

23:185-92 kalivala
advice tae the bride aboot livin in an extendit faimilie whaur thir 's no muckle food

This is hou the seilie feel
hou the blessit think -
lik daybrak in voar
the sun oan a spring morn.
Bit hou dae A feel
in ma doule depths?-
lik the flat brink o a clood
lik a derk nicht in autumn
a black wunter's day;
naw, darker than thon -
mair mirkie than a hairst nicht.

22:173-84 kalivala
the Maid o the Nor leavin her hame wi her bridegroom.

Owreset intae Scots bi Liz Niven

Nesting
Katy Ewing

The promised instinct never quite came true,
not as I had pictured it.
I'd stand over the borrowed basket
where my own small life had first been put safe,
had slept and squalled, a life ago,
under my mother's fierce unfailing care,
and try to feel.

I'd made it up with gender-neutral tiny sheets and blankets,
to be prepared,
and now came here to look, to try to wake some urgent hidden self
that wouldn't come,
hand on my belly feeling life twist and turn, kick out, fearfully silent.

What did I expect?
That something tangible would happen, some strong harsh magic,
that suddenly I'd fit the mother skin I'd visioned for myself?

But it just stayed remote like children's games,
playing dolls until the real work began.

Fox
Gordon Meade

Fox is sick of being
chosen as the subject
for so many poems,

all she wants is to be
left alone to get on with
her business of being

a vixen; of raising
the next generation of
inspirational cubs.

Seahorse
Gordon Meade

Seahorse is a great father. All
the mothers agree. Seahorse is so good
a father that he has taken over

almost all the mothers' roles. To begin
with, the mothers are happy for the help.
But, after a while, the more militant

turn against him. Seahorse, it seems,
is not a great father after all. Seahorse is
nothing more than a surrogate mother.

Ties
Lindsay Macgregor

I was told he was my father.
And, sure enough, he had my nose,
my mouth, my frown. Like me,

he always seemed too old,
spoke the language of elective
mutes. He shuffled round

the house, replacing fuses,
lagging pipes, sharpening knives.
I raised him as my own.

Island
Philip Miller

On Liung,
sleeping on your stomach,
my head dead, rising and falling
with your lungs
my ear to your belly button -

your mother is gathering driftwood
for her house.
Your womb lies empty,
my brain remembering:

that an umbilical cord
is born from woman
without nerves on its slippery flesh,
so that its severing
causes no pain.

The Light Is Soft This Morning As I Write You This

Kevin Henderson

Like I think a trout might see from a stream.
It's that cold as well.
A thousand frosted blades of grass quiver in the beat of a bird's wing.
My hands are filled with silence.
The coffee has gone cold in the cup too.

I'm watching the light change. The field changes colour
in complete stillness. Everything
held by fragments of light, by our sky.

I think of you sitting up in bed shaped by the light
listening to the birds sing.
The forecast is for rain later, perhaps sleet.
The light has already begun to falter.

Here is a land outwith where
the light is tender on our painful bodies.
A world takes shape
and then dies.

The rain didn't come in after all.

Morning You
Calum Maclean

Like me, you're not a morning person.
You have no time for those who whistle into their breakfasts,
And you find the concept of a runny egg quite distressing.

Like me, you get lost in the shower,
Delaying the future as long as you can,
'Til your toes wrinkle, your cheeks redden,
And the bathroom is shrouded in steam.

Like me, you anticipate an eight hour shift like a deserter against the wall,
With a pit in your stomach,
A shake in your hands,
One last cigarette as the blindfold descends.

Unlike me, you recover.
 You know it's just work,
That it's something we do but it's not who we are,
That it's not what defines us, there's no need for stress,
Then you walk out the door always looking your best.

Even
Seth Crook

all the flowers
sent by all the world's hungover
and so apologetic men,

accumulated,
wrapped in one big bow,
(not bought at the last garage,
at the last minute)

and ferried, with a tune,
by all the best dressed pipers
of the Lords of the Isles,

won't quite do. Not today.
I'll go to the shed, I think,
contemplate the life of mice,

creep to bed
when the light is out.
Keep to my side.

Threshold
Mark Russell

As an act of love
I promised to have
A crimson tattoo
Of little red hearts
In the softened wheals
Your teeth left behind.

The Princess and The Frog
David R Morgan

Once upon a time, upon a lily-pad in the middle of a sparkling pond, there lived a large, green frog.

One very rainy summer's day, a princess set sail across the pond. As she glided past the lily-pad,

the frog raised his head and called to her.

"Kiss me," said the frog, "upon my forehead, and I will turn into a handsome prince."

"Fuck off," replied the princess, wrinkling her nose, "I rule my own kingdom, I lead my own armies into battle,

I make my own laws. I need no prince, handsome or otherwise. What else do you have to offer?"

"Kiss me," said the frog, "upon my forehead, and I will grant you great fortunes."

"Fuck off," snorted the princess. "I maintain a balanced budget with good economic growth and sensible interest rates.

Your great riches will devalue my currency, send inflation soaring and cripple our exchange rates. Is that the best you have to offer?"

"Kiss me," said the frog, "upon my forehead, and I will grant you dazzling beauty."

"Fuck off," sneered the princess. "I may be plain but beauty does not last. Personality counts."

"What do you want then?" demanded the frog, used to altogether more old-fashioned princesses.

The princess thought hard. On the bank a fairy attempted to dry her wings under a dripping bush. "Fuck it, my fairy dust is fucking damp!"

A little mermaid trudged by in fishnet tights, popping a painkiller. "Ouch, my fucking feet are killing me!"

"I want to be happy," the princess whispered at last, and kissed the frog upon his forehead.

"Fuck off!" laughed the frog, diving clean into the clear, blue pond. "This isn't a fairy tale you know!"

Extract from the novel *All the Little Guns Go Bang Bang Bang*
Neil Mackay

COME THE NEXT Monday morning, Pearse is back at school for the day of the 11-plus, to find out if he's intelligent or not, and Mrs Boatman is running through those auld mathematical and logical questions they set – in preparation for the test that afternoon. He needs the practice or else he will never pass the entrance for the Grammar School. She looks at Pearse over her pointy spectacles as she sets a mock question paper down, and says, 'This is perfectly easy for you, Pearse.' She walks off, with chalk down the back of her black jacket, and chewing gum on the heel of her shoe.

There are daft problems like 'what fraction in its lowest term is equal to 42 per cent?' Who cares. Or they show the alphabet, as if no-one knows it, and then say 'PP is to SN as KL is to [__]', and you have to fill in the blank. How? What does it mean? And if it does mean something, Pearse has been away sick and missed it.

Nothing much else happened that week except for those 11-plus tests, and a fight after school on Thursday with Brian Blackwell, which Pearse never started. He tried to cripple the wee clipe in the fight, though, by jumping on his knee-cap a few times after he'd got him on the ground.

He hadn't seen May-Belle all that week either. She wasn't out and about in the estate, and she was never around in the morning or evening going to or from school, so she must have missed sitting her own entrance exam for the Catholic grammar – though it was highly unlikely she'd ever have passed it anyway, even in a million years of swotting up. It just wasn't her style.

The memory of Martin and the terror of the police had drifted away – for no-one seemed to give a damn what they'd done; it was never mentioned: no-one came knocking at home, there wasn't a word said at school. Nothing happened. Pearse missed her and was lonely and hated the fact he'd bailed on her; wanted to dump her. He couldn't call for her now, though, regardless of how he felt. He didn't want to see her horrible Ma; and he still couldn't be sure if the police had got to her, and if they had, then had she been able to carry off her lies to them, or had she caved but not squealed on him; he knew he shouldn't see her anymore, no matter what, but he couldn't resist the pull of playing with her either.

Pearse's mates didn't call for him on Saturday, the sleekit gits, and he wasn't going to go chasing after them like some love-sick wee girl, so he spent the morning watching Swap Shop bored off his tits. Fed up, he dandered out the door and took a wander about the streets, not doing much, kicking stones around and whipping bushes with a bit of a snappy auld branch. He was idling outside the gate of the last house in May-Belle's row, which ran along the top of his street, at a right-angle – as the auld mathematical 11-plus types would say. The people in that house – the last on May-Belle's row – were never in and had no kids, but they did have two big dogs that were always chained up in their backyard and surrounded by mountains of their own shite and pish. A terrible sight. The breed was indeterminable

➤➤

– they were mutants, about the size of Shetland ponies and a smokey-blue-grey, with red tongues lolling a yard out of their gobs and big bleary eyes. Pearse was poking his stick through the slats in the fence and making them bark, when he heard a big, 'Hi, Pearsey, fanny-boy,' right in his lug-hole.

He swizzled around and there she was herself, May-Belle, looking a bit puffy round the gills from whatever happened to her, but with her wee puckered up smile on her face and her eyes blinking.

Pearse says to her, 'What happened to you? I saw you at the hospital and it looked like you'd been in a car accident.'

She says, 'Ma beat the shit out of me for being late when we came in from robbing the orchard.'

'Jesus,' he says. 'She must have given you one hell of a hammering.'

'She did,' says May-Belle. They wandered about the estate not heading anywhere in particular or paying any heed to whether they were going left or right or east or west. 'She twisted my arm up my back and I thought it was going to break, and she held me by the hair and punched me in the face. That's why I've not been to school.'

'Was that your Dad with you at the hospital?' he asked.

'Aye,' she says. 'But he had to go away again, a few days ago, for a couple of months, I think.'

And Pearse said nothing, because he didn't know what to say.

'He wasn't there, though, when she hit me,' says May-Belle. 'He was down in Belfast. He can't stand the bitch, but she won't let us go away and live together as she says she needs us. She had one of her fellas at the house when she was laying in to me, and he did nothing to stop it, but when it was all over – and this fella could see that I could barely get up and I'd made a pretty bad mess of myself too – he goes to call the ambulance and Ma says, 'no, ring her useless fucken Dad instead,' so this guy runs out to the phone box at the top of the hill and makes I don't know how many phone calls until he finds someone who knows where to fetch Dad, and Dad gets a mate to drive him

up first thing in the morning, because by then it's late and he's no way of getting up here, and when he arrives I'm all fevery and being sick in my bed and near blind with a headache so Dad takes me to the hospital up in Ballymena.'

She pauses, and laughs, and says, 'Och, I'm outta breath talking. What happened to you? Why were you up at the Waveney?'

Pearse says, 'Oh, I was just swinging the lead and trying to get out of school.'

'Why?' she asks.

'Just,' he says, and she looks at him, smelling a fib. 'What did you tell the doctors?' he asks her.

'Dad said that I fell downstairs backwards.'

'Right.'

'On the way home, he said there was something wrong with Ma – that she was sick in the head and that's why he couldn't live with her.'

'Right.'

'When we got back, he threw one of her fellas out and told her that if she ever touched me again, he'd break her neck. He's said that loads of times, though, and nothing ever happens. This has all gone on before.'

Pearse said nothing. Just '…', dot dot dot – ellipsis – the way it's written in books when someone is waiting or struck dumb.

'Ma told him to get the fuck out of the house, and he said he was staying. She said no court in the land would allow a man like him to have me.'

Pearse nodded.

'And she told him he better watch his mouth cos she had plenty on him. He said, 'Try me'. And then she got her coat and her purse and left, shouting 'you can keep the fucken wee bitch'.'

'Where'd she go?'

'Och, she went to Belfast. That's where she works sometimes, or even down in Dublin or over in Glasgow. Once she went to Aberdeen for a month, but said it froze the knickers off her and she'd never go there again.'

'So who's looking after you now?'

'She came back the morning Dad had to go, so I'm stuck with the auld bitch now, til he comes home.'

'I hate that kind of stuff,' Pearse said.

'It's been like this for years.'

They sat down on a wall and started spitting on the paving stones and throwing wee pebbles into the gutter. 'Sorry I never called down for you,' she says. 'I was feeling better the last few days, but I didn't know if you were ill and I didn't want to see that Da of yours, to tell the truth.'

'That's alright,' Pearse says, 'you were sick.'

'I fucken hate her,' says May-Belle, and Pearse can see out of the corner of his eye that she's crying a wee bit so he doesn't turn to look at her in case he embarrasses her.

'There's plenty of dicks I hate too,' Pearse says.

'That Da cunt of yours?' she asks.

'I'd love to kill him,' he says.

'Fuck, I'd love to kill her too,' she says back.

'What about the police?' asks Pearse.

'I'd poison her so the cops would never know. Make it look like a suicide.'

'No,' says Pearse, 'I meant about Martin and the fire and all that.'

'I never heard anything. No-one gives a fuck round here.'

Pearse has a Sherbet Dib-Dab in his pocket so he gives it to May-Belle, telling her he can't stand the way it feels against his teeth, and as he doesn't want it, she can have it. She sits there sucking the sherbet off the lolly, while Pearse tells her how the same thing is happening in his house. 'Mum's going to leave Da one day – two sures about that.' She says, 'Dad'll one day get custody of me as well'. May-Belle's dribbling fizzy red and yellow spit out of her mouth onto the ground. Pearse can't get a proper slobber out of him. He's been gobbing and talking so much his mouth is dry. His throat is spikey, like a blade of grass is stuck in it.

Pearse feels a bit of a cry coming on him now, and is scared he'll start bawling if they don't change the conversation, so says to May-Belle, 'Come on down to my house. Mum's in, and she'll give us a couple of auld jars to go catching bees'.

May-Belle's up for that, so they wander back to Pearse's house, and she waits outside the garden gate while Mum huffs and puffs a bit because she's been asked to tip a whole jar of coffee into a tupperware holder, and wash out the tail end of the jam from a jar that's nearly empty; but after a few minutes she's fine and dandy, and they've got the jars and are away out the gate again and going up the road towards the common.

Pearse takes his penknife out of his pocket and digs air holes into the top of the jars. He's got the coffee jar and May-Belle's got the jam jar. They put a wee bit of grass and some nice smelling petals in the bottom of each jar to attract the auld bees – they add in a gob so the creatures will have something to drink – and then they go hunting on the flowers hanging off the bushes along each side of the common.

Pearse has always considered himself the King of Bee-Catching, but May-Belle gives him a pretty fair run for his money. Like the most practiced bee-hunter, she's not scared. She knows that the big bumblebees, the auld hairy fellas with the fat arses, wouldn't know how to sting a human being if you paid them. They're like fat furry flying cows – they are that gentle. They aren't like honey bees or hornets who'd dive bomb the bollocks off you and sting you half to death just for looking at them the wrong way. May-Belle makes sure she targets the right type for capture.

She's fast too when she's hunting and uses pretty much the same technique as Pearse: creep slowly up on the auld Bumbler, with the jar in one hand and the lid in the other, when he's perched on a flower having a drink of nectar and getting the pollen all over his wee black legs, and just slowly slowly bring the jar up and the lid down on Bumbler, flower and all. Screw the lid shut, snapping off the flower at the head as you do it, and Bumbler and flower are now trapped in the bottom of the glass going 'zzzz-fucken-zzzz-what-the-fuck-happened-zzzz'.

Then the Bumbler will start blattering himself off the inside of the jar, and you can feel him zzzz-ing through the glass until he gets knackered and just sits on his wee flower – beat. Even if you don't roll them over and over again down a hill in the jar, or spin them around,

➼➼

making them dizzy and sick and wobbly, the auld bees will eventually just fade away and die, trapped inside. There's never been a captured bee last more than about three hours inside a jar, even with air holes, without it just deciding to die for whatever reason – sadness or boredom or fear or confusion. And they'll die despite having other bees in the jar with them – so it's not loneliness that's killing them.

After they've nabbed about six or seven bees apiece, May-Belle and Pearse wander along to a nearby street and sit on a wall that surrounds a big tree outside an end house and shake the bees about and give the jars a bit of a spin on the ground. That shuts the bees up. There's no more zzzz-ing and they lie quiet among their flowers, just waggling the odd wee sticky leg in the air or stumble-bumbling into each other. They wouldn't even imagine trying to fly now inside the jar, it's all shaky-slow walking about or lying still – sick, groggy or sleeping. If you opened the lid, they wouldn't know how to escape.

Pearse and May-Belle haven't said anything for a wee minute to each other, which is fine. Although, usually, Pearse doesn't like the quiet and no-one talking, with May-Belle it's alright – and she prefers silence sometimes without the need for noise. A bit of a right bitey wind is getting itself whipped up now out of nowhere, so Pearse says to May-Belle, 'Do you want to come down to my house for a wee while to watch the telly and have some juice. Da's out down the pub and won't be back for ages, so it'll be alright as Mum's the only one in and she's dead on'.

'Aye,' she says, and then she picks up her bee jar and gives it a hell of a shake. 'What about these wee fuckers?' she asks.

'Just let 'em go,' Pearse says.

'Away on, Pearsey,' she says. 'Cmon, follow me.' And she races round the corner to a dark skinny path which runs up the side of a row of houses. Windowless bare brick back-walls line the tiny lane. Facing the bare brick walls, are the big tall bushes that run down the length of the common. It's a secluded lane – the path no broader than a man and a woman walking hand-in-hand. This is the kind of place where older kids come to smoke and write graffiti as it's all in shadow and no-one can see. On the walls there's writing saying things like 'Gary W fucked Pauline M' and a drawing of a dick with pubes and pimples and spunk. Glass is smashed all over the place, and there's graffiti on the ground too, saying 'Cunts look here'.

'You ready?' says May-Belle, twiddling the jar between her two palms real fast as if she's trying to warm her hands.

'For what?' Pearse asks.

'For chucking the wee bastards?' she says, and she mimes throwing the jar like a cricket ball or a bomb, right and loose and over the shoulder in an swinging arch.

Pearse gives the bees in his jar the auld twiddling routine to make sure they keep right groggy and tells May-Belle to hauld on til they're sleepy. Pearse usually keeps his bees outside on his window sill til the morning and then throws them away. Maybe if they're groggy and sleepified, though, the end will be easier for them. The landing won't be too painful – they'll be kind of anaesthetised from all the twiddling and won't suffer too much.

'Ready?' she says.

'Roger!' he laughs, and they pull back their arms like German grenade-men – aiming up the alley away. They count to three together and then fire the jars in a big swoop over their heads. Both jars arc in intersecting parabola – like you'd see in a maths paper – and collide in mid-air about thirty feet in front of them, smashing to smithereens; the silver sparkle of the shards raining to the pavement. Pearse lets a big whoop out of him when the jars kiss and explode, and spins round on his heel to race off before any adults come out of their homes – but May-Belle grabs ahold of him and says, 'Och, hauld on, Pearsey, come here'.

He hesitates for a wee second, and when he can't hear anyone coming allows her to pull him forward, towards the broken jars, by his sleeve.

'What you doing, daft faggot?' he says to her. 'Come on. Let's get the fuck outta here.'

'Wait a wee minute,' she says. 'Let's take a look and see what happened to them.'

'Flippen hell, May-Belle,' he says.

They scoot forward. The bees are lying among the broken glass and battered flowers. Some are well and truly dead – busted up or cut in two. Others, though, are wandering about, like survivors after a bombing raid; tottering around not knowing where they are going, a bit tattered and torn and shell-shocked but otherwise alive.

There's one who's made it away from all the wreckage, a good few inches from the glass and jar lids and flowers. He's heading for the bushes. May-Belle brings her big guttie down on the wee fella – bomp – and scrapes him about underneath her plimsoll. She lifts her foot and he's just a dirty wee hairy smear on the ground.

'Fuck, May-Belle,' Pearse said. 'Have you never heard of the Geneva Convention?'

Bomp. She splats another one. 'What you on about, Pearsey?' she says.

'You're not meant to kill prisoners. It's the law.'

'Bollocks,' she says, and wallops another one under foot.

There's only two left alive, so he says to her, 'Aye, you're right, I suppose', and he leaps high in the air, aiming down hard with his feet, and lands perfectly, flattening the last two survivors at the same time – one under each shoe. Blap. Blop. All squished.

She laughs like a drain, and the pair speed off towards Pearse's house yo-hoo-ing to each other. When they get there, they're just in time for The Basil Brush Show followed by the Pink Panther, the rinky-dink panther. Mum takes a good long look at May-Belle on the doorstep and after a second says, 'Hello, come on in. I expect people to behave themselves in this house, so no carry-on, please. Sit down and watch the TV and I'll get the pair of you some juice and a biscuit'. Mum comes back with a couple of Penguins and some coke, and Pearse and May-Belle sit on the floor and watch Basil Brush getting up to his auld boom-boom shenanigans and the Pink Panther being suave.

When the sports results come on, May-Belle brings the dirty dishes into the kitchen, where Mum is making Spagetti Bolognese on the stove, and says, 'Thanks very much, Mrs Furlong'. Pearse is repeating the football scores

to himself – trying to be like Mike Yarwood and copying the man's voice on the telly, saying the names of all the funny-sounding football teams – 'Blyth Spartans 4, Queen of the South 6' – but he's also got one ear cocked to what's going on in the next room and Mum says, 'You're welcome, dear,' and May-Belle comes back into the living room.

'I'd better be heading,' she says to Pearse.

'Aye, ok, then.'

Mum follows her in and says, 'Is that you off then, love?'

May-Belle says, 'Yeah, I'd better be going for my tea thanks.'

Mum says to her, 'Well, Pearse and I are away out tomorrow for a picnic up to the Six Mile River in Muckamore. Would you like to come along?'

Pearse goes, 'Are we mum? You never told me. Aww beezer, mum, beezer.'

'Shush, you,' Mum says. 'I just decided. It's meant to be a nice weekend, and your father is away tomorrow so I thought it'd be nice to get out in the sunshine.'

'Beezer, ma,' he says.

'Don't call me that,' Mum says. 'I hate that word. It's Mum.'

'Aye,' he says, leaping around on the sofa like a thing possessed. 'Brill, Mum. Can you come, May-Belle?'

'Your friend had better ask her parents if she's allowed.'

'Ok. Thanks,' says May-Belle.

'Can I go up with her, Mum?' Pearse asks.

'Yes,' Mum says, 'but don't be pestering her mother and father.'

They bomb out the door and peg it up the road. May-Belle says to Pearse, 'I like her – she's nice.'

'Aye,' Pearse says. 'Fuck, I love picnics.'

'Me too,' she says.

They get to the bottom of May-Belle's front path, and Pearse hangs back, waiting at the gate. May-Belle walks on, leaving him behind, glancing back as she rings the door bell. She waits twirling her hair round her fingers and swinging on her heels. The door opens and a blank-faced blonde woman stands there screwing up her eyes to shield them from the weak evening light. She's wearing a flimsy white top and no bra. Beneath are these wild vivid pink nipples that Pearse can't take his eyes off. May-Belle lets go her hair. The woman looks at Pearse and a clumsy uglified smile passes over her face. She pulls the door open and May-Belle walks inside. A few minutes later the door opens again and out walks May-Belle.

She nods her head, as she pulls the door shut behind her, not looking at Pearse. She gets to the bottom of the path, opens the gate and says out the side of her mouth, 'That's fine. I can go.'

'Top notch,' he says and they race back to his house, skidding down the flight of six steps that lead from May-Belle's row to Pearse's row – pushing each other and ya-ho-ing.

While they run May-Belle babbles, 'Ma even told me to say that it was very nice of youse to ask me along, and she'd like to return the favour one day.'

'Super,' Pearse says as they run up his garden path, and into the house.

'Grand,' Mum replies when they tell her it's all okay. 'Now weren't you meant to be off home for your tea, dear? I'll see you in the morning about eleven o'clock,' she says to May-Belle.

That night Da didn't get in til God knows what time. By the time he did arrive back Pearse was fast asleep. Before Pearse fell asleep, the evening had been top crack: Gran came over for her tea and told some of her auld stories; then she went back to her place at half nine, and Pearse and Mum settled down to watch the horror double bill on BBC2.

When they're going to bed, Pearse hid in the dark at the top of the stairs and leapt out on her – hissing, shouting 'vampyre, vampyre'. She screamed like he'd bitten half her face off, called him a wee shit and then laughed and chased him around his bed saying she'd eat him. Pearse hopped into bed and she gave him a kiss.

Pearse could smell her Harmony Hairspray as he fell asleep thinking about playing with May-Belle down at the river in Muckamore tomorrow afternoon. Playing was the wrong word – daft; they were heading for the big school soon – so they'd be hanging out.

By the time Mum wakes up that Sunday morning, the Morning of the Last Picnic as Pearse came to style it, he's already downstairs in his jammies making a fort out of a cardboard box, as there was sod all on telly except those auld Jesus Jones Holy Joe type of programmes with ugly types singing hymns. Praise the lord, and pass the ammunition.

Mum walks into the living room looking a bit baggy and saggy round the chops, says, 'Morning, Pearse love', and goes into the kitchen to have a cup of coffee with four sugars, and a couple of fags.

Pearse tootles on with the fiddly business of fort-making, using scissors to fashion wee battlements and a hinged portcullis.

A big holler comes down the stairs – Da shouting, 'Och, Josie, will you come here?' Mum grumbles to herself and walks to the foot of the stairs and shouts up, 'What do you want now, lump?'

He goes, 'Come here, Josie, please.' Pearse hokes his US 7th Cavalry men and some red indians – Crazy Horse and his Lakota Sioux braves – out of the toy-bag where he keeps his soldiers. He's arranging the cavalry boys and the Sioux in and around the fort for one helluva battle, when Mum comes back downstairs. Pearse was pondering over whether or not to take the fort and all the wee men into the back yard, allow the indians to win the fight and then burn the fort to the ground with the Americans inside, but Mum says, 'Your father claims he's ill and he's not going on patrol today.'

Pearse glanced up and then went back to playing because he couldn't've cared less. Lance-Corporal Lame-Dick usually spent his Sundays out with the UDR manning vehicle checkpoints, auld VCPs, on the road to Randalstown, which is a dump with one pub, no shops and a load of backward bumpkins. Gran says he hassles Catholics in their cars just for the hell of it and drags them out in the pissing rain to check their papers and call them fenians and such like, so he can act the big man in front of his Proddie pals.

Pearse is struggling to cut decent shaped sniper slots in the cardboard fort when a wee thought occurs to him that the auld turd being sick might mean they can't go on the picnic.

'We're still going on the picnic, right, mum?' he calls, while she's doing whatever she's doing back out in the kitchen.

'Of course,' she says. 'I have to go to the shops and get him a paper and some head ache pills and tomato juice cos he says he's got food poisoning. Rubbish. A hangover more like, and now the big soldier boy can't even get out of bed to protect so-called Ulster.'

Pearse asks her if she'll get a couple of Scotch eggs for the picnic because he loves those wee fellas, and she says aye she'll go when Gran comes round so there's someone to mind Pearse while she's away at the shops. Gran is coming to the picnic as well, though she says she hates the countryside as it's full of hidden cowpats and wasps and nettles, and she grew up on a farm and had her fill of the fields. The city is the only place a half-way sensible or civilised person would want to live, she says; even a town the size of Antrim is barbarian in her book.

Mum's moaning on – while she makes sausage sandwiches for brekkie – about having to take the car and go down the town because you can't get tomato juice at the local shops.

Crazy Horse and his Sioux braves charge the fort – in a big blood and thunder rush – and get shot to pieces by a volley of gunfire from the marksmen along the walls. They retreat and General Custer, Old Yellow Hair, sends out his dragoons on horseback – but the braves ambush them, cutting them down with their arrows, scalping the survivors.

Pearse finishes his sausage sandwich, sitting cross-legged on the floor, taking the dead off the battle field and rallying the troops, and drinks a glass of milk.

Gran comes in about ten o'clock and says hi and sits at the table in the kitchen with Mum. Gran has a cup of tea, with loads of sugar too, and Mum another cup of coffee and they both have a couple of smokes and a bitching session about Da being a worthless waste of space who Mum should leave at the first opportunity.

Crazy Horse sends in his braves in again to storm the fort and this time they scale the walls and slay nearly all the soldiers inside. Custer and his trusty lieutenant surrender and are captured. They're all that's left behind. Crazy Horse rides into the fort. He says to Custer, 'There will be no mercy for you, Paleface', and kills the pair of them with his tomahawk.

It would have been much better to stick pencils in the ground and tie the soldiers to these stakes and burn them alive, but Bagpuss was about to come on telly and so the war had to finish toot sweet.

Mum gets up and says, 'Right, I'd better be off, or we'll still be sitting here when your friend May-Belle comes round.'

She fetches the car keys and says, 'See you in a tick, love.'

And she kisses Pearse goodbye on the forehead. Her lips are soft and warm.

She walks out the back door and through the garden gate to where the car is parked in the wee concrete driveway. All the houses are the same: each one has a ten-foot drive, and each driveway is separated from the next one by a scrappy patch of thorny bushes.

From the kitchen Gran says, 'Damn', and then gets up from the table. 'I need ciggies,' she says. She hurries to the back door, saying, 'Hang on, Josie, will you get me twenty Sovereign, darling?'

Mum, it's supposed, didn't hear her, and Gran must have went outside after her. It seems she followed her all the way to the car and was talking to her through the driver's window about getting her ciggies when Mum put the keys in the ignition and switched the car on.

From the living room, Pearse heard the car chugging to life – the battery half flat. The engine going 'kerchicka-kerchicka-kerchicka-kerchicka-kerchicka-kerchicka-kerchicka-ahhh-oomm' as it tries to catch and start; and then it starts. And then instead of the rumble of the engine turning over, Pearse is picked up by a sound – the ground opening up and hell spewing out through it onto the earth – and flung across the room. As he spins through the air, he sees parts of his house flying through space with him – the windows of the kitchen blown in and glass whistling by his head. The garden gate sails in through the space in the wall where the window was a moment ago, landing on the lino on the kitchen floor. All of that happens before his body hits the far wall of the living room, and his head catches the window sill just above the right temple and he's knocked for six. Down and out for the count.

When he wakes up, Da is standing in the doorway to the living room, the air sick with dust. He looks knackered and stubbly and dirty and panicked out of his mind. He's wearing a tatty auld woolen dressing gown, but the tasselly cord around the waist isn't tied and it's hanging open – underneath he's in his blue y-fronts with white piping.

'Are you alright,' he says. 'What happened?'

Pearse's ears hum dull and vibrate. He shouts, 'What? I dunno. The house just blew in. I can hardly hear you.'

Pearse gets up, and Da screams, 'Fuck sake. Stay down.'

Da's trembling like a wee girl, and a breeze is blowing into the house through the hole in the kitchen wall. There's the smell of summer in the air, behind the smoke and burning. Da crouches down, the way a soldier under fire would squat; he makes a hunched run into the kitchen. He rises up quickly to see what's outside and then ducks down again.

'Jesus God,' he says.

'What?' Pearse says.

'Jesus Christ,' he says. 'Oh son.'

He holds onto the kitchen door frame. From where Pearse is – kneeling in the living room – he can see all the way into the hallway. The living room, the kitchen and the hall are layered in dust, carpeted with bits of torn paper and pieces of brick and scraps of metal. Everything that was standing is knocked over. If Pearse moved he knew the world would give way beneath him and he'd fall forever – just a spiral of arms and legs, vanishing down a hole, screeching all the way to eternity, and still never stopping.

'What's wrong,' Pearse says again. His mouth and brain feel like he's crying but when he puts his hands up to his face to wipe the tears away, there's nothing there – just a bit of blood

and white dust.

'Son, son,' Da says and starts to walk outside. Pearse gets up as if he'd just been switched on again and follows. The back door has been blown off its hinges, splintered over the hall.

Outside, Gran is lying in the back yard, on the concrete. She's got some of the fence under her body. She's on her belly, face down, and the top of her head is missing. So is her left leg. Her auld tweed coat is scorched at the sides and still smoking, and her right arm is twisted all the way around, with the hand lying palm up on the pavement as if she was waiting for someone to put a penny in it.

Beyond the remains of the fence – raggedy black teeth jutting out from the ground – sits the family car. A giant has taken his hands and ripped the roof of the car open to get at what's inside. The chassis has shifted about a foot to the right, as if the giant had picked the car up and put it down again, only a bit skew-whiff and slanty, after satisfying his terrible curiosity.

Pearse walks down the back garden path, and looks to his feet – where Gran is lying – and then looks up. Inside the car Mum is sitting in the passenger seat with blood covering her face and a big wound in her head. The giant had found her and tried to get into her skull with a tin opener. The car's squashed up into a crumpled pyramid; fire playing round the wheels.

Pearse shouts, 'Mum,' and runs to the car. Da says, 'Please, son,' and tries to catch ahold of him, but Da's moving as if he's in slow motion – he isn't quick enough to keep Pearse back.

'Don't,' Da says as Pearse gets to the car. There's no glass in any of the windows. The top half of Mum's body is in the passenger seat. The rest of her, from the waist down, is still sitting in the driver's seat. The bonnet has been blown off and it's propped up against the neighbour's gate. The engine is pushed up, out of its block, and into the car. It's sitting on Mum's feet, crushing them.

Mum's eyes are closed, and the light breeze catches the lapels of her jacket and dances them about in the bombed air for a moment. Pearse feels his head spin around and around on his shoulders, and Da's talking to him saying something that he doesn't understand and then he's just gone, out. Bang bang, you're dead.

Skin

Ewan Gault

ON HER DAILY commute, Katarina likes to count the number of cars that are anything other than grey. Every month, there are fewer of them, as if the cars like chameleons are trying to camouflage themselves amongst the concrete and colossal continent of cloud that covers the sky. It is with some relief that she glances at the famous old Rail Bridge. It is partially covered in scaffolding and she imagines the men working to keep this one part of the country in colour. Katarina has heard that their endless battle will soon be over, that they have been using an impenetrable paint which protects the bridge from the elements and will never peel or flake.

As the bridge's hump rolls into view, Katarina sees an orange scuttle between a car's tires. She turns to Charlene, who is plump and pouting in the passenger seat, to confirm that she is seeing this too. A van weaves drunkenly as she watches its fat, black tires unsure whether the driver is trying to squash the oranges or avoid them. There are hundreds, thousands of oranges on the road; a freak storm of fruit. Rolling away from wheels, trembling as lorries thunder by.

Katarina thinks they are beautiful. She wants to stop, and watch them getting crushed. But there is no place to park and the road clears on the far side of the bridge, the cars returning to their straight urgent lines. She scrunches her nose at her passenger who stares vacantly out the window. 'Well you're no company.' Charlene nods her perfect head, her lush hair and unblemished skin. Katarina gives her thigh a squeeze.

Tucking her motor away in the furthest corner of the car park she looks at the hotel. The engine ticks as it calms down, her heart beats with a growing panic. She always feels sick before work. With Charlene lying safely out of view on the backseat, Katarina climbs out of the car. She has to duck as she goes down the stairs, slaps the sign that says, "Mind Your Head," with the flat of her palm. The kitchen sizzles with fry ups, greasy pans for her to clean.

'Awright doll, how's yerself?'

She tries a smile for size.

'Cheer up hen, might never happen.'

'It already has,' she whispers, thinking that these Chefs would never dare call the waitresses, protected by their tight black skirts and white frilly shirts, 'doll,' or 'hen.'

Katarina takes her mother's oversized ring from her finger, puts on a pair of pink rubber gloves and gets to work. Radios tuned to different channels argue from the corners of the kitchen until she silences them with the sharp guillotine shut of the dishwasher's door.

That evening she drives home watching the orange lights of the refinery flicker in the darkness like an octogenarian's birthday cake. As they approach the tollbooths she makes sure Charlene is sitting up right, her hat slightly covering her face. Before summer, the radio had announced that the Road Bridge had almost paid for itself and so for the next year cars travelling with passengers would be exempt from any charge. She laughed, loving the idea of a bridge finally paying for itself like some spoilt twenty-something who'd finally got a job. Clapping his hands, Derrick, her boyfriend, had rushed into his studio before shouting, 'Let me introduce your new travelling companion. Your ticket to free trips across the bridge!'

Charlene was one of the leftovers. She'd been brought in by a man who had paid for an all over body patch up and never returned to collect her. This happened more often than one would have thought and Derrick had started to call his studio, 'The Abandoned Sex Dolls Retirement Home.' He would keep 'his girls' inflated, dress them up for Halloween, hang decorations on them at Christmas. Derrick, who had held onto aspirations that he would make it as a sculptor right up until the bitter end used to dismissively describe what he had to do to make a living as 'fixing fannies,' but it was more complex than that. Katarina shuddered when she thought of the state those dolls arrived in. Some of it was simply wear and tear but others had been burned, beaten and bitten with a savagery she found sickening. With each one Derrick lovingly patched torn PVC, wove artificial hair over torn out bald spots, replaced plastic eyes and sent them back to men who vented their hate on inflatable dolls that they couldn't bear to be parted from.

Katarina and Charlene pass through the camera's stare in the non-paying lane, neither of them blinking. Charlene is wearing one of Derrick's old jumpers. It doesn't suit her but Katarina hasn't done a wash all week and likes seeing it on someone. Leaning over she could probably smell him, lingering amongst the wool. His parents told her to get rid of everything. She sold CDs, donated books, but somehow can't get rid of his jumpers. She realises that this morning was the first time she had driven over the bridge without thinking of him.

The next day she drives to work over a road covered with white splattered stains, scabby remains of yesterday's fruit spillage. She sees one lone orange; bright amongst the cataract cat eyes, somehow saved from the passing wheels. She slows down to look at it. Crossing the bridge she spots two more half-crushed oranges. She smiles lazily at them.

At the highest point on the bridge she gives the railings one sharp look. It is all still there, the rustling cellophane, bowed flower heads, tattered Celtic and Ranger's strips hand in hand. She should untie the sleeves' fists, which cling to the railing like a crucifix and throw them into the river.

The kitchen at night is a: cutlery rattling, pot boiling, whisk beating machine. The noise of a constant earthquake. For the next six hours she plunges plates, soaks saucepans, lays broken down grocery boxes over slippery tiles. Andy the head chef screams that he needs the grill plates cleaned and she's over in a second scouring carbonized steak, imagining it was his scabby face she was attacking with a fury.

On the way home Katarina recounts the petty indignities of her night to Charlene, who with her pout, trout lips and always open mouth acts as a suitably shocked listener. As they approach the tolls Katarina gets her to sit nice. 'Not so pert now, are we doll face?' Charlene looks back with a manic stare, the ends of her lush lashes glued to her face. Katarina moves in close and licks her eyeball.

The following morning, Katarina drives towards the bridge at pensioner pace, scanning the lanes and the lay-by. A few pussy looking scabs on the concrete are all that remains of the spillage apart from the one loan orange. Its skin looks duller and dustier than before but it is still intact. She drives on past the football strips and flowers, flapping in the wind. 'What happens to them, Charlie?'

Katarina wonders if the strips will be allowed to turn to tatters, the flowers broke back skeletons. 'Maybe someone takes them away? Maybe I should bring fresh ones.' She sits in the car park, counting the last seconds of freedom. Some commercial pop that she'd normally hate blares from the radio and suddenly seems tinged with magic.

Maureen is working and Maureen is horrible. She has been here for decades, giving girls grim smiles that know they're not going to stick it, that their names are not worth learning. Maureen has a button nose with eight huge blackheads, ripe for squeezing. Katarina is terrified that one day when the old bitch is giving her a row for not stacking the plates in some elaborate way obvious only to herself that she will reach out and get that nose between her finger nails.

'Alright, Maureen?'

The woman gives a shrug as if it's the daftest question, as if her state of 'alrightness' is something far beyond Katarina's ken. Taking her mother's ring off, Katarina puts it in her pocket and pats it through the cloth. It seems like a sacred act. The water in the sink is boiling. Katarina can feel the shock sizzle up her arm. Maureen will be watching, so she eases a pan into the water holding the corner of it so that she doesn't get scalded. She scrubs away but the scouring pad becomes soaked in the water and is painful to hold.

'Is that water too hot, hen?'

'No. You need hot water to take away the grease.' She smiles at Maureen but they both know she's taking the piss.

'Well at least yer not like some Ah could mention, who have tae wear they daft gloves. If you're gonnae K.P. you might as well get yer hands used tae it. See these hands. Dinnae feel nothing.'

Maureen holds her red podgy fingers up to Katarina's face, one finger throttled by a wedding ring that you'd have to call the fire brigade to cut off. It's true though, Maureen feels nothing. Katarina minds seeing the old woman picking up trays straight from the oven, the sink water hissing as she dropped them in. She takes her own hands from the water, looks at how red they are. Her fingertips stroke the invisible down on the rim of her ear; touch the dry skin on her bottom lip.

'Here, let me in. You can load the washer.'

Maureen plunges her hands lustily into the suds. She starts scrubbing with a fury that makes the whole sink unit shudder.

By the end of the day Katarina is scunnered. Maureen is away flirting with the chefs who have nothing to do now that the last orders are out. She sneaks some cold water into the sink and puts her hands under the tap. She looks at the swollen veins on the back of shaking hands, which used to touch the skin of loved ones. After a few sob like breaths she starts again, cleaning knives and cutting boards.

Andy loves nothing more than striding up and down in front of the waitresses, sharpening the knives, telling them how dangerous these 'instruments' would be in the hands of an unprofessional. She feels the tip of the blade, thinks for the hundredth time about murder in the kitchen. Instead she presses the heel of the blade down on the red bloated hands attached to the end of her arms. Blood, always darker than expected twists round her wrist, falls into the suds that are white and bilious as clouds on a sunny day.

'What have you done?'

She holds up the bleeding hand, as if offering Maureen benediction. The old woman ushers her up to the staffroom and the First Aid kit that is kept in what looks like a green lunch box.

'It stings,' she whispers, half surprised that this hand which carries burning plates, dries with dirty dishtowels, washes in boiling water should still feel anything. She has watched it tear up boxes in seconds, crawl over a tray of cutlery, scooping up all the forks. She doesn't understand how it got so fast, so clever. It is a strange bony insect. Next time she means to cut it off.

'Go home, love. Don't want you doing anymore damage to yourself.'

She stops in the bathroom, splashes cold water on her face. Even her freckles have gone pale. She makes mad eyes, spooks herself.

The next day is wild and windy. She thinks that the lone orange must have been blown away or crushed but it is still there, splattered by motorway spray, slowly becoming the same colour as everything else.

Charlene is wearing a pair of Derrick's shades, chin resting on her chest like a person with a broken neck. Her face, which a week before had been plump and full, is now haggard, her cheeks collapsed. Derrick's breath is ebbing from her. Katarina doesn't know what to do. She checks up on Charlene during fag-breaks, spies on her as she sits in her dead boyfriend's studio. But she can't breathe life into her. Can't bring herself to do that.

There are camera's eyes all over the bridge. Do they watch Charlene's demise? They watched Derrick jump. He must have known that, must have wanted them to see. The post mortem declared: Death by Misadventure. Police said it was probably an accident; drunk and climbing about on the railing. The muscles on his arms were torn, his nails and fingertips showed signs that he tried to grab the bridge as he fell. Everyone looked at the ground, said it was a sad loss, a young life.

At work all is strangely quiet. Andy lurks, spouting jokes that might sound smart in the mouth of a stupid thirteen-year-old. Eventually he gets bored and makes her clean the already clean tiles round the sink. A delivery arrives, a chance for the men to do some *real*, physical work. Andy muscles to the front, attempts three large boxes that she can see contain tinned fruit. He waddles off with two of them, eyes staring psycho-like ahead.

'Walking heart-attack that wan,' mutters the delivery boy.

She takes a box of frozen baguettes. Andy returns for the second load, weighing up how much each person is taking. He tosses her a packet of tortilla chips with a, 'See if you can manage that darling.'

Katarina is left to pack the walk-in freezer. There doesn't seem to be enough air and she inhales sinus numbing blasts. She works quickly, standing back only when the job is done. Before leaving, she makes her hand into a claw and drags it down the boxes frosty fur. On the way back to the kitchen, ice thaws from beneath her torn nails.

A pile of boxes, like a shantytown after a hurricane, remain. She selects a knife, stabs it through sellotaped spines, breaks the boxes flat, stamps on them when they threaten to get up. She sandwiches the flattened boxes between two larger bits of cardboard and takes them out to a brick fire place behind the car park. They catch easily and she hides behind the flames, watching the hotel shimmer and shake. The smoke stings her eyes, fluffs up her hair. Three times round a fire, if the smoke follows it means you're going to die. She completes two laps looking over her shoulder but the smoke gives up the ghost.

Back in the kitchen a pile of dirty dishes awaits. The dishwasher keeps failing to drain, so she has to lean into its clammy jaws, shoogle the blocked pipe in a corner never touched by the mop. Katarina wipes her wet forehead, grease on the back of her hand like she'd been using a hamburger as a face cloth. Escaping to the toilet, she washes her hands and face in cool, clean water. She unpeels her once white hairband, now a pussy yellow like the inside of an elasto-plast. Letting her hair fall over her face she peels the lank strands stuck to her forehead and takes off the extra-large hotel issue T-shirt that hangs like a shawl to just above her knees and makes any body – fat and collapsed or young and beautiful – look the same. Proudly, she walks to the staff-room in her bra, before taking a black skinny cardigan from her locker and walking out the back door.

Driving with the windows open, the wind rinses the smell of carmallising onions from her hair. Near the bridge she steers her old rustbucket into a tourists' car park overlooking the river. She decides to cross the bridge carrying Charlene's deflated body. Tourists taking photos of the famous Rail Bridge don't notice her as she walks towards its uglier, younger brother. She remembers the first time she took the train over the bridge, all excited because she thought it would rollercoaster up and down the top of the diamond shaped peaks. Her dad explaining that it was shaped that way to keep it strong against the tugging currents, not to make the ride into town more fun.

The bridge had frightened her anyway. The round red girders and thick rust cords reminded her of a picture she had seen of the human body, the skin stripped back, revealing muscles, tendons and veins. She dreamed for weeks that the bridge pulsated, tried to flex and move, longed for a skin.

She squeezes Charlene tight. The walkway shudders as lorries pass by. They reach the highest point on the bridge, the rustle of cellophane, the football strips twisting and dancing. She doesn't read the smudged writing in the cards, look at the names of all these friends she hadn't met until he was dead. Charlene rests against the handrail, the bar folding her body in half. Katarina sniffs Derrick's jumper one last time, picks up the near weightless doll and throws her to the wind. Her body flops and tumbles, hits the water with barely a splash.

Katarina feels the stare of the camera's eyes. Is a man in some distant office reporting a murder? Is anyone watching? She doesn't hang about to find out. Striding away from the bridge she focuses on the one loan orange, dirty and abandoned at the roadside. She picks it up, tries to clean the dirt from the skin and puts it in her pocket. She climbs the caged cliffs at the side of the road, stops at a vantage point.

A body floats down river, past the water that swirls and curls round the Rail Bridge's feet. Unblinking eyes stare up at the tendonous tangle as the deflated doll, like a human that's shed its skin, begins to sink. Katarina unpeels the orange, its spurting smell stinging her nostrils. She discards the dirty old skin, bites down on a segment. The fruit is juicy, tastes full of life.

Bikes

Mike Russell

THE BIKES DROVE everyone crazy. They would race up and down the streets, whizzing out of nowhere as people left for work or went for a walk. At night, the bikes with bells on their handlebars would ring them, non-stop. People yelled from their windows in protest, but the ringing didn't go away. The bikes were having too much fun, not being malicious or dangerous, just enjoying the fact they were alive.

China had the worst problem, with reports saying that 3 per cent had already been knocked off the year's growth rate because people couldn't get to and from work: their bikes, by the tens of millions, were wheeling wild and free.

At first people had panicked because they didn't expect to see bikes moving around by themselves, pedals turning and chains ticking. We ran away from them and hid indoors. But once it became clear that they posed no real threat, we came back outside again.

Scientists captured a few to examine them, taking them to bits, drilling holes in them, but there didn't seem to be a definite explanation for why they moved around by themselves. There were various theories doing the rounds, to do with cosmic rays, ticklish neutrinos, confragilistic magnetism, and the devil. Most people discounted the devil, as invoked by the sulphurous volcanism of crackpot TV preachers. I mean, if it really had been Armageddon, then getting bikes to move by themselves didn't seem a very evil or effective way of ending the world.

It was when the kids started to sit on them that the trouble started. No one really owned bikes any more; it was more like they owned people. Like wild horses, they seemed to only let certain people sit on them. Kids, mainly, but a few adults as well.

Most adults weren't happy with the situation. They fretted and plotted, fed up with the nuisance and noise. And when the first kid got injured it was the perfect excuse to attack.

The bike didn't mean to hurt the boy. It had carried him 12 miles from home, out into the country, on a lovely sunny day and didn't seem too inclined to go back the way they'd come, or even stop. So the boy, hungry and tired and scared after be carried along for hours, was left with no option but to jump off, breaking his arm and cutting his face. The bike just whizzed away, did a wheelie across a field, and sped back and forth until it found a gap in the fence. Other bikes drifted by but the boy was too frightened to get on any of them. He eventually found his way back to the main road and a bus home. His parents were frantic, but he recovered. They assumed he had been abducted by a paedophile.

After that, the adults started destroying as many bikes as they could find. The great cull began. First of all we penned as many behind fences and walls as we could. Those we couldn't trap were blown apart or captured and cut into pieces with blowtorches. A kind of napalm was developed to melt them. Before long, the threat to our security had been neutralised.

There are still a few bikes skulking around, keeping to the countryside. I've even heard that

➤→

there are people who protect them, give them sanctuary, and that the bikes are grateful.

Now that everything is more or less back to normal, we're afraid to make any more bikes. It's rumoured that the military are secretly trying to weaponise the ones they didn't destroy. And China still can't get to work.

Karelian Anniversary

for Aila Juvonen

Liz Niven

A can see ye
in thon scrievin class
thirty year ago.

Scrieve in a Finnish dialect,
they said.
an ye telt them ye had nane.

Mindin thon hate
yer parents had warned ye aboot,
no tae speak yer ain tung
ootside yer hame.

The hame yer faither
focht fir;
his clachan loast,
his hoose brunt doon.

His faimilie sent tae squat
in anither faimilie's ferm.

An independence socht in vain,
a culture caucht up intae anither kintra's laws.
Caucht up an swallied hail.

A can see ye
in thon scrievin class
thirty year ago,
an ye kent richt then
ye did hiv a vyce,
aw yer ain,
floodin oot wi the memories.

Rekindlt ilka sixth
December lik the caunles
burnin in windaes nou,
tae celebrate lives loast
in thon wuid lang ago.

Jethart snails

Bridget Khursheed

Sweets for funerals: would you like one of the last
from the paper bag he left behind;
each boiled drop wrapped in cellophane,
every day could be a Christmas.

These came in a tin. There's one still
in the back of the cupboard with the grocer's
logo dreamed up by a Frenchman.
Hence the snail or was it the shape?
In the old factory – the back of a shop -
an apparition clung to the walls.
Forget Wonka.
Here is where it all started.
The toffee mentholated hung from a hook
each Monday
and pulled down by a week of gravity
to get the fine texture;
the escargot swoop and roll.

And when you left that shop
you were a little candied too,
following the road through the snow
up to the gaol and museum closed today;
ghosts at your shoulder
that you walk through like the flakes
that leave no footprints;
suck and mould with your tongue
until the tin is empty
not even sold here anymore.

Niagara
Brian Johnstone

Mostly you flop,
tired from the twelve hour days
that brought you to lodge here,

marooned. Shame
that there's nothing to read but those tracts
she so tactfully

placed by your bed;
nothing on telly she'd countenance
if even she owned her own box. She does not.

Take your cue from her habits
and watch where you place all four feet:
move a chair

and the carpet will mark in a moment,
give you away;
or spend time in the garden

cat-teasing the walls,
or picking dead leaves from the shrubs
lest they fall,

untidy the soil;
even go to the wee room,
get some practice at pulling the chain

the exact way she has shown you
over and over again.
It's her tread on the gravel, her key in the lock

and you've done it
this time: moved every table and chair
half an inch from its spot,

shaken dead leaves from each shrub
till they drop,
pushed the cistern beyond its known limit,

got it to live up to its name. That's your game.
Now she's climbing the stairs
and you're leaving the back way,

silent with suitcase in hand,
while Niagara pours
from the landing she's footing it for.

Made in Glasgow
Graham Fulton

Death Watch starring Harvey Keitel
as a man with a camera behind his eye
so he can film a dying woman
for a prophetic reality show
is on
at the GFT
featuring surly1980 Glasgow skies
the colour of TCP
and nice shots of the City of the Dead
and wet streets going downhill
in the general vicinity of Blythswood Square,
and there are
25 people in the cinema
who sit in an evenly-spaced-not-
too-close-or-not-too-far-from-each-other way
for the shared experience
with their fellow human beings
and with
fifteen minutes to go,
at the exact moment Max Von Sydow says
Not everything has to mean something,
somebody
lets rip with a sharp fart,
and everyone sits really quiet
not wanting to say anything in case it spoils the mood
and wondering if
it was only them that heard it
in the first place.

To Postwar Tinned Salmon

A C Clarke

You made your entrance
at family gatherings
sometimes a solid round
straight from the tin
a grey film toning down
your lurid pink
sometimes forked
into chunks
either way
flanked with pale slices
of peeled cucumber
served with lettuce
on which Heinz salad cream
was poured
like a libation.

Doused in vinegar
to ward off germs
your tart flesh harboured
spinal bones
like necklaces of tiny
transparent cotton reels.
Soft enough to crunch
for calcium
they wouldn't stick
in the craw.
You were the only fish I'd eat
without sifting each flake.

Highdays and holidays
you came into your own.
We tasted in you
luxury of food unlimited
freedom of seas
no longer gunshipped
the glamour
of the dollared
unconquered West.

The Big Velodrome in the Sky
Graham Fulton

Reidy posts an email
to let us know
     he was knocked down
          while riding his bike
by a car overtaking
          a lorry on a bend
which glanced
    with its mirror
and kept on going,
        he flew to the ground,
   he stood
  okay,
but now
     he's got bruised ribs
       and a bruised mind
   and it's hard to communicate
which makes me
       dwell on
   the delicate path
we pedal
each day
   with its dunts and bumps,
       its small collisions, and all
I can manage
to reply is
      Sorry to hear that old pal,
   and I hope you get better soon,

and it isn't until
this very second
   I realise
    I could have typed
something insightful like
Look on the bright side,
      if you'd reacted
  half a thought slower
you'd already be on your way
   to the Big Tour de France in the Sky
      or the Big Lycra Shop in the Sky
or The Big Velodrome in the Sky
      or something else
  equally unhelpful, but the moment
is gone

The Gull in the Dunes

Mark Russell

This is no way to carry on, it cries.
Lying here with your Player's No.6
a punnet of strawberries and Mick
Naismith's girlfriend. Shame on you.

It's true, Mick Naismith's girlfriend is eager
to learn how the resulting erosion
of silicon dioxide provides meagre
purchase for feet, knees, elbows and bottoms.

But please, take your hand from inside her knickers,
her bra off your head, get straight back to school.
You're missing double RE and the story
of the fig trees that summer too soon.

Benedict

Lindsay Macgregor

Ladies and Gentlemen, with regret,
I must inform you, Benedict
cannot attend.

Benedict insists his innocence
a propos the ransom note,
the bungled coup, the prostitute.

For Benedict, as you recall,
has allergies to acid rain, ruminants
and Parsifal. On top of which,

Benedict cannot resist
cavalcades, croupiers, mulatto
boys. Benedict's the real McCoy.

'It is very queer, but not the less true, that people are generally quite as vain, or even more so, of their deficiencies than of their available gifts.'

Nathaniel Hawthorne, *The House of the Seven Gables*

Of Fish and Men
Tom Bryan

I SIT BY the river. As rivers go, it is not mighty but strong. It is too wide to swim across safely. I know how deep it is in places. It is muddy, the colour of milky coffee. It turns back into itself, making eddies and whirlpools. It is overhung by willow and cottonwood; its banks are eroded into small sandy cliffs. Beyond the river are a row of hunched cottonwoods, beyond them, endless cornfields. And beyond that the sky, blue grey, a few moving clouds. It is late summer. To my back is a small dirt track, leading through a forest to a few houses beyond.

I finger the bait, dough in balls the size of small grapes. I boiled them up this morning, in water laced with garlic salt. My fishing line ends in a large lead sinker, to keep the line on the bottom. The baited treble hook is about six inches above the weight. I can imagine it in the muddy river, sitting just above the bottom. Spinning reel. Strong rod. Heavy line. I cast it half way across the river into a quiet eddy. I set my pole upon a forked cottonwood twig and wait.

I have known this river for years so know what might go on out there. Big catfish. Flatheads, blues, channel cat as big as your forearm. Snapping turtles, soft-shell turtles, gar. But most likely, carp. Carp fishing means waiting.

I take a flask of coffee from my pack. I pour into its plastic cup. I watch the river. There is a lot going on. A great heron spears in the shallows in the creek on the opposite bank. Redwing blackbirds gargle from the reed beds. The river has its own pace. Painted turtles sun themselves on a bleached cottonwood tree. Now and then, a big fish flops sideways. I sit, back to the sand, and wait.

The line twitches, in between the moves caused by the current. The small loops will increase as the dough melts small enough to be swallowed. When it is swallowed, the fish will swim out with one final loop; the one that doesn't return.

This happens about an hour later. The loop goes out. I jump up, grab the rod, and set the hook by snapping the rod back over my right shoulder. The rod stays bent. At first, I think the line is snagged on a tree root or on the flat stone slabs that line the bottom of the river. The early tribes called this river 'the River of the White Stones' – the huge natural limestone slabs over which the river formed millions of years ago. However, the line keeps moving and I let out some slack. Fifteen minutes later, the line is still running deep, cutting zigzags across the middle of the river. I have never had a fish run this deep for so long and the weight of it is a moving fish weight, not the dead weight of a large turtle.

Instantly I am aware of someone watching me from the bank above, unusual since I heard no footsteps or greeting. I steal a look.

It's all in the eyes, or not in the eyes in this case.

It is the man, Sterno, twice my age but curiously ageless. His nickname comes from 'Canned Heat' – a red flammable jelly that comes in a tin. Take the lid off, light the tin and place it under the small folding stove supplied

➤➤

with the tin. Years ago, desperate men filtered the mixture for alcohol and drank it. Sterno drank a lot of it until something went out in his head. His eyes now don't seem connected to anything.

I need to watch my line, and the fish, which is finally surfacing.

It is a huge silver carp (rare in this river) and it is at least three feet long. It is tired though and comes side up, close to the bank. Its eyes swivel to mine, it is spent. Fish eyes don't say much, but they are at least connected to something.

'Some fish,' mutters Sterno.

I play the fish onto the sand and it is mine. A silver shining bar, outshining everything on or near the bank. I am aware of three lives going on. The fish is lying still, I unhook him; he doesn't move.

I miss my opportunity. The fish should be accidentally freed, flipped back into the current before Sterno registers; before his eyes relay the message.

'I could sure use a big carp right now. Take em up to the house. Nice meal.'

I look to the quiet fish. No oven big enough. Carp are difficult to clean, prepare and eat. They have a long mud vein which sours the flesh; they also have more bones than any fish. They need kept in a clean running pool or enclosure until the muddy flavour leaves them. This takes a few days. I doubt Sterno's ability to do this properly.

This big fish might be as old as Sterno. It belongs back in the river.

Sterno's eyes, like the fishes, are also moving. There is no fear in them. There is probably some fear in my eyes and some in the fish's.

Sterno knows no fear. It is beyond him. Way beyond him. Dead men walking don't fear anything.

'Can you clean and cook this fish?' I ask him.

'Yeah, sure, hey man, I really do like carp. We live on the river too. Ate my share of carp'.

I'm not convinced. I should flip the fish in. Ease it in with my boot

What am I afraid of?

It is my fish. I am young and Sterno is old. He can't take it from me. Am I frightened for the fish or for me?

Ages more pass. The heron flies up from the creek. A huge catfish splashes in the current. A few thin clouds float over.

'All right,' I hear my zombie voice saying. 'It's yours to carry up to the house. Say hello to your parents from me.' He only stares. He smirks.

I carry the huge bar of fish half way up the bank, cradled in my arms like a child. Sterno gets down on his knees, like a supplicant, to receive the fish. The fish doesn't move. It is struggling to breathe. Its eyes are closed.

'Thank you kindly,' mutters Sterno but his eyes are still disconnected.

Sterno walks up the dusty track towards his house, only its chimney visible above the trees in the distance. It is a long way to walk for a man whose eyes don't really see.

I have given the fish away to gain favour with a man who talks to demons and trees, whose eyes have no faith or meaning.

I have given one life away to make mine easier somehow.

Dusk comes to the river and I am still sitting there.

I have heard Sterno swear *fuck* and *fuck* again, until his cigarette has disappeared like a firefly in the woods.

I know what has happened because my eyes are connected to my head, to my thinking worrying brain.

Sterno will have dropped the fish repeatedly until he lost interest in it. It will have choked on the dust he dropped it in; its blood will by now have attracted crows, rats and foxes. The fish will be shredded to bits during the night, its silver scales strewn in cruel confetti.

Sterno will have forgotten about all this as he falls into his own chemically untroubled sleep.

I will lie awake thinking of the fish looking toward the river and the man above me looking toward the fish and my own eyes not settling anywhere, giving away what was not mine – but allowing it to be taken from me.

Extract from the novel *Choose Me*

Tracey Emerson

THERE SHE IS.

Sitting by the window in Her favourite café on Islington Green.

Grace Walker.

Unaware that I am here, above her, at a small table on the café's mezzanine level. Watching. She comes here every Monday before work to drink green tea and read. Today's choice is a book with a blue cover. *The Power of Now*.

On the wooden table in front of me is the red pocket diary devoted to her. My name across the front – **Anna**. I open it to today's date – **January 24th** – and put a red tick at the top of the page, to show she is following her usual timetable.

Something in the book makes her smile and shake her head. Last week I could see the grey coming through her brown centre parting, but there's no sign of it now. Dye job. She had it done last Thursday. She's had a bit taken off the length too, given her bob back its definition. When we were together she wore her hair long and wavy and almost to the waist. Just like mine is now, although mine is slightly darker.

Today she wears a grey batwing jumper. Dark blue skinny jeans over her long, slim legs. That navy coat she seems to like the best – trendy, with drawstrings at the waist – is slung over the back of her chair. Her jeans are tucked into grey Ugg boots; identical to the ones I'm wearing. I freaked about a bit when I first saw her in them but I told myself so what? Everyone wears Uggs. Doesn't mean anything.

I sip my Earl Grey. Five months ago, when my surveillance started, I couldn't have coped with us being this close. The first time I saw her, I'd been waiting outside the entrance to her block for nearly five hours. She strode past me, headphones trailing white from her ears, humming to something. When she was out of sight, I bent over and threw up all over the place. At least I got all the drama out of the way then.

A young waiter with a goatee beard swaggers over and picks up her empty cup. She knows all the staff in here. He stops to chat.

'No fucking way,' she says in response to the story he's giving her. 'That's unreal.' It's embarrassing, the two of them flirting like that; he doesn't look much older than me. She's not bad for her age, considering she'll be turning forty-three soon. There are lines though, tiny grooves near the corners of her mouth, markers of her smile's perimeter. Faint creases fan out from the corner of each eye – the brown one on the right and the green one on the left. The waiter is transfixed by her odd-coloured irises. When she tilts her head to the side, his follows. When he leaves her, he glances back over his shoulder, but she is already lost in her book, flicking through the pages, searching for something.

When she's finished here she will walk to Angel and take the Hammersmith and City line to Edgware Road. From the station it will take her about eight minutes to reach the Capital School of English. Her first class is at ten-thirty. Beginners.

I doubt English language teaching is the career she once imagined for herself.

➺➺

Usually I'd follow her but there's a busy morning ahead. Before going to Bedford Square I need to make a quick visit to her flat to deliver the flyers.

Finally it begins. Me planting myself like a seed.

Besides, I know her movements well enough by now. As well as work, her week will include two Ashtanga yoga classes and one contemporary dance class. Intermediate. Sometimes she goes out for drinks with her fellow dancers after class, or with students and teaching colleagues. On Wednesdays she meets Siggy for coffee at eleven a.m. in the British museum. Wednesday nights she goes to the cinema alone. Only a single, childless woman would have time for all that.

A short, scruffy man clutching a stack of Big Issue magazines taps on the window to get her attention. She looks up. They exchange laughs and waves before the man trots off.

Her smile fades and she rubs her eyes. She always looks tired. Even though it's six months since she buried her mother, she still goes down to Folkestone most weekends. I suppose there's still a lot to sort out. Mothers are very time-consuming, dead or alive.

She checks her watch and closes her book. Time to go.

What am I doing? If I start this how will it end?

It comes over me as it does occasionally, that traitorous urge to rush to Her and place my ear against Her heart. I grip the sides of the table and wait for it to pass.

It always passes.

Striding down Tottenham Court Road on my way to Bedford Square, flyers delivered. I kept Her letterbox open to hear them land in a fluttery rustle.

Can't stop smiling. Cassie's right. You feel much better when you act on your beliefs. When action and conviction are aligned, she says, nothing can stop them.

I pull out my iPod and scroll through the tracks, looking for something to walk to. 'Mama' by the Sugarcubes will do. Bjork starts to wail. I've made a playlist of mother related

songs. 'Mother' by Tori Amos. 'Three Babies' by Sinead O' Connor. 'Mother's Ruin' by Kirsty MacColl. Strictly speaking, it's Her iPod, not mine. Found it in the handbag I took two months ago when She left it unattended in a bar in Soho. People's music collections are so personal, an insight into the soul. Hers includes Joni Mitchell. Blue. Joni gave her child away. Not ready for motherhood, more important things to do. At least she had the decency to go through with the birth. At least her daughter can listen to her mother's back catalogue and think that perhaps the pain wasn't for nothing. They're reunited now.

Only two people are holding vigil outside the abortuary today. A bald man in a beige jacket stands in the centre of Bedford Square and a thin, bespectacled woman is in position on the pavement outside the 'clinic' doors, her back to the iron railings, fingers worrying a rosary. Only one protester is allowed outside the abortuary at a time. The woman has gaunt cheeks and I wonder if she's fasting in protest. Some of them do. Her lips move in silent, fervent, prayer.

Above us all, the sky is a grey lid, sealed shut.

The man has set up a stall of sorts. Leaflets pinned down by paperweights cover a trestle table. Two poster-bearing placards rest against the table's rickety legs. One shows Jesus, radiant under a rainbow, blessing the collision between sperm and egg. The other, a rosy-cheeked baby floating on a cloud.

I take a picture of the man and his offerings with my mobile and store it to show Cassie later. Then I open my blue pocket diary to **Monday January 24th**. Underneath the date I write **2**.

Two isn't enough. Workers file past on their way to the offices in the square's Georgian buildings, or carry on to streets elsewhere. Tourists meander along, looking at everything and seeing nothing. No one pays any attention to the praying woman and, at best, they treat the man to a dismissive glance. They don't stop to consider the destruction going on behind the abortuary's glossy red door. They won't be so dismissive when they are old and frail and a doctor or relative decides it's time for lights out. That's where we're headed, Cassie says. The Culture of Death is upon us, it is taking hold and, one day, people will wonder why their lives have so little value. They will wonder where such disrespect for human life began.

It begins at the beginning.

A quick check through the notes on my previous five visits reveals 10 as the highest number of vigil-keepers. Cassie's right. It's time to *make* people care. We need to do it like they do in the States, she says. Flood the streets with graphic images; force them to look at the carnage.

Totally. Rainbow Jesus out, dead fetuses in. It might shock them; like seeing images from a war in a far-off land they've never paid any attention to.

Vigils are frustrating. I've done enough of them to know. Free Life is mostly a Catholic organisation and the trouble with Catholics – Cassie agrees with me on this – is they think prayer and guilt will be enough. Prayer and guilt and lobbying and petitions. That's why I left my three-day a week voluntary placement as Free Life's youth-outreach assistant six weeks ago. They were surprised to see me go. I beat loads of other applicants for the post, winning on the strength of my commitment to the organisation and my prize-winning essay comparing abortion to slavery.

Prayer and guilt won't save lives. Cassie says the Saviours of the Unborn will and I believe her. The Saviours aren't an organisation like Free Life. Not really. I belong to a cell and the cell responds to information from a control centre. I like that idea. Every human life starts with one cell and all the information for that life is contained within it. When people don't want to face the truth about abortion, they tell themselves their child is only a bunch of cells. As if a cell isn't everything.

There are others like us, Cassie says. Spread across the country. Ready to strike. We will only stop when everyone faces up to the Killing. When it is outlawed, criminalized, as all Killing should be.

I'm only supposed to be observing today, gauging the mood, but the cruelty of the passers by is too much for me. I march over to the man at the table, show him my Free Life membership card and ask if I can hand out some leaflets. He nods, busy with incantations he dare not interrupt.

I clutch my batch of leaflets. Talking to strangers is not something I enjoy, but when it comes to saving the innocent I can conquer my shyness. The message on the front of each leaflet is simple – **THE TRUTH** – but no one I approach is interested in that.

One middle-aged city type, smart in a black-belted overcoat, doesn't hold back.

'Don't give me any of your religious shit,' he says.

'I don't believe in God.'

'Oh.'

That gets him. He hesitates, confused. I've often thought more people would listen to us if God wasn't involved, but non-religious objectors like myself are rare.

'Why are you anti-abortion then?' he asks.

'Because I want to stop this Holocaust.'

'That's a totally offensive and inaccurate comparison,' he says and marches off. Even an offensive interaction is better than apathy, which is what I usually get.

Ten minutes later I see a girl approaching, her head hung low. I know she is a Killer and I know where she is headed. I run up the street, block her path and offer her a leaflet. We're not supposed to 'harass' people on their way into the abortuary but I can never stop myself.

'Get out of the way,' she says. She looks a year, maybe two years younger than me. Her eyes are red-rimmed and puffy. I can see she's upset but what I feel is the fear radiating from her womb, from the little person about to be torn from his or her cosy hiding place.

'You'll regret killing your child,' I say. Very important to refer to the fetus as child or baby. Never call an Unborn 'it.'

'Shut up,' she snaps. Clearly she feels no Connection to the life inside her yet. I take out my phone.

'Let me show you a 4D ultrasound image of a baby smiling in the womb,' I say.

'Just... just fuck off.' She pushes me out of

the way. When she reaches her destination, rosary woman offers her a leaflet. The Killer flicks the advice away and hurries through the abortuary door. I cannot breathe. As if it is my life in the balance.

Rosary woman returns to her beads and her mute, pointless prayer.

Caravan of Love

Jim Taylor

YOU'RE SITTING IN the lotus position on the hilltop overlooking the campsite, the dunes, the sea and the isles, with your long hair and bum fluff beard, wearing the heavy crucifix you've just shoplifted from the gift store way below us. I'm peering down nervously, waiting for the manageress to run out and raise the alarm, but nothing happens.

You got me to ask the lady about an Airfix model on the top shelf back in the toy section, while you nicked the jewellery out front. I know the drill by now and, I've got to admit, take a helluva pride in displaying a form of competence even you would have to acknowledge. Obviously it's terrifying – just not as much as saying no to you would be. I usually play decoy while you lift fags or booze, but you've got higher things on your mind on this trip. You're concerned about your spiritual development, and about your new relationship. As well as the pendant for yourself, you've pinched a smaller piece to take home to Joyce. And you've sent her a postcard with 'love and peace' scrawled on the bottom – the catchphrase you've adopted to go with your new style, though some of the skinhead paraphernalia is still intact, like the flick-knife hidden in the secret pocket of your Wrangler jacket.

You were describing Joyce's vagina to me the other night, while we lay in the bunk room. I didn't need that, to be honest. The caravan was already rocking gently back and forth, while I tried to block out any mental image of what might be going on in the master bedroom. You were sniggering and throwing sweets at me, the hard boiled ones Gran always sends wherever we go on holiday, along with the lucky dips and comics, in what she calls our 'red cross parcel'.

I think I heard Mum and Dad shagging once before in the house, but I've never actually been shoogled around by the vibrations of it up to now. It made me feel sick, but sad as well. I feel sorry for them, especially Mum, that they feel they've still got to do that sort of thing, even though they're virtually fossils. It's probably just a holiday treat cum chore, like the books they buy whenever we go away (Mum and Dad read one book apiece per annum – a romantic novel and something about spies or war).

I don't mind the thought of sex entirely, only not if it's too close to home or involving the elderly. To be honest, the idea of you and Joyce going at it like rabbits doesn't exactly fill my heart with joy either. I suppose I mainly don't mind thinking about it just if it's me doing it with someone decent, like Natalie Wood, or one of the Biggerstaff twins from regi class – the quiet one. Even then, I would rather not talk about it. But you want to talk about it non-stop. And, as with everything else, you are so fucking angry about it, you're staring at me like a psycho played by Jack Nicholson. You could be a famous actor yourself with those eyes, I reckon, if only you would broaden your emotional range.

'Listen to this,' you say, picking up Dad's novel. 'This is what turns the old bastard on.'

'It's just a stupid war book,' I say.

But you make me listen to every word

➤→

of some rape scene you've found, involving Japanese soldiers and a young girl, even though you can hardly read and it's the last thing you would want to do normally.

All this talk about Joyce's squelching fanny and gang bangs and Mum and Dad – it's too weird. Thank God the thought of the old ones at it is so utterly bogging, otherwise I'd probably get a stiffy, as I do most of the time these days, and I know that is what you want, so as to prove what a hypocritical mutant I am.

Towards the end of last term I had to permanently position my Adidas bag so as to shield my groin from public view. Barry Kerr, who was next to me in Biology and is very mature about these things, admitted any tree with a skirt wrapped round it would almost be enough to get him going at the moment, and that's pretty close to what actually happened to me when Mrs Reid's skirt rode up her leg while she was sitting at the front of the English class. So big and ancient is her thigh, it was like being turned on by a glimpse of the Birnam Oak.

Still cross-legged on the hill, you start glugging from the half bottle of vodka you've bought with money from Dad's wallet. You say they can't smell it if it's vodka and if you go back late enough when they're in bed it won't matter about being half cut. We can say we've made friends on the site. We have actually been talking to a gang of boys you sarcastically call 'the heavy mob' because they are younger than you. They are a bit older than me though and look cool in their pilot's sunglasses and college jumpers, like Showaddywaddy. It's the first time I have ever felt protected by you, because they are the sort of lads who would normally have beaten me to death if you hadn't been there. They said I am the spitting double of you, which makes me feel great.

You get friendlier after a drink and put your arm round me.

'Faithful soldier,' you call me. You tell me you're going to leave home now you've turned seventeen. You're already doing an apprenticeship and Joyce has started her first job too. You're going to get a flat together. You tell me I can come and visit. I am excited because I think having an adult brother makes me cool. I am also relieved because it means I will no longer have to be scared of you round the house, or generally feel terrible all the time about being a snob, a tit, a spastic, a sook and a specky, useless, fat, poofy, wee cunt.

You stagger down the hill with me by your side. It's dark and we fall through all sorts of bushes and bogs, being bitten to death by midges. When we get into the caravan, Dad is sitting up waiting. I am scared, but he just looks depressed. He sends me off to bed and I listen through the door while he tells you he's going to run you home in the morning and leave you there. By the time the rest of us come back at the weekend you've to be out of the house. You can learn the hard way what it means to be responsible and we'll see how long you survive if you think you can pish everything you earn against a wall.

Nothing is said while we lie in the dark or the next day over cornflakes. I've always liked the Kellogg's selection packs Mum buys for going on holiday, but even the choice between Frosties and Ricicles fails to cheer me up. Me and Mum watch you and Dad drive away and Mum cries and tells me to go for a walk, so I wander around on my own, hiding from Showaddywaddy, until I'm too hungry and go back for a sandwich. Mum has composed herself and tells me that you have a long road to travel but there is nothing any of us can do because they've already tried everything. At least I am not like that, though – I will make something of myself.

I go into the bunk room and find a tiny box on my pillow. It is a St Christopher's medal you must have taken from the shop. I hide it in some bushes, under a stone, nowhere near our caravan, in case the shop phones the police and they come with sniffer dogs. But I'll go back for it just before we set off home. And when I'm wearing it I will try to make my eyes go like yours – scary but beautiful – though I'm not sure if it'll work through my glasses.

Penguins Eulogy

Sally Evans

Penguins, pulp-paper rough-paged set-books
matched the texture of duffel-coat pockets,
cost threepence on streetside stalls, fuelled
the Robbins generation socially mobile
redbrick universities welcoming freshers,
Beatle music blaring in bun rooms and writing rooms,
common rooms and bars, sounding in satchels
wherever we carried our three-guinea hardbacks.
Penguins served bravely, the purple Latin,
sky-blue sociology, Psychology
not Today but Fifty Years Ago,
smooth red of politics, old grey Huxleys,
cherry-coloured Cherry-Garrard never on the course.
The brown of the great Greek dramas. Call no man
happy until he is dead, buried and forgotten.

Call not Penguins happy yet. They saw a time
of hope and education, striving more than strife,
opportunity without the clawing back
of non-existent money, but poverty
for a purpose. Students neither
arrogant zombies nor lost souls,
nor best advised to skip degrees, to stir
the dirt and fog of moneymaking
so as to be in with a chance. Of what?
Heritage, the past translated
in stored neat woodpulp shelves,
those block coloured covers, those back adverts,
sanserif headings and old style poster scripts,
disintegrating photo sections, line
diagrams interchangeable between subjects.
The inky names. The thumbed bookmarks.

O Penguins, if I could ever go back in time
I would use you as tardises, your light bright
newness and hopefulness, the mindful glow
of your expectations. You did it,
you hung on for a century, just as alive
and as limited as those who read you.
By solemn necessity I have outlived you,
to be a guardian of your influence and power,
as your small even shapes, your memorials,
gravestones of past pernicketiness
and overflowing detail, a dated store,

still line my shelves, till the glue crumbles,
paper falls apart, and all you and I have said
fade with us, our share in worlds gone,
all diminished in this last perspective,
our failing yet satisfactory lifespan.

Magpie (ii)
Gordon Meade

Magpie does not like books,

although, once, he was drawn to

the shininess of a particular

cover. Magpie does not care

much for music either, but likes to

see the occasional row of

discarded CDs, strung up

and glistening in the noon-day sun; no

doubt, a makeshift bird-scarer.

Magpie (i)
Gordon Meade

Magpie is black and white

but, unlike that dreadful riddle

for a book, Magpie is

really blue all over. The only

things that make Magpie happy are

the sorts of things that shine.

Sunlight, or moonlight, on

water, at a push, will do it for her; but,

mostly, costume and paste.

Be the first to like this

Theresa Muñoz

kicking pine cones down the street
climbing the backyard cherry tree
lying in new sheets
waking in darkness   waking to snow
how your chest thickens when you're scared
how your voice bubbles when you're pleased
be the first to like
view of wind turbines from the train
golden tint on a glass of wine
gliding on rollerblades by the sea
waking so warm   waking on the beach
how your eyes flood when you're tired
how you laugh when you're relieved
like bridges creeks frisbees
silly cat videos and Instagram photos
like strolling with a friend
between folds of trees
and your heart rolls out a big pink wave
and your lips recall something sweet
like skiing and ice-skating
zip-lining above trees at seventy clicks
blood thudding in your ears
like every new experience because it was new
to you   pocketed in your memory
like the first time you fed the ducks
at Stanley Park
and they stormed like villagers
to your feet

Could be
Iain Matheson

Another time you'd be out walking and
you'd meet a straight line, it seemed to have been
drawn by a pencil, you'd invite it home
for a bite to eat with some friends. You'd say
to the straight line, "You know, you could be a
much more interesting shape, the shape of
a man, sitting by a river maybe,
capable of love maybe." Your friends would
say nothing. The straight line wouldn't make a
sound. "How about it?" you'd say, "or you could
bend yourself into the letter L, start
a Library, Lepidopterist, some
word like that, what do you say?" Thus you would
rattle on. The others would smile sadly;
in their hearts they would know it was just a
line which could lead anywhere or nowhere.

powder
Claire Quigley

spilled like mothdust at the mirror
pale gold, irridescent, in this
echo chamber where the music
throws its body at the door.

squeezes its hand around the heart -
beating it for her - of a girl caught
in the air rush from the speakers
strobe-white stuttering the scene

spinning higher, faster
closer to the light.

First draft of a zebra
Alison Grant

Under the chestnut trees
he is *pianissimo*.
Both nostrils flex,
one ear snatches at flies,
his mouth chews obliquely.
Later
he will shake the dust from his neck and break into a canter from a standing start, testing
the length of the paddock, easing into a gallop beneath the bridge
and for one,
two,
three
seconds,
he is pounding the savannah,
invisible to the crowds.

Dactylography
Andy Jackson

I looked for you in what was left behind;
The programmes that you Sky-plussed,
the recipes that only worked for you

though I assiduously followed every line.
I hoped to find you, latent in the dust,
so swept each surface for a residue,

resorting to my fingerprinting kit,
its stock of powder, magnifying glass,
the little book to keep my findings in.

I thought I might find evidence to fit
my theories, chance impressions, lost
among the corrugations of your skin,

but in looking for a pattern in the stripes
I missed the lonely speck of blood,
the pillow with its single strand of hair,

the glass you drank from, partly wiped
of prints, the version of events that said
how you were not there, there, not there.

The Jaws of Wasps
Brian Johnstone

A tinnitus so small
it barely murmurs in the ear,

this steady graft
that rasps behind my back:

the jaws of wasps
fast wedded to these planks

flaked paint
has bared to their desire.

Each scart of timber they collect,
the work of seconds only,

leaves a track
dead wood can not repair;

but every second builds
to minutes, hours, in time to this:

the bone-white byke
they'll hang from someone's eaves

to fizz with life,
an airy simulacrum of the brain.

Free advertising for a Neuro Linguistic Programmer

Jon Plunkett

At first I stayed on the surface
spreading weight so I wouldn't
sink into the sponge of your mind.
At the chasm between spheres
I braced myself across the walls,
hand and foot on each, edging
my way down among electrodes,
so deep into your sub-conscious
you barely even felt me.
There between left and right
I staked my claim. Just enough
on which to pin suggestion.
The climb back up was tricky
but I found a way, breezed through
your ear like a whisper, knowing
that, at a certain trigger,
you would sing my praises
left, right and centre.

Core beliefs
Jon Plunkett

Sometimes I find myself thinking
that inside each of us – me,
you, others, exists a tiny coliseum.
Maybe it is tucked away behind the ribs,
or set on a piece of waste ground
between the liver and the lung. Maybe
the walls of the large intestine
form the dusty floor where two
tiny figures are locked in battle.
Swords clang, and every breath
we have ever taken gives them strength.
Small puffs of dust fly from the skirmish
and the ground is all sweat-spattered.
One - the one in black - advances
and we feel exposed, as though
he will win and run amok, cutting
small windows that will reveal us.
We clutch ourselves so the clangs
will not come out our mouth,
stifle a cough into the crook
of an arm, hoping no one
will see the flurry of dust.
And when we sweat we know
that the battle must be heating up.
While we wave it away with a comment
like *anyone else hot in here?*
we wonder if it is just us
who feel a clot-sized coliseum
somewhere near our heart.

Middle-of-the-Night Poem

Sally Evans

How long ago and far away
and how dead everyone is
you thought about that day

yet how real it is after all
that scene that came to life
in a set place, that crowd

you could go there tomorrow
and they would all be there
thinner than the air

their clothes fluttering,
their speech slightly old-fashioned,
well before they fled.

Signs of Life

A P Pullan

Ever had the time in the day
to take your own pulse,
plumb the depths of carotid
or ulna?
　　　You cast into the currents
of that other world where life fits
and flits into every cranny, where
something will bump, knock.
　　　But even here, you tread slowly
to hear only your own shallow breathing
just to make sure, just so you know.

Wait and I Will Follow
Zoe Venditozzi

SOFT-FACED AND VULNERABLE looking, he poked his toe at the edge of the car tyre. I could see him clearly from where I was sitting and if he cared to look towards my unlit house, he could see me well enough. But he wouldn't think that anyone was watching. I could tell looking at the worn down-state of him that he wasn't somebody who was noticed much.

It wasn't my car he was working up to kicking. It was Philip's. Philip had left it behind and he wasn't due back for two more days.

I was bored.

No, not bored – waiting.

The boy brought his foot back then gently nudged at the wheel. He looked up then down the street.

'Come on!' I felt like shouting. 'You can do better than that!'

He dragged his sleeve across his nose and tried again. Much better – this time he definitely kicked Philip's tyre. I wanted to open the window, lean out and applaud him. I wanted him to draw a key out of his pocket and decorate the silvery wing of the Audi with his frustration.

But perhaps he wasn't frustrated. Perhaps *he* was waiting. Or perhaps he had a perfectly nice family sitting at home, anxious for him to return. Maybe they were hostages to his whims and emotions. But I doubted it. He looked like he'd walked out of the advert for the NSPCC. He was pale and sunken-eyed. His shoulders sloped. His laces were probably undone.

He looked like a cat torturer.

I wondered what I would look like to him. Nothing probably. Some woman. Some mum or teacher or something.

It was starting to get dark but the weather was lovely and still. I'd spent the day in the garden digging holes and hiding things. My shoulders felt tight and warm. It was the most exercise I'd done for ages and I felt well for it. Whether it was the action or the act, I couldn't tell. Perhaps I'd regret it later, but I doubted it.

I'd been sitting for ages in the kitchen chair that I'd dragged through to the lounge window as a kind of test. I'd placed the chair in such a way that I was facing the window so I could count how many people passed. There was an extremely comfortable wing backed arm chair right next to me, but I knew I would fall asleep there. I was so ridiculously tired all the time that I needed to set myself challenges to keep on the ball. Hence the unpadded seat with its ladder back and the hunt the objects game in the back garden. – which I'd failed somewhat at – two spoons and a brooch were in the future hands of domestic archaeologists now.

I brought my attention back to the boy again. Now he was eyeing the aerial. He looked up and down the street again then his attention was brought to me. Or at least to the window. I automatically raised my hand in a wave. He nodded or maybe twitched. I stood up and, ignoring the pins and needles in my feet, watched him walk along the street. He pushed something through the post box at the end of the road and turned left up the hill and out of sight. I scrambled out of the house, determined not to lose sight of him. There was a fine, minutely needling rain which I hadn't seen from the house. I was coatless and was wearing flip flops but the ground was dry enough and I didn't think I'd be going too far. The boy moved at a good pace but I was able to keep him in sight whilst hanging back far enough that he wouldn't see me. If he turned I was prepared to walk up someone's path as if going home. But he didn't turn and I didn't need to hide.

I wondered if he had a plan for where he was going or if, like me, he was adept at wasting time. I looked into people's windows as we walked up the hill. Most houses had a blue light flickering out into the darkening village. Perhaps they were all watching the same show. I had no idea what was popular anymore. Not since I'd cut the plugs for the TV and radio. All that chatter. I could get that anywhere.

I stopped in front of the curtain-less living room and watched the family inside eating from plates on their knees – all transfixed on a big TV attached to the wall. They lifted food from their plates and slotted their cutlery into their mouths. None of them spoke. A baby standing in a playpen looked out at me with menace, its upper lip curled around its dummy.

I remembered what I was doing and hurried off again. I couldn't see the boy. I decided to see where instinct took me. If I couldn't find him I'd head home. I kept going up the hill and turned along the last street which curved around the brow ending in a small wooded area. At last I could see him. He was sitting on a wall right at the end of the street. He got up and began walking. I hurried to get closer to him, then he disappeared again. I almost ran to the end of the street to where the woods began. There was no sign of him. I wasn't sure what the best course of action was. Should I keep going or go home?

But home to what?

I stood still for what might have been a few minutes, my heart speeding and slowing.

'Why are you following me?'

He had appeared at my side and was peering up at me. He was smaller than I'd thought, but his voice was older, like he smoked.

'Following you?' I tried to laugh. 'Don't be ridiculous.'

'You are. All the way from your street.' He smiled.

'Don't be a silly boy.' The smart-alecky look on his face was infuriating. 'I'm just out for a walk.'

'Up here?'

I thought quickly. 'My dog's run off.'

He tipped his head back. 'You don't have a dog.'

'I do.' My voice rose.

'What's it called then?'

I thought of the only pet I'd ever owned – a tortoiseshell kitten that I'd grown tired of immediately. 'Mitzy.'

'Mitzy? That's a gay name.'

I didn't know what to say to that.

'Where's its lead then?'

'Its lead is at home. It's very well trained.'

He laughed in a loud, ridiculously excessive manner. I half expected him to slap his knees.

'Anyway,' I said. 'I need to go home.'

'Why? What are you going to do?'

'That's none of your business.'

'Won't you need to find your dog first?'

I nodded grudgingly.

'Shall I help you?' He bounded off into the woods shouting, 'Here Mitzy, Mitzy, Mitzy!' like he was being filmed.

I had no choice but to follow him and play along. 'Mitzy' was a stupid name. I'd regretted it as soon as I 'd said it. But it was too late. I was a lonely woman with a dog called Mitzy. Hopefully Mitzy had been run over and I'd be free of her.

The boy's voice bounced around the shadowy woods. He sang out the dog's name, throwing it away from himself and gathering it back in. It was like he was everywhere and yet I couldn't see him. I probably should have gone home at that point. The course of action I'd chosen wasn't proving fruitful.

Then he was beside me again. His eyes shone up at me in the gloom.

'Can't find her.'

'Oh well.'

Nobody knew where we were.

Anything could happen.

He was waiting for me to act, I think. He was giving me the same look that Philip was inclined to give me. Blank but pointed. I could hear rustling in the bushes around us but couldn't see anything. The boy kept looking steadily at me.

'What?' I asked, trying not to sound spooked.

'You're the one who followed me.'

'I didn't follow you.' I took a breath. 'I told you – I've lost my dog.'

He leaned in towards me. 'You shouldn't tell lies, you know.'

I shook my head as if it was all some silly joke.

'Should you?' His voice wasn't loud, or rude. He was talking to me patiently as if I was the child. I should have been outraged. But he was right. My head dipped.

He leaned towards me and snuggled his head into my breast. I stood stock still, frightened to move. Then he nipped at me with his teeth. It wasn't sore, it was the sort of thing a lover would do. Everything went silent. My hands half rose but then stilled. He pulled back and looked at me calmly.

'Go on now,' he said, his hand hovering near my arm. 'You should go home. Maybe he's waiting for you.'

He smiled and then disappeared into the trees. I stood for a few minutes and then, sure the child was watching me, I went back the way I'd come.

A Case of the Puncs

Andrew McLinden

AT THE LIBRARY I hand back two books that I didn't read. All I did was score out all the punctuation marks in both of them. When I finished I felt better than I had done in weeks. The woman behind the counter is hook nosed and cruel. If I knew a better word for cruel I'd use it. Because she's cruel I can't place her. I think that another word for cruel might be vicarious. She's vicarious, I say, trying the word out in my mouth.

The woman hands me back my library card and smiles. As I walk out, an old man holds the door open for me. I can't decide what kind of Punc he is either. We pause and stare at each other, him with his watery eyes, mine dry, both of us sword fencing bad breath.

'Is anything the matter?' he asks me.

'A Comma,' I say, finally.

Dave starts up the car and indicates. 'It wasn't hit and run,' he says. 'I waited a hundred yards down the road and the kid got to his feet, you know? I watched him shake himself down.' Dave slips the car into second, then third. Fences start to flicker by. 'The kid looked unsteady. Sure, I'll give you that. But there was no indication things were going to turn out the way they have. That's why I drove off. And now there's this court case.'

He turns off the radio and turns on the window wipers. The car slows and we sit in silence at a set of traffic lights. A Question Mark walks across the pedestrian crossing dragging a collie behind him. The lights turn green and we start off again. I look at Dave as he drives: those Quotation Marks around his head. They look like earphones.

'The doctor's no help,' Dave says. 'I get these pills and a pat on the back and I think, what am I supposed to do with these pills? Will these pills bring the kid back? Where is the pill that brings people back? That would be something worth inventing. Nearly every patient in the world would be cured with a pill that brought someone else back.'

Quotation Marks are the easiest of the Puncs to spot. It will say 'War Vet,' or 'Lesbian and proud' or 'Anti-social Goth.' It will say 'Religious,' or 'Earth Mother,' or 'Cam Girl.' It will say 'Quiz Show Watcher,' it will say 'Academic.' It will say 'Hit and Run Driver.'

Whatever is in between those quotes dominates them: it dictates the clothes they wear, it dictates the places they go and it dictates the friends they keep.

'I lay these useless pills out in a line and then I put them back in the bottle. I lay them out in a line and then I put them back in the bottle. This goes on for hours. I think, is this doctor telling me to take them all at once? Is that what he's saying here? Then I pop one in my mouth. It tastes of night. I turn out the light. But those pills don't stop the dreams. All they do is chain me to my bed so I can't wake up and scream. All the screaming's inside.'

He points to his temple then shakes his head. As I watch his Adam's apple bob I think that Dave might be turning into a Question Mark but say nothing. Puncs can change throughout their lives. That's something you need to understand. A couple can be happily married for thirty years – he's a Semi-Colon and she's a Comma. Then one day over breakfast the man announces that he's a repressed Hyphen. He's known it all along – known it since he was young. He always wanted to be with another Hyphen but married to cover his tracks.

'Last week I went up the grave,' Dave says. 'Just to tell the kid I was sorry, you know?'

I tell him that graveyards need to move with the times. I say we should be using electronic headstones, linked to social media sites, lighting up those dark cemeteries at night: 'Miss you forever,' flashing above a date of death in red. Twelve people like this.

My wife is doing exercises to her Zumba DVD as I push through the front door.

She waves, like I'm on the opposite side of a river, and stops the music.

Sweat blurs in a V down her chest.

My wife is an Ellipsis.

...no way did we forget to pay that... and then this kid, well he says: let me get the manager... after my father died I swore... two for the price of two it should say... but there was a foam party on the island... it's repeated after eight...

As I lay back on the sofa, trying to get comfortable, I can hear my wife crying in the bedroom. I think of what a let-down life is, and how you never find a woman as perfect as your mother, who gives you love unconditionally, and how it's all back to front that you find that first and afterwards you meet all these women who will only ever be mothers to other people.

Next morning Dave picks me up again. He seems down and we travel to the doctor's in silence. This time it's me who's going in to see the quack. I turned forty four weeks ago. The only card I got was from the Health Centre inviting me in for check-up.

Already seated in the waiting room is a pair of Brackets and a Colon. The Colon is rocking a baby in a pram. 'Coo chee coo chee coo,' the Colon says. A doctor walks by. He stands erect as he talks to the receptionist. I wonder if he's Dave's doctor. He's an Exclamation Mark and this to me is right. Exclamation Marks are important Puncs. They're tall alpha males who live in the best parts of town. They're go-getters

and jet-setters. They become Presidents, Popes, and Prime Ministers. They fly planes; they manage banks; they go to schools that look like castles. Sometimes, if you're out and about, you can see them pogoing down the street on their Exclamation Marks, knocking people out of the way.

The nurse calls and I follow her white slip on shoes down a carpetless corridor. I roll up my sleeve as my body finds shape in the green leather seat. The nurse straps something around my bicep and it tightens. Something beeps. My nostrils flare.

'I don't like that first reading at all,' she says. 'It's way higher than I would expect for a man of your age. Does anyone in your family have heart trouble?'

I tell her my family's trouble is that none of them have a heart.

'Ah,' she says. 'We have to rule out any underlying health issues. Something might be causing this. You might be a Full Stop.'

I ask her to repeat herself.

'I said the fight is to get this blood pressure to drop.'

'Ah,' I say.

Frankfurt
Miriam Vaswani

NOT LONG AFTER I arrived in Frankfurt, still surrounded by half-empty boxes and eating dinner most evenings with utensils borrowed from my landlady, I started sleeping with a Belgian-German war correspondent. He'd spent a month in an Afghan jail, so I was confident he wouldn't find my biography exciting.

This was a problem I'd had with men, particularly after the Almaty incident which, though I don't publicise it, fills the first two pages when my name is typed into a search engine. A thing people don't understand about Kazakhstan; you don't have to be anyone special to get in trouble. Another thing; there are some kinds of notoriety that cannot be spun into a book deal.

He had a rough beard, which I liked, though it gave me a rash. It was white, unlike the rest of his hair, which was blond. His eyes were blue, and surrounded by an outline of weather-creased skin. His university nickname, a long time before I knew him, was Viking. He was nearly two decades older than me and had two teenage children. I saw photographs of them, but none of his wife, who he mentioned occasionally but not by name. He had the courtesy not to bother me with his guilt, assuming he felt any.

We met in a press office in Berlin, under the shrewd eyes of a woman called Ute who ran the place. She wore a crackling headset over a swirl of red hair, and granted me mild favouritism after she saw me talking to him. Everyone knew him, and he worked for everyone, whereas the only publication I'd managed to get a job with after the Almaty incident was an underwhelming financial weekly that littered bankers' desks in Zurich and Frankfurt.

About once a month he drove to a city an hour from mine to meet with his editors, then to me. In the trunk of his car he carried a bottle of wine chosen from his cellar three floors below Brussels. He presented it to me after we kissed, after I let him into the parking garage under my flat, filled with shimmering German cars with Swiss and Italian license plates, insect corpses smashed on windscreens. There was always drama surrounding the wine.

I don't know if he survived the journey.

I'm sure it's fine, Marcus. How was the drive?

The Autobahn was clear. I think the temperature is... yes that's good, hold it carefully like that. This scarf is beautiful on you, Farah.

I cradled the bottle like an infant. He'd give me instructions on how to care for it from car to kitchen counter. When we were inside he'd retrieve the corkscrew from my drawer, pour, let me taste first. He'd seek my opinion before relaxing. He was attentive to the sort of wine I liked, and might like. Amongst my possessions I still have the business card of his supplier in Strasbourg, who I never contacted.

We'd drink his wine with the dinner or lunch I made. I'd rarely cooked for men, and I haven't since. Not with such regularity and one-sidedness. I liked cooking for him. He complimented me justly while we drank and talked about work, the decline of our profession, how I was settling into German life. We were concerned about the increasing influence of the far right, after Le Pen's party gained 18% of the vote in the French election. I told him about the Islamaphobic landlords I'd encountered while searching for a larger flat in Frankfurt, who seemed to regard me as a better class of Muslim because I wasn't Turkish. He was furious, not only for me, but for his country, which was not the modern Germany I'd expected. He told me about his sister's boyfriend, an African-American financial analyst who'd moved to Paris to work for a prestigious bank, who couldn't lease a flat without a white countersignatory. The occasional sputters of bigotry of Ottawa were beginning to feel like a pleasant play I once saw.

Then we'd move to my bed, still talking until we kissed, sometimes still talking between kisses. Eventually we'd forget what we'd been talking about. We'd pick up the conversation a few hours later, lying curled together, too hot for blankets, candlelight on our skin, my short hair grazing his scarred chest. I allowed myself time away from my main worry; while some of my colleagues were witnessing the Arab Spring, I was analysing the Euro crisis in a money-obsessed backwater.

At the small of his back was a patch of skin so smooth it seemed to belong to a baby. He'd worked in Siberia and Afghanistan, two places I hadn't. I'd worked in Myanmar and St Petersburg, places he'd never seen. We each spoke three languages, but had only one in common. So we were equals, but with an exception. He'd worked in Lahore, the ancestral city I'd never visited thanks to a family rift that began when my Pakistani mother married my Indian father.

What's it like?

It's a hard place.

But what's it like? His hand on my breast, both floating in the candlelight, connected to nothing.

Boring and agitated, both. The place is full of anger. The men are insane. The women are hard and...

...is there more wine?

...intélligent. It was impossible to interview the women. But they know the story, so I went away with half a fucking story.

Sometimes he was patronizing. That was

a consequence, I decided, of sleeping with a man old enough to be my father. I'd begin to describe a worry, and he'd attack me with a solution before I'd finished my sentence. It was a habit that reminded me of the useless advice given by women of my mother's generation, about men and women and our different brains. It annoyed me that he was behaving exactly like men of his generation are expected to behave, by women of his generation. I didn't mind fucking a man with nearly grown-up children, but I had no intention of turning into an Ontario housewife.

...it's due at the start of business on Friday. I have the stats and I've talked to the people in Bangalore, that's done. But I know it's all different in the countryside, and my only contact has no email, no phone, she might be...

Well, ask someone in the city. They must know a colleague or someone in...

...no, listen. It isn't so easy, they have no contact with each oth...

...your editor should know...

...you're not listening to me. I've only got three days and...

...well the magazine can send you to...

...just shut the fuck up Marcus, please. Let's talk about something else.

He understood, with minimal fuss, that I must be entered slowly. He listened to my instructions. He honoured my stipulation that my knees must always be bent and my back arched in order to orgasm. He was adding the shape and taste of my clitoris to a private collection, not unlike the one in his beloved wine cellar. I was the sort of liquid that leaves an ache in the drinkers jaw. If I was to be stored three floors below Brussels, I would be the dark bottle in the corner.

I was collecting the curve of his shoulder, the top of his head, the smooth patch of skin. The sunburns that permanently scarred his shoulders in the late 1970s before a shadow on an x-ray sent him to buy cotton shirts and sunscreen. A stab wound from a security guard in Lebanon which halved a chest muscle. I could put my fingers in the gap; it no longer hurt him.

His willingness with the crook of his arm

surprised me. He invited me in after we fucked or as we paused our elaborate games, panting with thirst, to drink his wine. Later, he'd pull his arm tight around my waist and keep me there until I wriggled away in sleep.

We both smoked pretentious cigarettes. His were long, thin, French. Mine were longer, thinner, Russian. Since Almaty and St Petersburg, I haven't been able to hold a short cigarette without feeling inelegant. The Du Maurier's of my adolescence seemed far away. I never smoked in the flat unless he was there, and then we'd tap our ashes into an empty pesto jar he always left on my window ledge.

You think you know how it ended. I fell in love with him, or he with me, and because of his wife and children or my need for solitude it had to stop. I'll tell you how wrong you are.

But first, imagine him today. He sits at a wide desk made of Finnish pine, polished and worn and pockmarked with ten or fifteen years of droppings from his pretentious cigarettes. None of my cigarettes, though, because I've never been in his study. Probably he's made love to his wife on this desk, or let the children perch on the edge while he repaired skinned knees and dried tears.

It's a sunny day. He's drawn the curtains so the light doesn't interfere with his laptop screen, where he types. The document will be emailed to a Canadian editor today, before lunch. It'll be handled by subs, and unlike in my childhood or his, it will be delivered to the public long before tomorrow morning. Hopefully a few facts will be checked, because he doesn't know all of them.

He's never met my parents, for example, so doesn't know how closely I resemble my father, or why I don't get along with my brothers. He knows only the stories from my youth that I can remember, and those of course are unlikely to be accurate. He's met few of my friends. He's never been to my country, never walked through the Laurentians or swum in Lac des Bois with water weeds around his ankles. He knows I can hoist a canoe onto my head and carry it for an hour or more, but doesn't know how ordinary this is.

He knows I had a bicycle with blue streamers on the handlebars when I was seven, which I rode to the corner store to buy twisted black licorice, which I paid for with a coin with a picture of a caribou on one side and a meaningless queen on the other. He knows I have a broken coccyx from a fall on the ice when I was a teenager that still aches when I menstruate. He knows what really happened in Kazakhstan, and he will tell, one way or another. He knows my side and breast are scarred by the acid a relative tried to throw in my mother's face when I was an infant, exposing the bone of the arm she used to shield me. He knows she didn't put me down until she reached a clinic. He knows other things, which he won't write, at least not here; that I like to be fed wine while I'm still lying on my side, weak, letting him wipe the liquid from the corner of my mouth. That I am still a little bit in love with a Scottish engineer in Baku who photographs wooden doors as a sideline.

That's why I gave him this job, several nights before I left for the first interesting assignment I'd had in two years, gained thanks to a word of approval from Ute. I would witness revolution after all; I would make up for lost time. We lit candles. The room was full of sweat and flames. The windows steamed and the bottle of white wine he insisted on keeping in a bucket of ice water made me convulse when he placed it against my skin. I was bleeding; on his beard it looked savage, like he'd ripped me apart with his teeth. It was the only time I saw him take his wedding ring off, to wash it carefully in the bathroom sink, to remove the last of my blood.

I still hadn't bought my own cutlery. I will never buy my own cutlery. Some of my clothes were still in boxes, though most of the books were piled around the room, along with the flatpacked shelves I intended to assemble. The sight of those shelves would have wrecked my father beyond repair, which is why I instructed Marcus to take them to Brussels and put them in his study, a room I've never seen, where they will clash with the antique furniture he and his wife have gathered over nearly three decades. Nearly my entire lifespan, as it turns out.

It's a hard place, Farah. Stay with the camera

crew.

This is my small justice; the Almaty incident won't be the first thing to appear in a search of my name. Now, somewhere near the top of the page, will be my name next to his in print, a significance he will explain, carefully, to my parents and brothers, who should remember the way I lived rather than the way I died. Not good, not pretty, but remarkable.

'aye Dagoo, his spout is a big one,
like a whole shock of wheat, and
white as a pile of our Nantucket wool'

Herman Melville, *Moby-Dick*

Contributor Biographies

Simon Biggam's first novel *These Are Only Words* was shortlisted for the Saltire First Book Award. From a number of years he was the Literature Development Officer for Glasgow and is currently working on Arts and Heritage projects in the East End and is an Arts Development Producer for the City.

William Bonar's latest publication is a sonnet sequence in *North Light: The Anthology of Clydebuilt 3* (Dreadful Night Press, 2012). His first pamphlet collection, *Frostburn Steél*, appeared in 2004; his second will be published in 2013. His poems and short stories have been widely published in anthologies, newspapers and magazines. He lives in Glasgow and works in education.

Nick Brooks is a final year PhD student at the University of the West of Scotland, completing a thesis on Scottish Contemporary Gothic, and has also been teaching Creative Writing and Screenwriting there for the last 3 years. He is a published novelist and poet, with two novels in print (*My Name Is Denise Forrester*, and *The Good Death*, both Wiedenfeld and Nicholson). He has recently completed his third novel, *Indecent Acts*. Nick has twice been a recipient of a Scottish Arts Council Writer's Award.

Elspeth Brown lives in Dunbar. She writes poetry, short stories and plays. Plays performed include *The Siege of Haddington*, *Also Dynamo of the Twenty First Century*, and *The Spectrum*. One of her significant influences has been working with the Solway Poets. She provides editing and criticism and runs creative writing workshops.

Tom Bryan was born in Canada, but has been long resident in Scotland. He is a widely published poet, fiction and non-fiction writer. His short story collection *The Bridge Keeper's Log Book and Other Stories* is available from Biscuit Publishing.

A C Clarke's latest collections are *A Natural Curiosity*, shortlisted for the 2012 Callum Macdonald Award, and *Fr Meslier's Confession*. She is a member of Scottish PEN and has won several prizes, most recently the 2012 Second Light Long Poem competition.

Dan Coxon lived in Edinburgh for ten years and currently resides in the Pacific Northwest. His publications include the travel memoir *Ka Mate: Travels in New Zealand*, the anthologies *Daddy Cool* and *Late-Night River Lights*, and pieces in *The Nervous Breakdown*, *Monkeybicycle*, *3:AM*, *Third Wednesday* and *Two Hawks Quarterly*. dancoxon.com

Seth Crook taught philosophy at various universities before moving to the Hebrides. He doesn't like cod philosophy in poetry, but likes cod, philosophy and poetry. His poems have recently started to appear in such places as *Other Poetry*, *Ink*, *Sweat and Tears*, *Snakeskin*, *The Journal*, *Antiphon*, *Northwords Now*, and *Message in a Bottle*.

Paul Deaton was runner-up in the 2010 Arvon International Poetry Prize judged by Carol Ann Duffy. Most recently he has had poems published in *The Spectator* and the *Cockermouth Poets* and *Ice* anthologies. The first chapter of a novel (in progress) was published by Freight in *Tip Tap Flat*.

Tracey Emerson has just completed a PhD in Creative Writing at Edinburgh University. Her short stories have been published in anthologies and literary magazines and her short film, *The Crimson Chairs,* is currently in development with the independent company Monumental Studios.

Sally Evans is known for book length poems as well as being Editor of the long lived broadsheet *Poetry Scotland*. Recent work has appeared in Stirling Castle writers exhibitions, anthologies such as *Starry Rhymes* (on Ginsberg) and *Split Screen*, in which she has performed in Manchester, Callander and Pitlochry. *Penguin Eulogy* touches on her other life as a bookseller.

Katy Ewing is currently in the honours year of a Liberal Arts MA at the University of Glasgow (Dumfries). As well as winning joint first in the 2012 Kirkpatrick Dobie poetry prize, she has had poetry and prose published in *From Glasgow to Saturn*, prose in *Earthlines* magazine and poetry in *Southlight*, *Octavius* and the forthcoming *Far Off Places*.

Alison Flett is originally from Edinburgh but spent much of her life in Orkney and has been living in Adelaide, Australia, since 2010. She has published two pamphlets of poetry and a longer collection *Whit Lassyz Ur Inty* (Thirsty Books) which was shortlisted for the Saltire Book of the Year Award. She is poet-in-residence at the Adelaide Botanic Gardens. botanicpoetry.blogspot.com.au

Graham Fulton lives in Paisley. His publications include *Humouring the Iron Bar Man* (Polygon) *Open Plan* (Smokestack) *The Ruin of Poltalloch* (Controlled Explosion Press) *Full Scottish Breakfast* (Red Squirrel) and *Upside Down Heart* (Controlled Explosion Press). New full-length collections are to be published by Roncadora Press, Smokestack Books, Red Squirrel Press and Salmon Poetry.

Ewan Gault's short stories have been widely published and have won a number of awards. His debut novel *The Beaten Track*, which follows the misfortunes of two British athletes fleeing from a Kenyan training camp as a violent election engulfs the country, is due to be published this summer.

Rodge Glass is the author of three novels, *No Fireworks* (Faber, 2005), *Hope for Newborns* (Faber, 2008) and *Bring Me the Head of Ryan Giggs* (Tindal Street, 2012), and *Alasdair Gray: A Secretary's Biography* (Bloomsbury, 2008) which won a Somerset Maugham Award in 2009. Rodge is a Senior Lecturer in Creative Writing at Edge Hill University. He has edited a number of anthologies including *A Year of Open Doors* (Cargo, 2010) and *Second Lives* (Cargo, 2012). Rodge's story collection, *LoveSexTravelMusik*, will be published by Freight Books in April 2013.

Alison Grant lives in rural Angus and is currently pursuing a part time MLitt in Writing Practice and Study at Dundee University. Her writing has appeared in journals and anthologies, including Red Squirrel's *Split Screen* and *A Wilder Vein* published by Two Ravens Press.

Audrey Henderson was a finalist in the 2008 Indiana Review 1/2 K Award and took second place in the 2008 River Styx International Poetry Contest. She has new work in *Magma, The Midwest Quarterly* and *Tar River Poetry*. Originally from Edinburgh, she was a contributor to BBC Radio Scotland. She now lives in Boston, Massachusetts.

Kevin Henderson (b.1963) is a visual artist, mountain bike guide and writer. He lives in Perthshire.

Izabela Ilowska is a PhD student in Creative Writing at Glasgow University. She is working on a novel about a Polish immigrant living in the UK.

Andy Jackson is from Manchester but moved to Fife twenty years ago. His poems have appeared in *Magma, Blackbox Recorder* and *Trespass*. He is editor of *Split Screen* (Red Squirrel 2012), an anthology of film & TV poetry. His debut collection *The Assassination Museum* was published by Red Squirrel in 2010. An anthology of Dundee poetry entitled *Whaleback City* co-edited with WN Herbert is due in 2013.

Simon Jackson is an award winning writer of poetry, plays, films and music. His recent short films with Scottish poets and with Billy Bragg have been screened by the BBC and in film festivals round the world, and his last play, *Turning to the Camera* was The Guardian's Pick of the Week for Scottish theatre. He's never come close to making a living through art and teaches in an international school in Cairo.

Vicki Jarrett is a novelist and short story writer from Edinburgh. Her short fiction has appeared in print (including *Gutter 04*), been broadcast by BBC Radio and shortlisted for the Manchester Fiction Prize and the Bridport Prize, among others. Her first novel, *Nothing is Heavy*, was published in September 2012. She is currently working on a short story collection and a second novel. vickijarrett.com

John Jennett completed a Masters at the Edwin Morgan Writing Centre at Glasgow University. He is the son of a famous brain surgeon, despite which he studied music, became an hotelier and then a commercial sailing skipper. John lives in the Scottish Highlands.

Brian Johnstone's latest collection is *The Book of Bélongings* (Arc, 2009). His poetry has appeared throughout the UK, in America and Europe. His poems have been translated into over 10 different languages. In 2009 *Terra Incognita*, a small collection of his poems in Italian translation, was published by L'Officina (Vicenza). He is at present working on a memoir, *Twice Shy*.

Brian McCabe was born in a small mining community near Edinburgh. He has lived as a freelance writer since 1980 and has held various writing fellowships. He is currently Royal Literary Fellow at the University of Glasgow and was Editor of Edinburgh Review 2005–2010. He has published three collections of poetry, the most recent being *Zero* (Polygon, 2009). He has published one novel and five collections of short stories, the most recent of which is *A Date With My Wife* (Canongate, 2001). His *Selected Stories* was published by Argyll in 2003.

David Kinloch is from Glasgow and is the author of five books of poetry including *Un Tour d'Ecosse, In My Father's House* and *Finger of a Frenchman,* all published by Carcanet Press. He is Reader in Poetry at the University of Strathclyde where he teaches creative writing and Scottish Literature and currently holds a Fellowship from the Arts and Humanities Research Association. His personal website is at davidkinloch.co.uk

Bridget Khursheed is a poet based in the Borders; she also edits poetandgeek.com; recent work in *The Eildon Tree, Stravaig, Poetry Scotland, Northwords Now, Valve, Message in a Bottle, Ink Sweat & Tears, Up the Staircase* and *Southlight,* and on the Scottish Borders Council website; otherwise obsessively logging the A68 over Soutra and birdlife on Easter Road.

Lindsay Macgregor lives near Cupar and is studying towards an MLitt in Writing Practice and Study at the University of Dundee.

Neil Mackay is a multi-award winning investigative journalist, newspaper executive, non-fiction author, radio broadcaster, film-maker and playwright. He has won around two dozen national and international awards for his newspaper journalism. Mackay was a launch editor of the Sunday Herald newspaper, and has subsequently been the paper's Crime Editor, Investigations Editor and Head of News. He is currently working on a commission from the National Theatre of Scotland. *All the Little Guns Went Bang Bang Bang* is his first novel and will be published in June by Freight Books.

Calum Maclean is a twenty three year old writer from Glasgow. He is in the second year of a Creative Writing MLitt at the University of Glasgow, and is currently co-editor of the University's online creative writing showcase *From Glasgow to Saturn.* His poetry has been published in *Octavius.*

Ruth Mainland is a 22 year old Shetlander in her final year of studying English Literature at the University of Edinburgh. Her work has previously been published in *The New Shetlander* and *The Inkwell.* In 2012 she was the winner of the University's Lewis Edwards Memorial Prize for poetry.

Anneliese Mackintosh is based in Manchester, with an MLitt in Creative Writing from the University of Glasgow. Her fiction has been broadcast on BBC Radio 4 and BBC Radio Scotland, and published in various UK and US lit magazines, including *Edinburgh Review, Gutter, Causeway/ Cabhsair,* and *Citizens For Decent Literature.* She was shortlisted for the Bridport Prize 2012, and has just completed her first novel. anneliesemackintosh.com

Iain Matheson grew up in Glasgow and now lives in Edinburgh, where he works as a musician and composer. His poetry has appeared online, and in *The Scotsman.*

Bet McCallum was born in Dundee and studied at Duncan of Jordanstone College of Art before training as a teacher. After ten years as a Headteacher, she worked at the University of London as a tutor /researcher in primary education and assessment until she retired. She has published widely in academic research journals and co-authored three books. She has only recently started writing fiction.

Marion McCready was born on the Isle of Lewis and lives in the west coast of Scotland. She has had poems published in a variety of magazines and anthologies including *The Glasgow Herald* and *The Edinburgh Review.* Her poetry pamphlet collection, *Vintage Sea,* was published by Calder Wood Press (2011). Marion is a recent recipient of a Scottish Book Trust New Writers Award.

Kirsten McKenzie is 37 and lives in Fife. She has published two novels, *Chapel at the Edge of the World* and *The Captain's Wife*, both by John Murray, as well as various short stories and poems. She is currently working on a novel and a collection of short stories.

Andrew McLinden lives and works in Glasgow. He started life as a lyricist and his work has been used on a variety of film and TV projects from Irvine Welsh's Acid House Trilogy to a recent episode of American drama One Tree Hill. He's had short fiction published in a number of online and print journals. He hopes to finish 2013 by completing his first novel.

Hugh McMillan's last poetry collection was *Thin Slice of Moon: selected and new poems* (Roncadora Press). He has received several awards and been anthologised widely. He is currently writing a libretto for an opera.

Gordon Meade is a Scottish poet at present living in exile in East London. He has recently become a member of the Eastside Educational Trust creative team. His seventh collection of poems, *Sounds of the Real World*, is due for publication in September 2013 with Cultured Llama.

Philip Miller is a journalist and writer based in Glasgow. He is currently working on his debut novel.

David Morgan is a writer, teacher, arts worker and literature officer, organiser of book festivals and writer-in-residence for education authorities, Littlehay Prison and Fairfield Psychiatric Hospital.

Theresa Muñoz is the online editor of the *Scottish Review of Books* and recently finished her PhD thesis on outsiderness in the work of Tom Leonard at the University of Glasgow. Her poetry has appeared in *Poetry Review*, *Canadian Literature* and numerous other journals. Her pamphlet *Close* was published by HappenStance Press in 2012.

Anne B Murray is a Glaswegian poet who works as a creative writing tutor in various adult and community learning settings in Glasgow. She has had poems published in *New Writing Scotland* and *The Herald.* Her poetry pamphlet *Galilee to Gallicantu*, a record of her journey through the Palestinian territories, was short-listed for the Calum Macdonald Award in 2010.

Liz Niven is a Scottish poet based in Dumfries. Her most recent colection *The Shard Box* (Luath Press) was a Scottish Libraries Summer Read 2011. A new collaborative book, *Anything You Say*, (Taigh Chearsabhagh, Uist) will be published in 2013. She is a creative writing facilitator, delivering workshops to Scottish Poetry Library, National Galleries, and has appeared in Literary Festivals around the world.

Jenny Paine was born in Germany in 1983. She studied at Edinburgh College of Art and Edinburgh and Glasgow Universities. An artist and poet, she lives and works in Edinburgh.

Jon Plunkett currently lives and writes in Scotland. His work has featured in a number of online and in print poetry magazines and literary journals. In addition to writing Jon is currently leading the development of a poetry trail in the Highlands of Scotland that will see lines of poetry carved in stone and placed along a two mile trail. More of Jon's poems can be read at jonplunkettpoetry.weebly.com.

Stav Poleg's poetry has appeared in magazines such as *Magma*, *The Rialto* and *Horizon Review*, and her theatre work performed at the Shunt Vaults, London Bridge. Her poem sequence on the goddess Athena was performed last year at the Traverse Theatre as part of Words, Words, Words. She lives in Edinburgh.

A P Pullan was born in Yorkshire and now lives in Ayrshire. Poems have been published previously in *Poetry Scotland*, *Iota* and *New Writing Scotland* as well as online magazine *Pank*. She is currently writing a children's novel which is a lot harder than all that poetry malarkey.

Claire Quigley's poems have been published in a variety of magazines including *Magma* and *Other Poetry*. She lives in Glasgow where she works as a photographer and programmer.

Elaine Reid is a Glaswegian writer and second year student of Glasgow University's Creative Writing MFA programme. Elaine is a previous winner of Strathclyde University's Keith Wright Literary Prize and has been published in *From Glasgow to Saturn* and *Valve Journal*. Currently working on a collection of short stories, Elaine also writes monolgues and has performed at Edinburgh International Book Festival.

Tracey S Rosenberg won a Scottish Book Trust New Writers Award in 2010, and her debut poetry collection, *Lipstick is Always a Plus*, was published last year by Stewed Rhubarb Press. She's a committee member with Inky Fingers, and Bookstalls Manager for the StAnza Poetry Festival.

Mark Russell lives in Glasgow. His poetry has appeared in a variety of publications including *Poetry Salzburg Review*, *Cake*, *Bliss* (Templar), is forthcoming in *The Frogmore Papers*, and in 2012 he was shortlisted for the Bridport Prize. He has an MLitt in Creative Writing from the University of Glasgow, and is a St Mungo's Mirrorball Clydebuilt Poet.

Mike Russell is deputy editor of the *West Highland Free Press* newspaper. His short fiction has recently appeared in *Fractured West* and *Polluto* magazines. His first novel, a dystopian journey through a near-future Highlands, is currently looking for a home.

Maria Sinclair is a graduate of the MLitt at Glasgow University. She has written one novel, and is currently working on her second. She also writes and performs poetry, and has been accepted onto the Clydebuilt poetry programme.

Rob McClure Smith has published fiction in *Chapman*, *Manchester Review*, *Gettysburg Review*, *Barcelona Review* and many other literary magazines. A former winner of the Scotsman Orange Short Story Award, he teaches Film Studies at Knox College in Galesburg, Illinois.

Simon Sylvester is a writer, teacher and filmmaker. His work has been published by *Cargo Crate* and magazines including *Gutter*, *Smoke*, *Pank*, *Valve* and *Fractured West*. He lives in Cumbria with the abstract painter Monica Metsers and their daughter Isadora.

Jim Taylor is 50-odd and lives in Shetland where he combines two part-time office jobs. His stories have appeared in *Chapman*, *Edinburgh Review*, *Rebel Inc*, *West Coast Magazine*, *New Writing Scotland* and *New Shetlander*. He has written two novels and is currently working on a graphic adaptation of one of these.

Zoe Venditozzi's darkly funny debut novel *Anywhere's Better Than Here* came out in October 2012 with Sandstone Press. She is currently working on a short story collection and a novel about an unsettling relationship between a neurotic new mother and a psychic teenager.

Miriam Vaswani contributes to literary journals and news publications as a fiction writer, journalist, columnist and poet, and is fiction editor at *Outside In* Literary & Travel Magazine. She has lived in Canada, Scotland, Russia and Germany. She blogs about books, politics and global citizenship at miriam-littlebones.blogspot.com

Mark Waddell is a new breed of comedy-poet-libertine for a modern generation, with a fanbase including beat legend Michael Horovitz. Published in the UK and the Philippines and appearing in *Great Poëts of the 21st Century* by the Imaginary Press, he is fast gaining quite a reputation with his spicy, irreverently wicked humour, hilarious stunning live shows and hare-brained illustrations. markwaddell.com

Mairi Wilson was born near Glasgow then dispatched south of the border and beyond at an early age. Mairi has recently returned to Scotland and now divides her time between Edinburgh and Ullapool. She writes poetry to avoid finishing her novel.

Kirstin Zhang spent her childhood in Papua New Guinea. Following periods in America and Japan, she attended the School of Oriental and African Studies in London and took a MLitt in Creative Writing at the University of Glasgow. Her short stories have appeared in various publications, including *The Scotsman*, *Soho House Magazine* and GQ. She now lives in on the west coast of Scotland, where she is writer-in-residence to Creative Communities creativekilmacolm.org